More Praise for The Circus

'*The Circus* pulls you in. Beautifully written, with a compelling heroine. A story of survival, family, friendship – and fire.'

Patrice Lawrence, author of *Orangeboy*

About the Author

Olivia Levez lives in Worcestershire, where she divides her time between teaching in a secondary school and writing. *The Circus* is Olivia's second book. Her debut novel, *The Island,* was published by Rock the Boat in 2016.

You can follow Olivia on Twitter **@livilev.**

the
CIRCUS

Olivia Levez

ONEWORLD

A Rock the Boat Book

First published in North America, Great Britain
and Australia by Rock the Boat, an imprint of
Oneworld Publications, 2017

ISBN 978-1-78607-094-4
ISBN 978-1-78607-095-1 (ebook)

Printed and bound in Great Britain by Clays Ltd, St Ives plc

Oneworld Publications
10 Bloomsbury Street
London WC1B 3SR
England

Dedicated to my boys, Sam and Louis

- Rule #1: Don't stay in the same place too long. Keep moving.

- Rule #2: Alter your appearance. Use a disguise.

- Rule #3: Never spend money unless you absolutely have to.

- Rule #4: Never tell anyone where you are. Never contact home. Don't rely on friends.

- Rule #5: Have no plan. Be spontaneous.

- Rule #6: Never display interest in other people. Do not draw attention to yourself.

- Rule #7: Always be prepared to leave at a moment's notice.

- Rule #8: If possible, hide in full view.

- Rule #9: Never give in to paranoia.

Act 1

Aerial

I suppose you could say it begins with the buttons. That's when I have the idea; I mean, with the first snip. Because you can't go back, can you? Not after doing something like that.

There is a row of buttons, satin-covered, from the throat of the dress (low-cut, of course, the way the Handbag likes it) down to the lowest point of the bodice. Then there are handfuls of ivory silk, the dress heavy and new out of its plastic case, but I don't touch them. I want it to be subtle, what I'm doing.

I take the point of the scissors and ease it beneath the nub of the button, wiggle it until I get it to meet around the thread. And then, *snip*. The button pings over the carpet. I note where it lands, by the mirrored dressing table. It will go in my keepsake collection, to mark a Significant Moment. There'll be more of those to come.

It is easy then, to do the rest.

Have you ever felt like that, Beanie? Like your life is finally going to start over, like you've taken it by the reins and headed firmly in a different direction? It's a rush. My heart's skittering by the time I finish cutting off the last button, and I wonder whether I should take one of my tablets, just to calm down.

I don't, in the end. I decide to go with the buzz. I'll need that spike of adrenaline soon.

I hang the dress up carefully in its wrapping, place it back on the door and walk across her dressing room to look out of the window. They're arriving already, in twos and threes. A horrific pink limousine belches out a tumble of her shrieking friends, shocking high shoes in various colours of candy teetering on the gravelled drive.

Trust her to invite half of Southside. A whinny from the back makes me crane out further, but not too far. I don't want them to see me in the Handbag's room. It's Spook and Spotty, all dolled up like they're in a pantomime, feathered pink plumes bouncing on their heads. I feel another sting of rage. I told Daddy not to use Spook for her carriage. I *told* him.

But it doesn't matter now.

None of this does, I remind myself. I am dealing with it. I have a plan.

I leave the Handbag's room and make my way past the stink of lilies (funeral flowers – not for weddings, surely? But the Handbag likes them, so of course the house is full of them) to my own room. Inside, I slide off my strappy heels, look around for my trainers. There's no time to change properly, not while they're all arriving. I leave my necklace on; it might come in useful for selling later. I grab my black jacket and put it on over my cocktail shift dress.

Next, my bag, which is already packed and ready. I tug my journal from under the window seat and stuff it in too. Then I take your Little Kit of Happiness. (Yes, it was me who took it from your dressing table that time. I'm sorry, but I need it more than you, don't you think?) I take the first ivory button that I cut off and place it inside the yellow drawstring bag.

As I make my preparations, a wild-eyed mad girl keeps catching my eye in the mirror.

Today I'm supposed to be a bridesmaid.

I look more like an assassin.

One Arm Hang

It's easy to swing myself down the wisteria outside my bedroom window. I have thick wrists and thick ankles, and they are made for moments like this. Our wisteria's not going anywhere. It's as ancient as the rest of our house is new, gripping the stone ledge and reclaimed bricks with fleshy little claws. From below, I hear chattering and laughter. It's a sunny day, perfect for a wedding. The Handbag's friends are grabbing champagne and wheelie cases to fit all the make-up and hair extensions that she'll need to use to transform herself into Cinderella.

I hang from the side of the house and from here I can see right over our grounds. Far away, behind our summer house, one of the gardeners is doing something to the rose trellises. Over the lake, the willows sigh and hang their heads. My mother named me after them, did you know that, Beanie? Daddy said that she was sitting at her favourite window, stroking the bump that would become me, and the delicate branches silvered and shivered so beautifully in a sudden breeze that she named me after them, right there and then.

A delicate, slender tree. How wrong she was.

There's nothing slender about me. I'm not exactly the fairy tale princess in the picture books, am I? Not like you. But I'm strong, and I can cling to the sides of houses all day if I need to. I can climb and swing and cling to things. What fairy tale girl can do that?

Anyway, there I cling until the last of the Handbag's friends giggle their way into our house. I wait until Martyna, our housekeeper, sighs and heaves herself back inside, after shouting something at the new Polish girl who grooms for us. I am glad of my Hi Tops. The wisteria is sturdy and strong, and I have climbed it in bare feet before, many times, but not in clumpy trainers.

Below me, the Polish girl rakes over the gravel where the gigglers have scuffed it, muttering and probably cursing under her breath. I wait until she straightens the headdresses on the horses and kisses them on their noses. She starts talking to one of the caterers and they disappear into the ridiculously big marquee on our lowest lawn. No doubt to admire the pink swags on the gold chairs, or to watch the events staff blow up yet more balloons for the love arch.

I swing myself down the wisteria before I literally vomit. I think of the Handbag knocking back Daddy's champagne and letting her friends glue on her fake nails and eyelashes. I wonder if she'll notice all the satin-covered buttons stuffed in the plant pot by the window. I think of her rising in her too-tight shoes and taking the dress from the back of the door, easing it out of its plastic casing.

The thought makes me shiver.

My dress is too long, and I hitch it up as I run, past the lake, past the willows, to where the woodland starts. I pass the copse where my au pairs would sometimes take me to play while they smoked dark-smelling cigarettes and texted their boyfriends or sisters or mothers.

There's the Goblin Tree, ridiculously small now, but the first tree I climbed, trying to reach for the clouds. There's Snake Pit, where I performed death-defying feats with my dolls and teddies. I once stayed the whole night in this wood, but I don't want to think about that right now. That was one of the first times I tried to run away before, but of course I was far too young.

I didn't know the rules, not then.

I know them now, of course. I've spent a long time preparing.

Rule #1: *Don't stay in the same place too long. Keep moving.*
Rule #2: *Alter your appearance. Use a disguise.*

I expect the police know all of this, don't they, Beanie? Scally will, naturally – she'll have been on courses. Probably raised an ironic eyebrow and enjoyed the free lunch, made sarcastic comments under her breath about the newbie course presenter, because she's been around the block; she knows a thing or two.

I have everything I need for #2, but will need to do that properly later. I'll use the train toilets. For now, I wriggle out of my bridesmaid dress and shove it into a hole in the Goblin Tree. Shivering in my bra and pants, I pull on a dark sweater and black jeans. Stuff my hair into a hat.

Now I really look like an assassin.

I grab my jacket and reach the road, bursting out of the secret world of our land into ordinariness and traffic.

Then I stick out my thumb for #1.

I keep walking, keep my thumb out, but pull it in when I see the catering vans and string quartet arriving for the wedding. There'll be press too, probably. The Handbag's biggest ambition is to get into *Hello!* magazine.

After twenty minutes or so, a lorry stops.

'Where to, love?'

'London,' I say.

It's a man. Early sixties and looks like Santa Claus. Or a fisherman. He puffs out his breath when he sees me. He has a gold stud in his ear.

'I can take you as far as Oxford. That'll do you?'

'Fine,' I say. 'Thank you.'

I ignore his outstretched hand and climb up into the cab, squeaking around in the plastic seat until I find the seat belt. I put my backpack by my feet. In the wing mirror, I can see Daddy's car arriving, his red Porsche with its blacked-out windows and personalised number plate: *GAS 1*. Gary Allan Stephens. I used to cringe on the few occasions he would pick me up for exeat weekends.

All the other girls' parents drove beaten-up Land Rovers that had been in their families for decades. Like yours, for instance.

'You all right, love?'

The driver's staring at me, a concerned look on his face. He has photos of his kids plastered all over his cab, stuck on the dashboard and on the ceiling. There are ones of teenagers on family holidays; a young man and a woman in graduate gowns; photos of them with melty looks on their faces as they hold babies of their own. I turn away.

I wriggle round, stare at Daddy's car as it moves slowly down our drive. He's gone. It's over.

I make myself smile brightly at the driver.

'I'm fine. Perfect,' I say.

The driver's a talker, but not a listener, which suits me fine. I gaze out of the window as he talks about his daughters, who are both studying to be doctors, and his latest grandchild – who was born premature but is a real trouper, a fighter, tough as nails – and his wife, who has just been diagnosed with Parkinson's but doesn't let that get in the way of their dream, which is to do up a narrowboat and retire on water, under the stars.

'Beachy Head,' he says. 'Best canal system in the world. Wake up to see a heron on your deck and a fox through your bedroom window.' He rustles inside his glove compartment and pulls out a much-folded picture.

'That's her,' he says. 'That's our *Brown Betty*.'

I take it and make ooh-ing noises at the reclaimed wood and the stripped and tarred hull and the log burner found in a French street market. But I'm not listening, not really.

I refold it and pass it back, turn to look out of the window.
We're passing through the Cotswolds, juddering past choc-
olate-box villages and green, summer-soaked fields.

I fiddle with the button in my hand and wonder whether,
back home, all hell has broken loose yet.

I drift off, and when I wake up the driver is pulling his
lorry into a lay-by.

'This is it. Oxford. I always stop here for a fry-up and a
snooze.'

He's indicating a bus that has been converted into a snack
bar. *MAUREENS BITES* it says, no apostrophe.

I unsnap my belt and get ready to open the passenger
door, but he's already out and opening it for me. I watch him
swing my bag down onto the tarmac.

'You take care now,' he says. 'Always stop for young girls
like you, I do. To prevent undesirable types picking them
up. I'd like to think the same thing would be done for my
daughters and granddaughters.'

He's staring at me with sharp blue eyes.

'Thank you for your help,' I say stiffly. I take my bag. 'I'm
afraid I can't pay you.' Rule #3: *Never spend money unless you
absolutely have to.* I withdrew all my savings for my gap year a
week ago, and have them in a padded brown envelope stuffed
down the lining of my bag. I can't let anyone – even someone as nice as this driver appears to be – see me take it out.

He looks hurt. 'Wouldn't dream of taking your money,'
he says. I feel his eyes on me as I cross the road to the train
station.

Another adrenaline spike.

Because this is the part where I travel all the way to
London without buying a ticket.

*Remember you are an accustomed fugitive. You have run away
many times before.*

The first time I ran away, I was nine.
That first time, it was all because of the mouse ear.

Schoolgirl Missing, Aged Seven

Sheila chatters all the way home. She's interrupted all the time by her satnav, which tells her to turn down lanes in some old Doctor Who's voice, which Beanie's brothers say makes her a saddo.

I don't really listen, because I'm thinking of Daddy and Storm's faces when they see me back home. It's an exeat weekend and Daddy has promised he'll drive me to his offices with him and take me to Hamleys and I'm so looking forward to seeing Storm again. On the way home I've imagined over and over his face and his whicker when he sees me; how he'll leave his grass-pulling, and come trotting over to nudge and snort and probably knock me off my feet, he'll be so excited.

Daddy's paid for Sheila, the house mistress, to drive me home. They do that sometimes. Get paid by the parents to do extra duties. I mean, they probably don't earn much looking after us, do they? Even if they get their own flat and everything.

Martyna lets me in. She's our housekeeper. She's in charge of food and me. She's bad at both, but Daddy hasn't sacked her yet.

'Oh, you're back,' she says, as Sheila waves me goodbye

and sails off down the drive with Doctor Who. 'I thought it was tomorrow.'

'Where's Daddy?' I ask, pushing past her. This isn't easy because she takes up most of the doorway. I leave all my bags for her to take upstairs and run from room to room, breathing in all the smells of home. New carpets and new LG TVs and Martyna's scented plug-ins. Beanie says that those sort of things are naff. Her house smells of beeswax and cut flowers and coal ash.

Daddy's not in the drawing room or library or kitchen. He's not in the games room.

Martyna is standing in the hall, scowling down at my bags. 'Where is he?' I demand.

Her eyes narrow so that they disappear into her sullen face. 'We thought you were coming tomorrow,' she repeats.

Daddy's country office is in a converted stable. I crunch over the gravel and hum to myself as I stroke all Spook's rosettes in the stable lobby. He'll be in his field, of course, waiting for me. I frown at the dollops of dung in his straw. Nobody's cleaned him out yet. I hurry past the other stalls to the new stable block, which is all glass and steel and cedar cladding.

Daddy's office.

The door's not locked. Inside, it smells of new-sawn wood, because it was only completed a few months ago. Daddy has his main offices in Greenwich in London, but he often has meetings at home too. That way, he can still spend time with me when I'm back from school. I know that his work makes him an awful lot of money (more than both Beanie and Miffy's parents put together) and it has something to do with entertainment.

'Daddy?' I call. There is a scuffling noise from upstairs. I climb the glass steps to the mezzanine and poke my head round the reclaimed brick partition.

Daddy is fighting with a lady.

He has her over the desk and they are wrestling with each other. They are both struggling and snorting, and it looks like neither of them is winning. I watch until I can't stand it anymore, and one of them knocks a paperweight off the desk.

'Daddy, stop it!'

They swing round. All that fighting has made some of their clothes come undone.

Daddy's face is red so he must be really angry at the lady. She has her hand over her mouth and is straightening her dress.

'Oh, god,' she says.

I stand firm. 'Daddy, what are you doing? You knew I was coming home today.'

Daddy whispers something to the lady, and she gives me a strange smile and hurries out. I am glad she is gone. The air in the room smells funny, sort of hot and urgent mixed with the new wood.

'Did you remember the tickets, Daddy?'

He comes over and gives me a hug. He smells strange and I wriggle away. 'Willow,' he says. 'And how is school?'

I look at him. 'You haven't remembered?'

'I'm sorry, Willow.'

'You promised!'

~~Daddy always keeps his promises.~~

~~He never forgets to pick me up from school on an exeat weekend.~~

~~He is never too busy to take me out.~~

I watch him pick up his phone, which has been knocked to the floor. He jabs at the phone buttons with one hand, and does up his shirt buttons with the other. On the phone he speaks rapidly. It takes him two minutes to book tickets to the ballet at Sadler's Wells, and another two minutes to organise Martyna to go with me.

12

'There,' he smiles. 'All done.' His tie's still crooked from where the lady pulled it.

I stare at him, and then I run away.

The mouse has been on our mantelpiece for as long as I can remember.

It sits with its tail coiled round its haunches, and every detail is painted carefully, from the delicate long toes of its feet to the thin hair-like flicks of its whiskers. The mouse is clutching a china cotton reel, and it looks just like it's sniffing the air, nose quivering.

It is probably a priceless antique or something, because literally everything in our house is. Daddy pays someone to buy all our china at auction in Mayfair. The mouse is made of porcelain and has huge ears so delicate and thin that it would take a puff of air to snap them. Martyna, who is so clumsy she'd knock down a tree if she wasn't looking where she was going, is not allowed to touch it. Nor am I, nor is anyone.

Daddy used to tell me stories about the mouse. He said that it belonged to Mummy when she was a little girl like me. That her mother gave it to her, and her mother before that. But Martyna sniffed when I told her and said that it came from the auction house like everything else.

After I run from Daddy's office, I sit in the drawing room, which is cold because this is the older part of the house, the bit Daddy hasn't extended. No one comes here because there isn't a TV in this room. I sit on the sofa and watch the mouse. Sometimes, if I really look hard, I can make its head move and look at me.

Today, though, it's not working.

'Stupid mouse. Stupid Martyna. Stupid Daddy,' I say aloud.

Then, heart skittering in my chest and head feeling hot so that I can hardly breathe, I stand up and walk over to the mouse.

I look at my hands and they are rising up towards the china figurine. I watch my fingers as they curl over the mouse's ear.

Snap.

There's one.

Snap.

There's the other. Easy as that. The bits of porcelain in my hand are tiny and frail like pieces of broken seashell. The mouse looks really stupid now, with no ears. Its head looks shrunken with little broken spikes.

I am glad.

I start off by hiding in the car.

It's not far, but it still counts as running away.

I choose Daddy's Jag, because it is the comfiest, and climb into the back seat. Daddy's cars are hardly ever locked because Simon, his chauffeur, doubles up as a security man. He's almost as lazy as Martyna, and spends most of the time he's meant to be securing things and waxing cars watching box sets in his little office. He also smokes a lot of those flattened cigarettes he likes, the ones he rolls himself that smell funny.

I've packed my second biggest suitcase, so they'll know I'm serious. I've emptied all my drawers and wardrobe of everything I own: my spare riding clothes, my party shoes and party dresses, my second-best designer clothes, my spare wax jacket and Hunter boots and padded gilets. I've literally cleared my room.

So they'll all know that I've left home.

And Daddy will have to call the police and they'll put me on the news and even Martyna will feel guilty, for being so dull and boring and never paying me any attention when Daddy's away working.

I couldn't lift my case into the car, so I've hidden it in the space behind the pool machinery in the changing hut. I lie on the cream leather back seat, curled up, waiting. I chew on a sandwich that I took from Martyna's fridge shelf.

I can wait all afternoon and all night if I have to.

I want them to notice that I'm not down for dinner.

I want them all to notice that I've gone.

I want them to notice me.

Clown Face

My face ghosts in and out of the window. I breathe, watch it fade, watch it reappear. My face, but not my face. I'm losing who I am.

'Tickets, please.'

I jump, and stuff my journal back into my bag. I am sitting in the corridor, on a pull-down seat outside the toilet. I don't know what is wrong with me. I must have been on this train for ages and I haven't even done Rule #2 yet.

The loos are engaged. I glance down the corridor and it's all right: the conductor's busy talking to some students dressed as superheroes. Batman needs to buy a ticket, and so, it turns out, do all the others.

Superman and Batgirl are pulling out their money, swigging cheap white wine from a bottle. It's definitely not the sort of wine Daddy would keep in our cellar. Iron Man and Wonder Woman are sitting opposite them, laughing at something on their phones. Students. I think of the A Levels I'm supposed to be sitting soon. The future I'm supposed to have. My personal statement not filled in.

The conductor's looking a little harassed now; she's lost her good humour from earlier. The red clicks to green and the door opens. Spiderman comes out, smirking. He winks at me, and shakes his wet hands to dry them. Some of the water goes on me.

I hurry inside, slamming the door shut behind me.

My bag's so stuffed with the things I need, it will hardly squeeze in, and I don't want to put it on the floor, which is all wet and gross-looking. In the end I balance it on the lid of the lavatory. The train sways and grumbles. Outside the tiny window, trees fly.

First, my hair.

I rummage inside the front pocket of my bag and pull out the scissors I used to cut off the Handbag's buttons. They're just big enough for what I'm about to do. I pull my hood away from my head and plait my hair quickly, tying it with the hairband I have around my wrist. It's the last time I'll need that.

I stare into the speckled mirror above the tiny steel wash-basin, or, as the Handbag would call it, sink. I trace my finger over my high cheekbones, my too-heavy jaw.

'Goodbye, Willow,' I say.

Slowly I lift the scissors and widen them at the hinges. I let their little jaws close over the top of my plait, where it reaches the nape of my neck. There is a sort of crunching sound as the plait is cut and comes away in my hand. I am left staring into the mirror with my plait in one hand and my scissors in the other.

I take the plait, look at it for one last time, and drop it out of the tiny window. It whips past like a bird and disappears.

I rake my fingers through my hair. It's not bad. I cut away at my fringe too, so that it sweeps low over my eyes and makes them look wide and huge.

In the mirror, a teenage boy looks back at me.

I get out the liquid eyeliner that I took from the Handbag's dressing table. I draw out flicks at the corner of both eyes and then outline the inside lids, so that my eyes are dark and smudged and dangerous-looking.

Better.

I am the Runaway Bridesmaid. I am the Fugitive.

Humming under my breath, I wash my hands with tepid train water and slimy soap and wipe them dry on my jeans. I pick up my bag and shut the door with a click behind me.

The conductor's left Coach A, where the superhero students are. None of them gives me a second glance as I slide into an empty seat.

I stare at my new face until it disappears, ghoulish in my window breath.

I wonder whether they've called off the wedding yet.

I wonder which of them will notice that I'm gone first.

I could have killed the Handbag once. Saw her hair extensions floating over the water of that ghastly hot tub and it would have been so easy to have pressed both hands over her face and pushedpushedpushed her under.

I didn't kill her. But they kill me, every day.

Candy Crush Saga

I was prepared to go through with the wedding before everything changed.

I would do it for Daddy, I thought: smile and smile and talk and talk to the guests, even the ones the Handbag's in-

17

vited from Southside. There wouldn't be any need for me to hand out drinks or devils on horseback or the mini pizzas she's got the caterers to make. They have dozens of hired staff on call, hovering around in smart black skirts and trousers and bow ties. They're having the works: pig roast, the poor thing turning on a spit, a skewer thrust through it, mouth to arse. There's the string quartet, and the DJ for later. I'm surprised the Handbag's not got living statues scattering gold dust over everyone as they line up to pay her tribute. Maybe a couple of baby dragons perched on her shoulders as she simpers and air kisses and flutters those hideous eyelashes.

In my room, I have laid out my bridesmaid dress on my bed, and unballed the tissue paper from inside my new shoes. I've refused to match the rest of the bridesmaids, so my dress is black, which is obviously more appropriate than the baby-pink mermaid dresses she's making all of her friends wear. I suppose that I'd better shower.

I meet the Handbag coming out of the bathroom, look-ing pale and sweaty. For once, she's not tottering around in spray-on jeans and spike-heeled shoes, but is still in her dress-ing gown, a pink one with white love hearts all over it. She pushes her hair out of her eyes and gives me a sort of twisted smile. She looks awful without make-up. There's a spray of spots on her chin, waiting to be smothered in foundation.

'All right?' she says.

She's lost weight and it doesn't suit her. I don't know why she's nervous. I mean, it's not as if she isn't getting everything she wants, is it?

I give her a bright smile to freeze her out. One day, if I smile hard enough, I will magic her out of my life altogether.

We have three bathrooms, but this was always the one I used before she came, so I don't see why I shouldn't use it now. But like in the rest of the house, she's left a trail of pieces of her, like she's shedding skin. There are bubbles on the floor. Tweezers by the basin.

And she's left her phone on the side of the bath.

Probably for playing Candy Crush Saga, in between applying false toenails.

It's pink (of course), in her favourite zebra-print case in pink and white. A fluffy animal thing hangs from the corner like she's ten or something, not however old she is, which is at least half the age of Daddy. Turns out to be a penguin.

How sweet.

The Handbag's left it where it could slip and smash, and, remembering my plan to be nice, I sigh and reach for it, meaning to move it to a safer place. I'm not so nice that I'm going to trot after her and return it.

It buzzes. A message pops up in its green speech bubble:

Oh my godddddddd! Congratulations!!!!!!!!!!!!! Still can't believe it!!!!!!!!!!!!!!!!!

It's from Cheryl, her best friend from Basildon.

I frown, and pick up the phone.

There's a photograph attached to the Handbag's original message, and I tap it to make it fill the screen.

It's instantly recognisable: grainy, blurred, a black and white image that's out of focus. The Handbag's phone is the latest super-sized Android, and it seems that, as I stare, the bean shape in the middle of the photo shivers and quickens.

The phone buzzes again. Another text from Cheryl:

You'll be a GREAT mum!!!!!!!!!!!!!!!!!! xxxxxxxxxxxxxxx

Quickly followed by another:

Shame about You Know Who!

I have a spare box of my tablets in the cabinet. It takes me a long time to pop two out of their tiny blisters, and even longer to get my breathing back to normal. It won't do to collapse on the tiled floor. Martyna or someone would find me, and then there'd be a fuss, and it would be much harder to make my escape.

Because that's the only option left to me now, isn't it? They don't want me. Daddy will have a new son or daughter, one that's shiny new, not bitter and difficult.

There isn't a place for me here, not any more.

I know when I'm not wanted.

Now You See Me

I didn't think about the barrier at Paddington Station, but in the end it didn't matter. I just shrugged and looked sort of hopeless, and the guard opened the barrier and let me through without even checking my ticket.

I took my hoodie off and stuck on some lipstick, and it was that easy. But now there's a camera, watching me with its single eye, and I'm regretting uncovering my face. I feel hunted. I am hungry and tired.

I root around in my bag until I find some coins. I don't dare pull out the brown envelope because there are people everywhere, and I need to tuck myself away in some place quiet, to get my bearings, to decide what to do next. I've never got this far before.

I find enough change for a sandwich and a coffee, and eat slumped down on the floor, watching the station pigeons fight over a bag of crisps and listening to the hum of the passengers. In the end, I surreptitiously slide out the envelope and run my fingers over the crisp notes. One thousand, two hundred and eighty pounds. My entire gap year savings, from when I pretended to care about such things.

'You eating that?' a girl asks.

I flinch, and stuff the envelope back inside my bag. The girl is sitting with her back against the wall, dirty red bobble hat pulled low over filthy hair. She has broken teeth and sores around her mouth.

She could have once been pretty, but it is difficult to tell. In silence, I pass her one of my ham sandwiches. I watch her as she pulls out every bit of ham and feeds it to the pigeons.

'Veggie,' she explains. She yawns widely, showing off those jaggy teeth, and stuffs the bread and butter into her mouth in one go. 'Got any ciggies?'

When I shake my head, she shrugs and hollers at a passing man. He's not much older than me, bearded. He takes out a cigarette and lights it for her as she thanks him profusely. 'God bless you,' she calls.

The next time I look at her, she's fallen asleep, dirty parka swallowing her like a grubby duvet. Then I notice the paper cup. Her hands are filthy, blackened around the nails. The girl looks an awful lot like me: same firm chin, same dark eyebrows that almost, not quite, meet in the middle.

Looking at her gives me an idea. I take my pen and scribble on the paper napkin that came with my sandwiches. 7839. Daddy's pin number. I still have his gold card, left over from when I went interrailing at Easter. He lets me have it for emergencies, but of course I can't use it, not now. It will instantly inform anyone looking for me of my exact location. I know they have CCTV cameras behind every ATM machine; it's one of the ways they get you, when they're hunting you down.

Not that I've researched this or anything.

Heart hammering, I slide out Daddy's card, and wrap it

inside the napkin. Then I place both items inside her paper cup. She wakes then, when I am crouched over her. I see the flash of fear and violence.

'Have a good day,' I whisper.

Last time I checked, Daddy had over twenty thousand pounds in his account.

I break into a ten pound note and buy a tube ticket to wherever. End up at Charing Cross. Get off. Look around. Endless CCTV cameras. Hordes of homeless people gazing dull-eyed at other people's lives.

I get onto the first train I see, just because there's no way I can spend the night alone in London, and I need to sit down. I need to stop.

Stop.

Have you ever felt like that, Beanie? Like you want to step out of your life, just for a second, and take stock? I bet you haven't. You have a nice, normal life, with nice, normal parents. A father who is boozy and brusque and humorous. A mother who's something high up in some charity. A perfect home and a perfect life. You don't come home to find the Handbag's redecorated the drawing room so that it looks like Night of the Living Room Hell with matching swags and bows and cushions. You don't have to remove your dad's tart's hair extensions draped over the back of the brand-new hideous sofa before you sit down. At exeat weekends, when it's time to get collected, your family's car always arrives first.

This train is headed to Ashford, somewhere in Kent. I squash in behind a lady with a little girl and take out my Little Kit of Happiness.

A plaster to heal you when you hurt.

A diamond to bring a sparkle to your eye.

A Love Heart sweet so you know that someone loves you.

A rubber to erase those little mistakes you make.
A piece of string to hold it together in tough times.
A marble for when you start losing yours.

I place them all neatly on the fold-out table. Then there are the extra things, the ones I've added. There's your head girl badge. I don't know why I took it. Sometimes I just take things. It's like they're little pieces of other people that make me feel like I'm someone too. Wearing the badge makes me feel like I belong somewhere.

I unfold the newspaper clipping of me and my pony, Spook, cheek to cheek after winning at the gymkhana last summer. I try not to think of him, with those ridiculous pink feathers bobbing about on his head. Will he be pulling her Cinderella carriage at this very minute, with her all squashed inside like a giant jellyfish?

And there's the button, still with its little twist of silk thread where I cut it from the Handbag's dress. But what I'm looking for is at the very bottom, tightly folded so that it is no bigger than a stamp.

There she is, the image of me.

My mother.

She's staring a little past the photographer, as if there's something of unfathomable interest beyond. She has my face, my jawline. My chin. She's dark as a gypsy, beautiful and strong. You can't really tell from this photograph, but I am sure that she has strong wrists, thick ankles.

My mother is wearing a gold sequinned dress that looks like it is made of fire. She is smiling, dimple-chinned, with bare brown shoulders. Around her neck is a plump-looking python, its head cradled in her left hand. Behind her, a pier stretches out to sea. You can just make out a building on it, which must be the circus. There is a gold label in the corner, with one of its edges curled and worn. You can only read one word, which is: *stings*. I have tried and tried to make out the rest of the letters, but it is impossible.

I know this much about my mother:

I know that she loved the circus. It was her life's dream, and she gave it all up for me.

I know that her name was Bettina, and that she was partly Romanian.

I know that she named me Willow after the trees around our lake.

I know that, when I was three years old, she left us.

That's all.

There aren't many photographs of her. Daddy said he couldn't bear to keep any, but there is this one. It's all I have.

I have only one memory of her.

She is throwing me up to the sky, over and over again. Looking down, I can see her smiling face, the dark eyes half peering over my shoulder. I remember the rush of flying; my hands outstretched to find only air and space. I see the sun tilted on my mother's face, her red painted lips, the golden hairs on her cheeks and upper lip. My mother always wanted me to fly.

'Ready when you are, love.'

I jerk awake. My keepsakes from the Little Kit of Happiness are sliding over the pull-out table. I push them all back into the bag.

'Sorry – can you give me a minute?' I say. The ticket-checker shrugs and moves to the woman with her little girl. I grab my bag and slide out of my seat; hurry into the next carriage.

'Hey,' shouts the guard. 'Where d'you think you're going?'

So I jump out at the next station. Vault the ticket barrier. And this time I really do fly.

Contortionist

The first ones to stop are a family from Kent.

I feel relief when I see them. They look like they've just come back from Disneyland, Paris; the kids on the back seat are wedged in with Chip and Dale and Dumbo. The little girl's dressed as Elsa from *Frozen*.

'Rounded off the trip with a weekend in London,' says the dad.

Luckily, it's a people carrier, one of those vans that Happy Families usually take on holiday, so I find myself in the front with Happy Father. Happy Mother is in the back, trying to bottle-feed her baby. I am shoved between a pink broomstick and a flight case in the shape of a crocodile.

'Call me Julie,' the mum says. That's all she says before she shoves the bottle back in the baby's face and tells the boy off for wearing his sister's Elsa tiara.

'What's he like?' smiles the dad, rolling his eyes.

He asks me what music I like, and where I'm going.

'Anywhere south,' I say. I've decided to try to get a cheap ferry crossing to somewhere like Calais. Will I need a pass-port for that? I really don't know.

'And music?'

I tell him that I don't mind. He ums and ahs, and finally settles on Ellie Goulding, sitting back with a pleased sort of sigh when he's done choosing.

'So what's a well-spoken girl like you doing hitch-hiking, if you don't mind me asking?' he asks, in a low voice. 'Can't be too careful, you know.' He winks.

I stare out of the window. Behind me, the boy and the girl are having a fight, and the Good Dinosaur keeps shoving its head through the seat well. We're on the motorway, and I feel a surge of exhilaration at speeding further away from them all, from my old self, all the lies, the Handbag.

'I'm actually taking part in a sort of game show,' I say. 'Like the one that's been on television. I have to see how far I can get without being tracked. It's for charity,' I add.

I feel him rise to the challenge. 'Do you hear that, Julie?' he shouts, above the mayhem. His son's still got his sister's tiara. Julie, of course, doesn't hear anything, not with Elsa roaring to her brother to let it go. 'We'll have to see how we can help you, love.' He winks again. 'I'm sure we can think of something.'

'Something' is a sofa in their house.

The Carters live in a boxy-looking house on a housing estate. All the roads are named after detectives. It's all very *bijou*, the sort of thing the Handbag would love. I've told them my name is Beanie, and that I'm at uni.

After they've shown off their new conservatory, and pointed out the units in their new kitchen, Julie goes upstairs to put the kids to bed and Terry comes into the sitting room with two glasses of wine.

'How old are you, love, if you don't mind me asking?' he says.

'Nineteen,' I lie. I take a large slurp of wine. It's disgusting, cheap plonk. 'Yummy,' I say.

'Lovely,' says Terry, and I'm not sure if he's talking about the wine or me. I wish you and Miffy could be here, Beanie. You'd be pissing yourselves over Terry's attempts at seduction while all hell breaks out upstairs. Julie sounds like she needs some help. There are high-pitched screams over the sound of running bath water.

'Families, eh?' smiles Terry. He leans back comfortably, his arm laid loosely over the back of the cream leather sofa. I'm sure if I look at him he'd be winking again.

I sip my wine.

When Julie comes back down, Terry sends her into the kitchen to put some dinner on. I go into the kitchen to help her and to escape from Terry's trailing arm.

She's pouring a jar of pasta sauce onto some cooking mince, yawning.

I help her put the spaghetti on and pour her a glass of wine, because Terry seems to have forgotten her.

'So, how long have you got to be on the run for?' she asks. She's pulled on her night clothes, a horrible pair of droopy green leggings and a baggy grey T-shirt. She has a scratch on one cheek from where the baby's probably clawed her mid-scream.

Julie rips open a packet of garlic bread and shoves some in the oven. The mince is burning, so I turn it down. I am playing the role of high-flying student, doing something zany for charity. I enjoy it while it lasts. It helps me to forget who I really am.

In the night, Terry comes down, as I knew he would.

He's panting nervously, and there's a creak as he sits on the sofa. I feel, rather than see, his hand grope for me.

'Touch me and I'll fucking kill you,' I say in a clear voice.

Stupid old perv doesn't know that I'm an old hand at dealing with this. I've run away many times before.

Schoolgirl Runaway, Aged Twelve

The fifth time I run away from school, it is raining, so I don't stay out long.

By the time I get back to the school lodge, Mrs Threshbold is waiting for me by an unmarked police car with DC Scallion. I like DC Scallion the best. I call her Scally for short, because I feel like we're old friends, we've known each other for so long. All the girls at St Jerome's call each other by nicknames.

She puffs out her breath when she sees me struggling with my rucksack up the school drive.

Because she's a detective, she can wear her own clothes instead of police uniform, and her skirt is a bit too tight over her hips and tummy. There's something about her that makes me think that if she had a tattoo, it'd be a huge one, and if she could choose, she wouldn't be wearing those boring black shoes, but ones which are red and shiny and fabulous.

'Where the effin' heck have you been this time, Willow Bettina Stephens?' she asks.

She's the only person who ever uses my middle name. No one at school knows it.

'You've led us a right old dance.'

I open my mouth to speak, but my head feels swimmy all of a sudden. Mrs Threshbold looks like she wants to make me carve my punishment in my own blood, like Dolores Umbridge in *Harry Potter*.

'None of our girls has ever…' she splutters.

It's Scally who catches me when I fall.

'There, now,' she says, her arms all warm and solid. 'There

now.' I feel her large hands patting me on the back.

I squirm out of her grip. 'Where is he?' I demand. 'Where's Daddy?'

I can't see his sports car anywhere on the drive. They must have contacted him by now, surely?

Scally sighs. 'Let's get you inside, lovey.' Then, to Mrs Threshbold, 'Get this girl some hot cocoa, will you?'

Scally stays while I have my hot chocolate and biscuits, and then she checks her phone again.

'My kids will wonder where I am,' she says. 'I've left messages for your dad, love. He knows you're safe and sound, don't worry.'

She starts to lecture me on safety and risk and responsibility. I'm not listening, though.

All I can think of is Daddy, and why he never comes to catch me.

Night Owl

When Terry's gone, I tuck up my knees under my borrowed duvet, and stroke the picture of my mother. I try to uncurl the tight roll of the label at the corner, but if there were any more letters, they have long faded away.

At four in the morning, Julie comes down with the baby. I hear the ping of the microwave and several huge yawns. The baby's making strangled kitten cries. Another yawn.

I find Julie leaning against the worktop with her eyes closed. The baby's shoved under her T-shirt, and she's holding a bottle under the tap.

'Too hot,' she says, without opening her eyes. 'I'm trying to get her used to formula, but I made it too hot.' She begins to cry. She shifts the baby to her other breast with a loud plop.

I make her a cup of tea.

'He never helps,' she sobs, letting me sit her on a bar stool. The kitchen's too small for a table and chairs. I decide not to mention the little night episode with Terry. She wipes her eyes with the kitchen roll I give her. 'Will you take her a minute? I need the loo —'

And I am left holding a hot, heavy bundle. The baby is an ugly one, I decide. But then it opens its eyes and gives a wide, gummy smile. I smell the top of its head and breathe in its sweet, warm milkiness.

I wonder if my mother ever did that to me.

It is as Julie is taking the baby from me that I see it.

The pictures on the kitchen wall are pretend-vintage railway posters in cheap black frames, advertising different places to visit. The one in the centre shows a pier and a wide beach and a plump, jolly couple with two plump, jolly children in tow. The pier is long and strutted with a large white Victorian building in the middle. Beneath it, curly letters invite passengers to *Visit Hastings*.

It looks exactly like the one in my mother's photo.

I stare at the reddened cheeks of the father with his knotted handkerchief, the mother with her picnic baskets. I stare again at the pier, and at the script beneath it. In front of me, the baby gives a gentle burp.

'Are you OK, Beanie?' Julie is looking at me curiously. 'You've gone really pale —'

Hastings.

Ha — *stings*.

I know now where my mother was a circus girl. I know what the missing letters are.

Because snakes don't sting, do they?

Of course they don't.

Street-Walker

Next morning, Julie makes Terry drive me to Hastings.

He is tight-faced on the way, and there is no Ellie Goulding this time. I make sure that I sit in the back. There is something digging into me. I pull it out, and it's a broken Elsa tiara.

Terry drops me off by the seafront. *St Leonards*, a sign says.

'This is as far as I'm going.' It's the first time Terry's spoken to me since I got in the car. Ellie's been replaced by Talk Sport; I've had miles of middle-aged bores ringing in and giving endless analyses of endless football matches. 'I'll be late for work now,' he tuts, rummaging in his briefcase. He's wearing a pink shirt, red tie combo that does nothing for his pot belly. Disney Dad has been replaced by Business Man.

He doesn't help me with my rucksack, and slams the door shut the moment I am outside.

'Bye, arsehole!' I call after him. He doesn't look round.

I watch as he drives off with a rev of testosterone.

Fine. I don't care.

I try to get my location. The rain spits and I am by the sea. I hitch my rucksack higher and follow the promenade. The sea is a muddy olive, kicking up little white curls. The wind ruffles my hair.

Rule #5: *Have no plan. Be spontaneous.*

I am free and I have money and can do whatever I want.

I shift my rucksack onto my shoulders and, keeping the sea on my right, head for Hastings.

There are Georgian houses on my left, and a long, pebbled beach to my right. Some girls pass me, about my age, in spotty wellies, wearing flowery shorts and quilted jackets. They seem a world away from me. I sit on a wall and eat the packet of crisps I stole from Julie's cupboard for breakfast. There's a box of crackers too, and a banana, still with its label on.

A police car passes, and I duck my head instinctively.

I expect that Daddy will have called them now. And our intrepid Scally will be hot on the trail. She'll be wondering, won't she, where I've headed to this time?

I pull out my notepaper, and shake the rest of the crisps into my mouth.

First, the pier. I can see it in the distance, old and grand and regal-looking even from this far away. It's where I'll go to next, to see if it still has the circus shows, like the one my mother must have performed in.

I feel like I have come home.

Dear Beanie,

You'd like Hastings. It's all sea air, Victorian street lamps and promenades.

I mean, I know my mother's not going to still be here, obviously. She'll be in Las Vegas now probably, or somewhere exotic, like Russia or China, twisting and somersaulting and back-flipping over the scented sawdust, spinning in that gold dress.

There'll be a reason she never came back home. But, just to be here, breathing the same air, and getting an idea of the world she lived in before she had me — it makes me feel closer to her, as if she's my guiding spirit. She's in the clouds and the sky and the sea. I'll feel even more connected once I've achieved my aim.

Because I've decided that I'm going to join the circus.

That's right, Beanie, I'm going to be a performer! I'm going to make my living by making people crane their necks, and suck in their breath and gasp in wonder. It's like it's all fated, somehow. Why I can climb and ride and do gymnastics: it's all for a reason. It's because it's in the blood.

I need to find a job first, I expect. I've never had one before, have you? I mean, I need to be careful with my gap year money, obvs. Mustn't use it up too soon. Don't worry about me missing my exams, Beanie. They're not important any more, honestly.

First I'll look for somewhere to stay, and then I'll ask around for where auditions and things are held for the pier show. Can you imagine it, Beanie? Me in a gold sequinned dress, spinning, spinning, at the top of the roof, with the spotlights and sawdust and glitter...

Just imagine.

Wills x

Foxtrot

I don't send it to you, of course. Wouldn't do to let anyone at home know my whereabouts. Rule #4: *Never tell anyone where you are. Never contact home. Don't rely on friends.* Three ticks for me so far then.

I hitch my rucksack onto the other shoulder and start to hurry towards Hastings Pier.

It is empty. A shell.

The wooden floor planks look newly oiled, and there is a little information hut at its entrance, but other than that it is completely empty: no Hansel and Gretel gingerbread houses with curly roofs, no shops selling seaside rock and popcorn and starfish. And there certainly isn't a circus.

I pull out my mother's picture, and trace the line of the grand-looking Victorian building at the pier's centre. That must have been where she performed, I think. It's the only building big enough.

I push open the door of the information hut and go in.

A man is painting his nails black and talking on his phone.

'What happened to it?' I say. 'What happened to the pier?' I push my photograph at him. I don't care that he hasn't finished his call. This is supposed to be his job, isn't it?

He glances at it, and waves his hand towards the back of the little shop.

There, on the wall, are several large colour photographs of the pier. In all of them, it is on fire: flames engulf the whole length of it, apart from the struts where it's planted into the sea. The grand central building and all of the shops along it are blackened skeletons. In one of the pictures, a crowd has gathered on the beach to watch.

'2010,' says the man. He's finished his call now, and has come to stand behind me. 'A couple of kids left their fags burning, and *whoosh!* Up it went. The council had only just raised the funds to regenerate it too.'

'What happened to the circus?' I say.

He raises a pierced eyebrow. 'There's never been a circus there. The ballroom you see in the middle was used for tea dances and stand-up comedians. That's about it.' He pushes the photograph back to me and suppresses a yawn. You can tell he wants to go back to whatever he was doing on his phone.

'Well, *are* there any circuses in Hastings?' I ask.

He shrugs. 'You could ask at the Art Café,' he says. He nods towards a leaflet on a stacked stand. 'Oh, and there's the grand opening of the pier, I suppose. There'll be performances and stuff then. I think there's meant to be a tightrope…'

He gets up and passes me a flyer. There's a clown on it with tufts of black hair above each ear. A leather-clad couple balancing on something called the Wheel of Death. Chinese acrobats on a unicycle. But what transfixes me is the beautiful lady in the gold mask and gold dress, swinging in a hoop. She is the image of my mother.

My breathing quickens as I read:

Walk on Air! Play with Fire! Find Your Inner Clown!
We are looking for talented performers to join our show for
the Grand Opening of Hastings Pier. The World's Only
Pop-Up Circus!
Come find us at the Art Café. Auditions at 9a.m., 10 May.

Then I frown. That's two weeks away. I'll need to find a job first. When I've found somewhere to live, of course.

But once I'm settled, I will become a performer.

It won't be long before I'll know how to fly.

Schoolgirl Missing, Aged Ten

We watch the gold lady fly.

Beanie likes her gold shoes and I admire her long shining hair. We each hold a lollipop as big as our heads and we are wearing matching glitter nail varnish and butterfly face paint.

Daddy has paid for this birthday treat. I squeeze up close to him, feeling the warmth of him through his business suit. He smells of the men's perfume that Nikki, his PA, buys for him.

Beanie didn't believe me when I told her I was having a circus in my garden. Now she has to. I hope she tells Miffy and Lexy and all of the others about this being the best birthday party ever.

The flying lady grabs the swing as it passes and flips herself upside down. Her wrists are trembling, but she manages to hold herself straight before she gracefully does the splits and swivels on one hand, high up in the ring.

'That's my mother up there,' I tell Beanie.

She turns round to look at me. Her breath is huffy with strawberries.

'Don't be silly. You told me your mother's dead.'

'No, it's true. Mummy's a circus performer. Daddy said that I have to keep it a big secret, but I'm telling you because you're my very best friend.'

Beside me, Daddy is shuffling. Nikki has her hand in his lap and is probably stealing his popcorn or something, which is a cheek after Daddy's paid for it all. Daddy breathes heavily for a while, and then murmurs something into Nikki's ear, but I can't hear what.

I keep my voice low. 'She had to leave because she got so successful. She's literally the best acrobat that Russia's ever seen. So, Daddy made me promise not to tell anyone, ever. But once a year, on my birthday, she comes back, especially to perform for me.'

Beanie breathes out a sigh, eyes shining. 'That's perfectly lovely,' she says. 'You're so lucky, Wills.'

I like it when she calls me Wills. All of the girls at school have nicknames for their best friends. Even the favourite teachers have them.

'She's beautiful, isn't she?' I whisper, and I feel her nod.

We watch her flip and twist, ending in a spin that makes us hold our breaths. I notice how the spotlight picks the acrobat out exactly. How it catches the glitter on her costume and turns it into fire.

I want to do that. I can already do the splits because I've been practising every day since the last time we had the circus in our garden. I stand on my points every day too, like the ballet dancers at Sadler's Wells.

There's a shifting movement next to me, and Daddy and Nikki are both getting up to leave. I wonder why they haven't taken their popcorn with them.

The flying lady is right up in the roof now, where the pigeons are.

'Your mother's bloody brilliant, isn't she?' sighs Beanie next to me. Her breath is all sticky-smelling from the lolly.

'Bloody brilliant,' I agree, but my mind's on Daddy and Nikki. I wonder where they've gone.

Then the gold lady somersaults through the air and does a perfect landing, bowing and smiling.

Beanie and I clap loudest of all.

Afterwards, we get to have a special tea party with the circus performers. A clown on stilts lifts Beanie high in the air as everyone claps, and I try to look pleased. Nikki has had to go back home to her babysitter, so it's just Daddy again, which is how I like it. I turn to ask him if I can have a go with the stilt walker, but he's off talking to the gold lady.

She's even more beautiful closer up. Her hair is piled in curls around her face, which is made up in shiny pinks and golds. Her costume has hardly any front, and plunges all the way down to her tummy button, which is pierced with a star. Daddy has bought her a tall, clear drink with ice and lemon in it. When she laughs, her teeth are perfect and white. Daddy has a moon-shaped lipstick mark on his cheek which makes him look silly.

Beanie nudges me. 'Go and say hello to her,' she says.

'I can't do that,' I say. 'I told you, it's a secret.'

But she pushes me towards them, and now they're both looking at me.

'It's the birthday girl,' Daddy laughs. His voice is slurry. 'Having a good time?'

'Can I have a picture?' I say to the lady. In front of us, Beanie is waving and holding up her phone to take a picture. The lady looks surprised, but crouches down and we both stare into the lens. I press up close against her and put my arm around her, so that she has to do the same.

I know at once she's not my mother. Her wrists are too thin, and she smells horrid, of too-strong perfume and cigarettes. The drink that Daddy's given her has made her breath all nasty. This close, her skin's marked with little holes where she's once had spots and her makeup's trying to cover them up.

She lets me go the minute the picture's done. I am glad.

'What will you wish for?' Beanie asks me, when we're all crowding around my cake. It's a big top one, and even has pink and yellow bunting around the entrance.

I look towards the open tent flap, where I can still hear Daddy and the gold lady laughing.

When I blow the candles, I watch them flicker out, one by one.

There's only one thing I ever wish for, and that hasn't happened yet.

Sea Spray

Rule #5: *Have no plan. Be spontaneous.*

So I literally choose a guesthouse based purely on the colour of its door.

Green, I think. I'll go to the next green one.

The door to Number Six, Portland Square turns out to be Shrek-green, and the paint's peeling at its base. The sign on the door says *Sea Spray*. Lace curtains hang at each sash window, tied with baby-blue ribbons. There are stickers all over the lower panes, saying *No Cold Callers here!* and *Say No to Europe!*

It doesn't look very nice.

The landlady is called Mrs Fox. She gives me a lipstick-toothed smile and says that I need to pay for the next week's accommodation up front – 'because of the holiday season just starting, dear. We do have a lot of bookings, and I'd hate for you to lose your room. What did you say you did again, dear?'

'I'm a performer,' I say firmly. 'Mostly in the circus. I'm in the process of looking for work, but I'll find some very soon.' I pull out my brown envelope to show that I'm serious about staying.

Her eyes slide to the crisp twenties that I'm easing out. 'Well, that's very nice, I'm sure. We don't tend to get a lot of those. We get a lot of artists, though, and writers – what you might call creative types – but no circus performers as yet.' She stops to draw breath. Taps something into her computer. Then tells me a figure which makes me swallow hard and wish I hadn't handed Daddy's gold card to the homeless girl at Paddington.

'That can't be right, can it?' I say. 'That's not what it says on your tariff.' I point at the list hanging above a doily-draped hall table.

'An extra week's deposit in the tourist season,' she says. Her tongue flickers over her lipsticky teeth. 'You'll find it's the same elsewhere, dearie.'

I decide I'll pay for a week. I'll have a job by the end of it and can afford to go somewhere better. I count out the cash while she watches me. I smile brightly at her.

'Well, I'll get your key, then,' she says. 'Please respect our house rules: no smoking, no radio, no baths after five, no showers before six, breakfast is from seven thirty – but there's no kippers tomorrow, not on a Thursday – no carousing, no canoodling, no coming in after eleven, no eating in your room – unless it's the bourbon creams we provide – no pets, no poker, no alcohol on the premises, no –'

I stop her in mid-flow. 'And my key?' I say.

Mrs Fox scowls, and reaches over to a rack of hooks. The key, when she passes it to me has a large see-through plastic tag with the number 11 etched into it.

'Upstairs and first on your left,' she says.

She goes back to reading her *Daily Mail*, but I feel her eyes tracking me all the way across the hall carpet and up the creaking stairs.

I spend a long time staring at the room that is my new home. Then I swallow, take out my notepaper, and sink onto the groaning bed.

Dear Beanie,

You wouldn't believe where I'm staying: a sort of bed and breakfast/boarding house. Beanie, you should see it. Hilarious! Think Bates Motel meets The League of Gentlemen and you get the general idea. My bedroom's next to a tiny bathroom that's smaller than the ones we have in our stable, and the bath's literally filled with curly black hairs. Like someone's killed a million spiders. There are rows of dolls, Beanie, staring at me with glassy eyes. And the landlady! She's called Mrs Fox (AKA the Fox) and she's like the one in the Roald Dahl story who stuffs her guests with sawdust and props them up on the top floor. I'll have to make sure she doesn't make me sign the guest book...

It's squashed in the end of town which is filled with tat shops and clapperboard houses and dab sandwiches. Dab's a sort of fish, which they fillet here and shove between two pieces of bread and butter. You're supposed to eat it with vinegar. You'd love it — I can hear your voice now. 'Wills — that's literally sooo pseudo-ironic,' you'd say.

Anyway, I'm off to find a job now — keep your fingers crossed for me. Love you!
Wxx

Street Act

Below me, the streets wind. Blue plaques on the houses state which poet or artist or writer lived there. Families tug each other along. Dogs. Toddlers. Friends. A girl sits in the sunshine, absorbed in drawing in chalks on the pavement, a tangle of friendship bracelets by her side. Seagulls shrill and wheel. Below, the sea.

Hastings Old Town is a maze of thrift shops. There are yards full of old tat cast off from people's lives. Rule #5: *Have no plan. Be spontaneous.* If you're random one day, be organised the next. Never know what you are going to do yourself, because if you don't know, how on earth is anyone else going to know? How will Scally know, if I don't even know myself?

So my new look is: no look. Totally unplanned. I end up with a long coat made of mustard-coloured velvet and a pair of battered scarlet Dr Martens. I also buy a stripy leotard and a ballet tutu. The only rule is: no rules. Things that I'd never dream of wearing in my past life. Things that the Handbag would never wear.

I think of the pretty, ditsy dresses I used to buy with Beanie. Willow wore what Beanie wore. Except that Beanie liked to wear stuff her granny had passed down from the forties and fifties, proper vintage finds from trunks lurking in her family's attic, whereas Willow had to buy brand new. She thought that made her better, before she realised that it was simply *nouveau*. That all the girls could see through her.

'*Oh my god, you're so nouveau, Wills. I love it!*' Beanie's voice, bubbling with glee.

I switch her off; realise that I am starting to think of myself in the third person. Does that mean I am going mad?

I pay the owner, a whiskery old lady smoking an antique pipe, and then sit on a bench in the sunshine while I tie up the laces on my cherry boots. I roll down the top of the brown envelope and push it back inside my bag's lining, deep as it will go. My new clothes cost me £22.50. I need to be really careful with what's left of my money.

I huddle into my yellow velvet coat, and wind my way to the seafront. I walk past the ghost train, along the shingled beach to where the rotten hulks of fishing boats wait, with their gaping sides and creepy names: *Rosa-Lee Returns, Strange Sally, Black Nancy*. I pass a little stall selling freshly caught fish fillets with bread and vinegar, and a miniature railway and the funicular. It is cold and bright. Early holiday-makers are bravely wearing sunshades and sundresses with winter coats and walking boots.

I think about posting my letter to Beanie, but I can't, because of Rule #4. Finally, I sit on the wall outside the fairground.

A girl is smiling down at me, tanned-skinned, yellow-dreadlocked and dirty-faced. She's taken hold of my wrist and is wrapping coloured silk round it, plaiting rapidly.

'You like it? It'll bring you luck. A gift of friendship.' She has an Australian accent, throaty and twangy.

She holds out my wrist, and it feels strangely disconnected from me, a floating body part. On it, a bracelet made from coloured silks, yellow and black and orange.

My new friend's smile doesn't reach her eyes. She's keeping a check on a battered top hat by her pavement art. Her eyes flit about, perhaps for the police.

'So you'll buy? It's two pounds,' she says, still smiling. Her teeth are short and yellow.

I stare at her hopelessly. 'I don't have any change,' I say.

When her smile hardens, I decide to pay. Reaching inside my bag, I rummage around inside the brown envelope and draw out a handful of coins.

'That's all I have –'

But she's gone, melted away into the crowds. When I see her next, she's binding her threads around the wrist of a little girl in fairy wings, while her parents look on bemusedly.

The first place I try is a coffee shop in the Old Town. I feel bright and confident in my yellow coat. I have a new role now: a performer who's just in need of work while she waits for her big break. There are rows of delicious-looking cakes behind the glass counter: macarons and Florentines and chocolate brownies with bits of gold leaf on top. Early morning business people are sitting over their laptops drinking coffee. Jazz music is playing through the radio. I feel at home here already.

'Good morning.' I smile at the girl who's just come in from the back, drying her hands on her apron. 'I'm looking for a job, and wondered if I could speak to your manager.'

I stand up straight, push my shoulders back. I can see myself adding various flavours of syrup to coffee, serving customers giant white chocolate and cranberry cookies from one of those jars on the counter.

But she's already shaking her head. 'Sorry,' she says. 'We have no job. We are all fully staffed for the holiday season.' She has a Polish accent like our groom, and a tiny tattoo of a daffodil behind her left ear. She lets me fill in a form anyway, and I hesitate over the name, nearly writing 'Willow Stephens' before I catch myself. I fill in Mrs Fox's address, leaving out the postcode, which I don't know.

'You have a mobile number?' she asks.

I shake my head. This is because of Rule #4: *Never tell anyone where you are. Never contact home. Don't rely on friends.*

Mobile phones are one of the easiest ways for police to find out where you are, who you've been in contact with. I have a vague idea that they contain some sort of tracking device, but, however they use them to find fugitives, I do know that they are a definite no for people like me.

'I'm only staying at this address for the next week,' I tell her. 'I'll pop back once you've spoken to your manager.'

I leave her looking doubtful. I know that once I've left, she'll stuff the form with a huge pile of others somewhere, or worse, shove it straight in the bin. I know that I won't come back.

The smell of coffee and homemade scones wafts after me as the door closes.

Money in	Money out	
£1280 (total gap year savings)	2 weeks' rent + deposit at Sea Spray	£490
	Yellow vintage coat	£12
	Red DMs	£5
	Leotard	£2.50
	Tutu	£3
	Friendship bracelet	£2
	Total spent:	£504.50
New total: **£765.50**		

A Little of What You Fancy

There are no jobs in Hastings.

I have scoured the town, and spent £3.75 on a local newspaper and a dab sandwich for lunch. I also spent £3 on a family-sized box of tissues, a multipack of crisps, and a triple pack of lip balm in the pound shop.

Places I tried first:

YumYums, a delicatessen and café.

The Naked Lunch, a vegetarian restaurant.

Birdcage, a vintage clothes shop.

Bill and Pippa's Plaice, a stall selling dab sandwiches.

The Mermaid, a pub by the seafront.

Leaving the Old Town, I walk to the newer shopping centre and try all of the high street shops. No luck in Topshop, River Island, H&M, M&S, Dorothy Perkins, Monsoon, Burtons or New Look. I cross the road by the train station, and try the independent shops along Battle Street. This part of town has a very different feel to the old part. It is full of pawn shops and nail bars and tattoo parlours. I make myself ask for a job in five of the least scary-looking places:

Shoopermarket, a discount shoe shop.

Buy Your Leave, a budget gift shop.

Hastings Famous Pound Shop, a store where everything's a pound or less. (This amazes me. I lose track of time, exploring all of the aisles. Twelve rolls of toilet paper for one pound! Imagine.)

In each of the stores that I go in, my voice rings out too loud and too posh and too confident. Eyes stare as if I've dropped in from another world, and I suppose in a way I have.

In the end, I walk across the pebbled beach to the edge of the sea. I take off my shoes and socks and ease my aching feet into the chilly water.

Afterwards, sitting on the pebbles, I take out my Kit of Happiness. The first item I pull out this time is the head girl badge. I used to take it from Beanie's bedside table and wear it around town when she was off on an exeat weekend and I was not. It made me feel important, I suppose.

Next is the button from the Handbag's wedding dress. I turn it over in my hand, and wonder if they went through with the wedding. Did Daddy even notice I wasn't there to hold up the veil? Absent from all the wedding photos. The absent guest. The missing daughter.

What did she do when she went to put on her dress and it was ruined? Got Martyna, I suppose, to stitch all the buttons back on again while she and her bunch of pleb friends drank Daddy's champagne and topped up their spray tans. I try to feel delight at the thought of the Handbag and her missing buttons, but all I feel is empty.

In a minute, I will sit down and open one of the bags of crisps and read the free ads in the back of the newspaper. If there are no jobs in there, I don't know what I'm going to do.

Dear Beanie,
    Job-hunting in Hastings is a real scream. You'd never believe the places I've been! The best place by far is Hastings Famous Pound Shop (apostrophe not included) which is INCREDIBLE. Truly. I don't know how people can say they're poor when they can buy literally everything they need for only £1 per item. We so need one near school (if I ever come back, that is, which obvs I'm not going to). Imagine

47

all the midnight feasts we'd have, all the biscuits!

And if you ever need a five-pack of plughole debris collectors, then I'm your girl.

I'm having so much fun, Beanie.

Wish you were here.

Wxx

Camera Obscura

'It's for a job,' I say, 'so it's really important that I use your phone.' Mrs Fox puts down her Sudoku puzzle and leafs through a little notebook.

'That'll be five pounds per minute,' she sniffs. 'Calling out on our landline is not in our house rules.'

'Five pounds?' I say. 'Surely you can't charge…'

But she's reached for her biro again, and is writing a number into one of the Sudoku boxes, hissing out heavy coffee breath. I unclench my fingers and draw out a five pound note. Handing it over to her is like a physical pain. I think how many drinks and bread rolls and biscuits I could have bought with that at the pound shop.

Without raising her eyes, Mrs Fox pushes the phone over to me.

I tap in the number rapidly. Should I or should I not wear my ballet tutu? Would it be too much at a first audition? I have dozens of routines I can perform, from all those years doing gymnastics and modern dance at county level. St Jerome's prides itself on its extracurricular opportunities, and it helped fill up the time if I had to stay at school for the holidays.

'Hello?' says a man's voice, with a strong local accent. There's the sound of breathing for a moment, and then a series of beeps, as if he's put his touchscreen against his ear.

'Oh, good morning,' I say. 'My name's Beanie, and I'm a performer. I'd like to audition to be one of your dancers, please.'

I can hear the Fox listening hard. You can tell by the way her pen's stopped scratching at her newspaper.

There's that heavy silence again. Then: 'Auditions, you say?'

'Yes,' I reply impatiently. 'It says in the advert you placed in the *Hastings Bugle*. "Dancers wanted". Well, I'm one. A dancer, I mean.'

I count to five this time. Whoever's on the other end of the line needs a lot of time to register things.

'Are you Tone?' I say, at last.

The man gives a sort of laugh. 'Yes, I'm Tone. So, you're a dancer, you reckon?'

'Yes, I am.' I list all of my awards and achievements, finishing with my grade eight RADA certificate. I wonder how much this call is costing me, whether it's been over a minute yet.

There's a *hoosh* of breath from Tone's end. I write down the address he gives me on a corner of my newspaper. Afterwards, the Fox shows me her phone screen, her fuchsia lips pressed together. She's been timing my call on her stopwatch: 2:58.

She smiles thinly as I hand her two more crisp five pound notes.

Number Five, Quarry Lane doesn't look like the sort of place you'd hold auditions. There are no obvious signs anywhere, and I have to walk up and down the street before I'm sure it's

49

the right one. A broken pushchair sits outside it, and a child's *Finding Nemo* plastic ball.

It's a Victorian terrace with a big bay window at the front, except you can't see inside, because someone's clipped the curtains together with a clothes peg. It must be because of the photographs, to get the lighting right in the room.

I push open the metal gate and walk up to the front door. It opens immediately, and a face peers through a chain.

'Are you the girl for the auditions?' A man's voice, light and high. It's a different voice to Tone's.

'I'm the dancer,' I say. I shiver, despite the yellow coat I'm wearing over my leotard, tutu and leggings.

There's a rattle as he draws the chain, then he stands aside to let me in.

'I was expecting Tone,' I say. I look around. The house is strangely bare; there doesn't appear to be any furniture.

The man in front of me hovers, smiling uncertainly. He's very skinny, with that shoulder stoop that tall people have.

'My name's Patrick.' He holds out his hand, and I shake it, trying not to recoil at its soft dampness. Under the bare bulb, his face glows orange. 'And you are?'

'Beanie,' I say. I look around for somewhere to put my bag. 'Is Tone coming soon?'

He giggles. 'Great name. It's great that you're a dancer. I'm a musician.' He points to the guitar propped up against the stairs. He looks like a musician, I suppose: straggly gingery hair and long thumbnails.

'What do you do – your act, I mean?' he says.

I look at him; he sounds genuinely interested.

He plucks a few flecks of tobacco from his black T-shirt. I notice that his fingers are long and pale.

'Let me guess…trapeze, right?'

I stare at him. Think of my mother, with her strong wrists and wide shoulders that are just like mine.

'I'm right, aren't I? Just that you look kind of strong to me. Strong and powerful.' He has a quick, soft voice, and I decide that he must be shy.

'My mother is a circus performer,' I say. 'And, yes, it was the trapeze. I hope to follow in her footsteps.'

He looks impressed. 'Really? That's really cool. My mother works in the arcade.' Again, that quick, soft laugh. A pause, then: 'Shall we go through?' He nods towards the front room.

I follow him into a room that's dark and empty, apart from a rail of clothes and what looks like a tank on the floor. A photographer's umbrella stands in the corner.

Patrick takes my bag from me. I try not to mind about his long white fingers.

'Is she here?' A voice from behind the umbrella makes me jump.

'Beanie, meet Tone,' says Patrick.

Snake Charmer

'So, are those the costumes?' I ask. 'For the audition?'

Patrick is smiling and nodding. Tone smiles too, showing teeth like hubcaps.

'Ah, the costumes. We have plenty of those, don't we, Patrick?'

Tone is as short as Patrick is tall, and wears shades indoors, which makes me wonder what his eyes look like. He has pale hair, so light it's almost silver in the gloom.

I don't like Tone, and I like Patrick even less. Something about his high voice makes my skin shrink.

Tone shows me a plastic brochure with pull-out photographs. The cover says: *Tony Daiquiri. Publicity. Photography. Promotions.*

'These are my stars,' he says, showing his grey teeth. There are lots of pictures of girls, in soft focus, wrapped in feathers and tilting their heads at the camera. They look strangely old-fashioned, like cigarette cards of forties movie stars.

'All my girls are performers,' he says, rubbing his thumb against the plastic.

'So, shall I dance now?'

Tone snaps into business mode. 'I'll take your promo shots while you, er, audition,' he says. 'A full set, different sizes, will cost you –' He names a price which is a week's lodgings. 'Or you can have the introductory package for fifty quid,' he says. 'Includes my services as your agent, your basic sell sheet, information on all the local gigs. Basically, it's your way in. Includes costume hire as well,' he adds.

'Fifty pounds?' I say. Although that would buy me two nights at Mrs Fox's, it doesn't seem so bad.

'I want to be a trapeze artist,' I say. 'Like my mother.'

'Yeah, yeah, this is your way in. All the shows around here will expect you to have an agent. Having photos gives you the edge.'

The photographs look all right. I riffle through them, and then freeze. One of them is a shot of a girl with a snake around her neck, both of them winking at the camera.

'Ah, that's Lizzie,' says the man. 'She'll cost you extra.'

'Lizzie?' I stare at the photo. This girl is blonde. She's got a bony face and wide pale eyes. She's definitely not my mother.

'Indian Temple Viper. Completely harmless, she's had her fangs removed. But we use her as a prop.'

'So, it's all a fake?' I say, staring down at the photograph.

He nods and laughs. 'You don't think they use actual poisonous ones in the shows, do you? Anyway, time's ticking on, I've got to go out and meet some of my, er, clients later, so you'll have to make up your mind pretty sharpish, love.'

'I'll take the fifty pounds introductory package,' I say, still gazing at the picture. *Maybe my mother came here too,* I think. *Perhaps Tone was her agent.*

'Sure I can't tempt you with the deluxe…? OK, sign here, and we'll take your money up front, please. In cash,' he adds. He has changed from being benevolent Tone. He's taken his shades off, and his eyes look rattish in the light from the anglepoise lamp. I don't want to ask him about my mother.

'In here,' says Tone. 'Take your pick. I'll get the lighting ready.'

I look doubtfully at the few costumes hanging on the rail behind the screen. They all look revealing: a shiny purple bra top with sequins, a cowgirl outfit with tasselled bra top and tasselled boots and not much else, a flapper costume with drooping feathers, a Jungle Jane outfit in snakeskin – no doubt to match Lizzie, who lies stone-like in her tank, looking bored with the whole business.

I choose the flapper dress, just because it seems to have more material than the other ones. Tone hands me a used lipstick in bright red.

'Put this on too, love – and for chrissake smile. Imagine you're in the ring.'

I stand shivering behind the screen, and slowly take my clothes off. I can hear Tone and Patrick talking in low voices. I don't want to be here. I want to be as far away as possible from this horrible place and these horrible men and back in my room at Mrs Fox's, curly hairs or no curly hairs.

But they have my money. And something about Tone's

smile makes me think that there's no way he's going to give it me back.

Slowly, I pull the zip up. This dress smells unwashed, as if hundreds of girls before me have worn it in this seedy little room. I pull off my socks and my cherry DMs and put on the strappy silver sandals that Tone has provided. They are too big, and have faint foot outlines inside, where other feet have sweated and rubbed against them.

Finally, I bend forward and drag the lipstick over my lips. Press them together.

Taking a deep breath, I come out from behind the screen and stand in front of Tone. He is fiddling with something on his camera. There's a rug on the floor that wasn't there before. Patrick is lounging against the wall, biting his nails. His face is in shadow.

Tone points to the rug. 'Lie on that,' he says. 'On your tummy. Tilt your head in your hands…that's right.'

I do as he says, feeling foolish. It's cold in this room, and my arms are nubbed with goosebumps. The rug doesn't smell very nice. 'Shall I do my dance routine now?' I say, when he has finished.

'Can you do any circus moves? Do the splits? Stand on your hands? Anything like that?'

'I can stand on my hands,' I say.

He nods behind the camera.

When I balance, I am aware of my skirt falling around my arms, the feathers tickling my arms. My ridiculous heels waving in the air.

'Good, good,' says Tone. He is a long time taking the pictures.

'Can I get down now?' I say.

'Sure, why not, lovey?' He sounds a little breathless.

I stand, scowling, and flinch when something heavy and

dry is placed around my neck. It is Lizzie. She wags her head at me, flickering her black tongue.

'We'll throw her in complimentary,' says Tone. 'That's it, smile, love. Hold still.' His hand crawls round to adjust her position, and I recoil at the feel of it against my throat.

'All right, all right. Twitchy little thing, aren't you? You'll have to get used to this, love.'

Tone lifts Lizzie from my neck, and starts to coil her around my arm.

I jump back. 'Stop. That's enough. I don't want you to take any more.'

'But what about the close-ups?' says Tone. His hooded eyes make me think of a lizard. In the shadowed corner, I see Patrick's thin leg tapping.

'No close-ups,' I say. I look around for my clothes.

Tone makes a sad face. 'Up to you, lovey,' he says, licking his lips with a spitty sound. I push past him, and start to get dressed. Behind the screen, I hear Patrick say something, and Tone laughs. It sounded like 'school-ish'.

'When do I get the prints?' I say, pulling my yellow coat on.

Tone winks. 'Call back in a couple of days. We'll have them for you. Won't we, Patrick?'

Patrick's leg jiggles.

Dear Beanie,
    So I finally got the publicity shots!!
    They are literally amazing— you wouldn't rec-
ognise me. I am wearing the most divine costumes.
Talk about glamour! A professional makeup artist
did my face, then it was the turn of the stylist to
transform my hair. Finally, the costume...

Let me describe it. Think gold, gold and more gold, and you get the general idea. You know the dress you wanted for the last summer ball, but Miffy beat you to it? Well, it's even better than that! There are about a million tiny glass beads, all threaded into the fabric, which is light as a spider's web, because when I finally get to perform, obviously I can't have anything too heavy, not when I'm doing a double toe-loop in mid-air!

Anyway, I've got to go. You wouldn't believe the amount of rehearsals they get us to do. All of my muscles ache. It's literally heaven to soak in a hot shower at the end of each day...

Love you! Miss you!
Wills x

Money in	Money out	
£765.50 (gap year savings)	1 *Hastings Bugle*	£0.80
	1 dab sandwich with vinegar	£2.95
	3 items from pound shop	£3
	3 minutes' phone call at Sea Spray	£15
	Tony Daiquiri Promotions	£50
	Total spent:	£71.75
New total: £693.75		

Transcript of Telephone Conversation between DS Tracy

Scallion and Willow Stephens, Monday 9 May 2016 at 4.07A.M.

Willow: Hello?

Scallion: Who is this?

Willow: Hello? [pause] Scally?

Scallion: [sound of movement] Willow Stephens? Is that you?

[long pause]

Scallion: Willow, love?

Call ends.

Inner Clown

The auditions are 10 May. Today.

I slide the circus leaflet back into my Kit of Happiness.

I have been practising my stretches and gymnastics exercises when I can, in my room. It is time, I think. Time to show them all what I'm made of. Because it's my life, isn't it? And it's high time that I was the star of my own show.

The Art Café is filled with hippies selling rip-off jewellery and nicely spoken families drinking freshly made smoothies and real coffee. A girl in a clown costume stands talking to a child in dungarees and a beanie hat.

I feel self-conscious in my leotard and tutu. A girl with pink hair and a nose piercing is stretching. When she bends down, she has a thigh tattoo: painted swirls and hothouse flowers. I look down at my stripy leotard. Wish it wasn't so prim.

I pull out a paper ticket from a machine like the ones on the deli counter in supermarkets, and sit down.

Music sounds, low and shuddering. I look up, wonder where it's coming from. A group of musicians stands deep in the shadows, their chins hugging violins, closing their eyes as if all the sadness in the world is in their hearts. A large woman in a gypsy dress comes forward, lifts up her face and starts singing. She stands, and gives herself up to her song, strange and pain-filled and yearning, arms clasped across her chest. Her voice kills me. When she's done, she drops her head, as if exhausted, showing the white parting in her black hair, curved like a crescent moon.

'Romany singers,' says a woman, brightly. She's wearing a coloured headscarf like a Russian peasant, but her accent is Home Counties. 'They're wonderful, aren't they? They add a real feel of authenticity, don't you think?' She claps enthusiastically when they're done, when the last haunting note has melted away. 'Are you here for the auditions?'

I nod, but she's already moved off to chat to a pair of clowns, who are dressed identically, except one is in head-to-toe black, the other in white. There is a makeshift stage rigged up, with real sawdust, and a few wooden seats. A girl in a sports bra and leg warmers is dancing with her dog as she plays the flute.

'Not very good, is she?' At first I think it is the child in dungarees talking to me, but then I realise that he's not a child at all, but a young man, his trouser legs rolled up at the ankles. I flush. He cannot be much over four feet tall. 'What is your act?' He has an accent that is somehow familiar. Then I realise that he sounds just like one of my old au pairs.

'Are you Bulgarian?' I ask, then kick myself. Rule #6: *Never display interest in other people. Do not draw attention to yourself.*

But he looks pleased. 'Yes, yes, I am. From Sofia, although my family all come from Plovdiv.'

Plovdiv. Sounds like a strange, alien place. I realise suddenly that in all the years I've known her, I've never once asked Martyna where her family's from.

He's leaning forward, this man, eyes twinkling in his ugly-handsome face. 'Your act?' he repeats. 'Clowning? Mime? Acrobatics?'

I consider. 'Gymnastics, and a bit of modern dance thrown in,' I say. 'I do a bit of everything, really.'

He nods, and his mouth twitches. 'And where did you train?'

I shrug my shoulders. 'Oh, here and there, you know – the usual places.'

Because I'm not exactly going to say 'at school', am I?

He gets up, and once again I am struck by how short he is. I meet his eyes, and feel that, somehow, he's laughing at me.

'I'm Kristiyan, Kit for short,' he says. 'No pun intended. Good luck with the show.'

I realise that he's waiting for me to introduce myself, and for an awful moment, I nearly say 'Willow'.

'I'm Frog,' I say. 'Pleased to meet you.' And I watch him saunter onto the stage, raise his hand to someone at the side, and catch juggling pins, one after the other. Once again, the music swells, at first low and heartbreaking, then zithering into a frenzy as Kit throws the pins faster and faster, higher and higher.

I stare at the number being chalked up on the board above the bar: 17. I am number 20. I begin to feel the signs again, the tingling palms, the racing heart. Close my eyes and take deep breaths.

'You all right, love? You look a bit peaky.' It's the barman, friendly-looking, bearded, carrying a clutch of glasses. 'Can I get you anything?'

I breathe out. 'Just water, please,' I manage to say. I watch Kit finish his act by juggling chairs.

When the water comes, I pinch out two of my tablets and swallow them quickly, watching the number being scrubbed out and changed to 18.

It's the pink-haired girl's turn. She has what looks like a wolf's tooth through her ear lobe, and a tattoo of Pierrot across her entire neck. She is very good. She performs a mime act, both clever and bittersweet.

'Trained in Paris,' Kit tells me. 'School of mime.' He's back from his performance, sweating and slightly red-faced.

I nod, quickly. My throat feels tight. Inside my coat pocket, I hold Mother's photograph, turning it over and over in my hand. I close my eyes and picture my her face, those laughing dark eyes, her warm, strong hands throwing me into the sun, the clouds, freedom.

'I said, it's your turn. Number twenty, yes?'

A woman is hovering over me. She wears a silver tracksuit and a scowl. Her long dark hair is scraped back into a high ponytail, and she could be either thirty or fifty. Behind her, two floppy-fringed boys are stumbling out of the ring, each holding a unicycle, laughing.

Numbly, I hand over my ticket. She nods at the musicians, who take their places around the ring. One of them spits on his hands.

The music is yearning and haunting, but I am not.

I try to remember my gymnastics routine from last year. Begin to mix in a few dance steps, then change my mind. I am terrible, and that knowledge makes me more so. I see Kit look away, and think, he is doing this to spare my feelings, and I am mortified. I slow cartwheel around the edge of the circle. I try to remember my moves from when I was in the gymnastic shows at county level. I stand on my hands and wobble.

In desperation, I go down into sideways splits. At least I can show them I am flexible, I think.

But even this fails dully. I seem to have seized up since I was last performing in class, and my thick, ugly legs in their black tights stick stubbornly halfway.

The dark-haired woman raises her arm. *Enough!* But I keep going, I won't stop. She's turning away, uninterested. I start to feel frantic. I need them to see what I can do.

'I haven't finished,' I call. I slide my feet further and further away from each other until the tendons in my inner thighs are protesting.

Burn. Snap. Stretch.

I force my legs to keep sliding. The silky, scratchy sawdust pushes between my fingers as I place them on the ground to steady myself. It smells like sun and rain and eucalyptus oil.

Squeeze. Push. Force. Tears squeeze out of my eyes as fire burns through my tendons. Lower and lower. Both Kit and the clown girl are looking now.

'Enough,' the girl says. 'You are not ready.'

But I don't stop, not even for the tiniest of breaks in the pain. If my legs do not snap, they will splinter. Still I press down. I groan, breath coming in shallow rasps. The ground is only centimetres away.

'I said, stop!' the girl yells. 'Next.'

The music withers and dies.

Lions' Den

A boy in a feather boa opens Tone's door. He has a thin, pointy face and bruised-looking eyes.

'Welcome to the party,' he says, and his voice is slurred. I push past him and into Tone's living room. This time it is full of people and a thick fog of smoke. Some are in a circle, sitting on the rug and bending their heads over a cigarette that they're passing around. There is a sweet, acrid smell in the room. By the curtain, a girl is dancing in slow motion, dressed in the Jungle Jane outfit. She has dirty hair and dirtier feet.

'Where's Tone?' I say. 'Where's Patrick?'

'Heeeeey, Beanie. Make way for Beanie.' It's Patrick's voice. He's sitting hunched over a bong. He waves at me, then looks at his hand, as if fascinated.

I push out of the room and cross the hall through to the back room. This may have been a kitchen, but now it is empty of units. There are two or three tanks like the one that contained Lizzie, and a battered old sofa. A couple are moaning and sighing on top of it.

One of them is Tone. I go up to him and tap him on the shoulder.

'I've come for the photos,' I say. 'You said you'd have them ready.'

He pulls his face away from the girl's hair, and bares his grey teeth at me. 'What photos, love? Can't you come back later?'

'No. I need them now. You promised.' And I listen to my voice, with its boarding-school vowels and petulance.

Tone points to a grubby poly-pocket on top of one of the snake tanks. There's a couple of pictures of me with a smear of red lipstick, tilting my head coquettishly, and a few leaflets spill out. They look just like the ones at the pier information centre.

'What's this?' I say.

Words mumbled into the girl's hair: '…introductory package…'

'Where are the rest of them?' I remember the time spent standing on my hands, and suddenly I don't want to know. I push the plastic wallet back at him, slam the glass on the floor.

'And my fifty pounds?' I shout. 'Where's my fifty pounds?'

But my words are lost in the fuggy air, swirled into the wreathing smoke along with my money.

Scramble and Twist

When I return to Number Six, Portland Square, Mrs Fox is waiting for me.

She's wearing a pink, quilted dressing gown and a frown. A newspaper lies open on the counter; beside it, a cup and saucer. It is clear Mrs Fox is an early riser.

'We are not accustomed to our residents dropping in at all hours,' she says. Her nose twitches. I wonder if she can smell me out like a sniffer dog: the layers of Jägermeister and cannabis and grime from Tone's place. The photographs he took nestle in my bag like dirty secrets.

'It won't happen again,' I say, pushing past her to get to my room.

But she's following me up the stairs, dressing gown rustling.

'Miss Stephens, in order for you to continue staying here,

I really need to see a copy of your passport.'

'That's fine,' I call. 'I'll let you have it as soon as it comes. I've sent for it…'

I push open my door and slide past her. Smile at her brightly and close the door firmly. It's only when I am inside that I realised what she called me.

Miss Stephens.

She called me Miss Stephens.

It was the newspaper, I think. Daddy and Scally must have told the press. Or maybe Scally was able to trace my call somehow. They are after me.

The name that I gave her was Sarah Bean. Beanie. I pick up the button, the head girl badge and the photograph with shaking hands. I need to go. I have to leave *now*.

I imagine Mrs Fox at her counter, letting her cat lick at the spilt tea in her saucer. Beside her, the open paper, the large picture of me in my St Jerome's uniform. I should have disguised myself more. It's not enough. Cutting off my hair is not enough.

'My dear, can I speak to you?'

Mrs Fox's voice. A rap at my door. I don't stop what I'm doing; I swipe all of my lined-up keepsakes back into the yellow bag, search around for the rest of my things.

Rule #7: *Always be prepared to leave at a moment's notice.* Well, this is that time.

'I'm afraid you give me no choice but to…'

I think of her leaning over her *Daily Mail*, fuchsia-painted fingernails following the print along with her magnifying glass. Looking up at me slowly, as I came in, gasping. Something in her eyes.

She knows, I think. *She knows who I am.*

Quick. *Quick.* I can't walk past her, not with her suspicious eyes following me. Daddy must have informed the police by now. It has been six weeks since I went missing. The longest yet. Her dolls watch me over their lacy doilies. I hurry to the window. It's one of those sash ones, clagged with decades of old paint, but I am strong. I clench my teeth, heave. With a groan and a shriek, it lifts. A rush of sea air. I lean over. It looks over a small yard, with neatly positioned bins of different coloured plastic.

The fumble of a key in the lock.

I throw my bag out, and it lands on top of the brown bin. Next, my yellow coat. A cat shoots out from behind the bin, yowling.

A creak. Footsteps in the room.

I lower myself out of the window, hands gripping onto the sill. There's a glass sunroom below, glinting in the dawn light. If I jump, will I break through?

I drop, land and roll. Manage to scramble and twist. Above me, Mrs Fox's mouth is an O of surprise.

I jump down and crouch. Scramble for my bag. I can't stay here, not in that doll-filled room, not any more. I can't let them catch me. I can't go back.

I'll die if I have to go back.

Money in	Money out	
£693.75 (gap year savings)	1 Challenger Trail sleeping bag	£39.99
	Total spent:	£39.99
New total: £653.76		

65

Smoke and Mirrors

At first I think that it's the same girl, the one I gave Daddy's gold card to at Paddington Station. But it's not; of course it isn't. This girl has more life. She is hurling burning pins into the air, juggling with fire.

Around her is a mad scribbled world of pavement art. Coloured chalks lie scattered next to an upturned top hat. I am flicking through a newspaper someone's left on a bench, hoping to find jobs at the back. *Migrant Crisis!* shout the headlines, next to *Fisherman's Big Catch*, with a photograph of a man with his arm around his new bride.

It's busy in the little square by the fairground: holiday-makers wander in and out of the arcades, families sit on plastic chairs outside the fish and chip café. There's a little shelter with a couple of benches, and public toilets, and a children's teacup ride. I perch on the edge of a teacup and turn the pages of my newspaper. The print darkens with a few early splats of rain.

The fire-juggler is bringing in a small crowd. She's not bothered by the rain, which has picked up, splattering the paving slabs with freckles. Her dreadlocks swing as she throws her fire sticks, face upturned to the sky. Beneath her, her chalk art swims and disappears.

A father watches and smiles with his children. They are holding matching animal umbrellas, his little boy's, a frog, his daughter's, a ladybird.

I am hungry; the sharp vinegar tang from the café is making me crave fish and chips. Coins lie heavy in my pocket, tempting me. In the paper I find jobs for drivers, carers, machinery operators. Jobs in telesales. Jobs in sales management.

All of them require an address. All of them need internet access to respond.

The rain is threatening to dissolve my paper now, so I run to the little shelter outside the arcade to take cover. I have to squeeze in, as everyone else has the same idea.

'Excuse me,' I say, when my rucksack bangs against someone's knees. 'I'm terribly sorry —'

I push up against a girl at the end, and we stand for a while, watching the rain.

I wonder how I will dry my clothes without anywhere to live. Wonder whether I could try to find a youth hostel, now that I have a sleeping bag. I wonder what I'll do when my money runs out.

'That's some accent you've got there.' The girl is speaking to me. She has short yellow teeth and one of them is missing. 'I love the English accent, especially a classy one like yours.'

It's the fire-juggler. I recognise her now as the pavement artist, the girl who sold me the friendship bracelet. It's still there, on my wrist, tatty and grubby now.

She is tiny close up, much shorter than she seemed when juggling. She has streaks of pink and yellow chalk dust on her cheeks and is wearing grubby Aladdin-style pants. She smells of something strong and unpleasant.

'You staying somewhere close?'

Her accent is vaguely Australian, a mixture of coarse and soft bits, like it's being pushed through a sieve.

She's jabbing a thumb at my rucksack, with its carefully tied roll of sleeping bag.

'Youth hostelling?' she asks. 'Like a Duke of Edinburgh thing? We get a lot of those round here.'

She talks like she's the ambassador for Hastings. I hesitate.

Rule # 6: *Never display interest in other people. Do not draw attention to yourself.*

But she's nodding. 'Thought so. Like, I could tell that right away about you. That you're not just any old holiday-maker. I love your style, by the way. I love your coat.'

I study her. It doesn't look like she's being sarcastic. She has an honest face: all smiles and chalk smuts and wide, guile-less eyes.

She goes to shake hands, and it would be rude not to.

'I'm Suz,' she says, showing again those very yellow teeth.

I look around for inspiration. The boy is spinning with his frog umbrella, even though it's stopped raining now and the sun is sucking up puddles like a Hoover. Beneath him, Suz's chalk drawings swirl in dirt.

'Frog,' I say. 'I'm Frog.'

'Cool name,' says Suz, and the space between us shrinks.

Up close, she's filthy. There's grime around her hairline, and in the lines around her eyes. It's hard to know her age; she could be twelve or thirty. There's something about her that suggests she's been in corners of human existence that I've only ever peeked at. Like she knows everything worth knowing.

The only beautiful thing about her is her eyes, which are the colour of sea glass.

'Smoke?' she says. She's offering me a battered tin of tobacco, and she's making herself a roll-up with rainbow-chalky fingers that have nails rimmed with dirt. I think of the Handbag's zebra polish, and wonder what fingernails say about a person. My own are bitten.

Suz is still pushing her tin at me.

I shake my head. I've only ever smoked Marlboro Lights, and those were with Beanie, back at school. We'd leave each other fags inside the mouth of one of the gargoyles on the roof of Founder's Building. That was our secret meeting place, where we taught each other to smoke, lying on our backs after Prep, sighing out smoke and whispering dreams and listening to the thwack of the balls on the tennis courts below.

Suz is staring at my bag, and I place a hand over it protectively.

'So, what's your story?' she says.

I stiffen.

'You have one, right?' she says without looking at me. 'Apart from the youth-hostelling thing, I mean.'

'I really don't think that's any of your business.' And I hate the way my voice sounds, posh and petulant.

She hold her hands up as if to say, *I get it*. Spits a glob of black tobacco onto the pavement.

'Well, I guess I'll be getting back to work,' she says. 'Stopped raining now. Nice meeting you, Frog.'

I feel an ache then, of something I can't put a name to.

'Wait,' I say. I don't know why I'm talking. I don't know what I'm going to say. I only know that I'm breaking the sixth rule.

She turns.

'I wondered if…I wondered if you'd teach me to juggle fire.'

The dirty lines on her face deepen into a frown.

'I mean, I'll pay you,' I say hastily. 'I wouldn't expect you do it for free or anything. Of course not. I have money –'

Shouldn't have said that.

Her eyes spark green. 'I'm very busy,' she says, indicating her chalk drawings. 'I have work to do. Like, I'm really exceptionally busy.' She breathes tobacco and something sour and foul over me. 'How much?'

I realise she's talking money. 'Ten pounds?' It's not as if I'm getting expert tuition or anything. I know that Daddy pays my extra tutors forty pounds an hour. Like the time when

I was tutored for Oxbridge. But they were always super-qualified, whereas Suz…

She smiles broadly. 'Look, I'm real tired right now, Frog. I've been on the move all day. My feet ache. My whole body aches. And now you're asking me to be your teacher. Look at that crowd. I could just get up there right now and they'd be hurling money into my hat. So long, Frog.'

'Twenty.'

Her back stiffens.

'For half an hour. Just give me half an hour to teach me the basics.'

A sigh, deep and heavy. 'We-ell. OK. But you have to buy me a drink after.'

'Done,' I say. I try not to recoil as I shake her grimy hand again.

She lights one of her batons with a *whoosh*.

'They're called devil sticks,' she says. 'You hold them here, like this.'

She shows me how to hold one horizontally so that the flames don't lick up and burn me.

'You have to soak the wicks first. I use Kerosene 'cos it's the cheapest, and lasts ages. Spin the excess off before you light it, or you'll get fireflies.'

'Fireflies?'

'Little splashes of oil that set alight and hit the audience.'

'Oh.'

'Wait till it dies down a bit, and then you're ready.'

We watch the flame flicker and dip, and then Suz takes the baton from me.

'First you make friends with the fire,' she says. Her face is soot-grimed, but her eyes are bright. 'Just twirl it like this. Look.'

She passes it from one hand to the other, then does it faster and faster, hollering like a wild thing, twisting and throwing her devil sticks, feet scuffling in the chalk.

'The shouting's just for effect,' she hisses. 'Now it's your turn, Frog.'

I take off my yellow coat and pass the baton from one hand to the other, feeling its weight, the roaring dry heat of it. Through its vapour, the pavement shimmers.

Suz passes me the other.

'Come on, dance,' she calls, dreadlocks shaking.

So I do. I spin and swoop the fire sticks through the rain-spilled air, one in each hand, feeling the heat soar, seeing people's faces spin and sparks shoot like burning sawdust.

This is what I'm here to do, I think. *I've finally started. It's really happening!*

Time shudders and rainbows fly.

Around us, people shout and clap. At last, I stop, exhausted. I'm flushed, exhilarated. Suz is grinning at me. 'Whoo-oo,' she shouts. 'You've brought me luck, Frog. Look in the pot.'

A little crowd has gathered. Someone leans forward and tosses in a coin.

'Next time, I'll teach you the tic-toc,' she says.

'Tic-toc?' I ask. And inside, I'm thinking: *Next time?*

'It's the first step in juggling with devil sticks. You pass the big one between two smaller sticks. It's heaps cool. Looks great at night.'

She shows me how to blow out the flame and dip the wick in fuel again, 'so that it doesn't dry out'. She ties up the ends in a plastic bag and wraps the sticks up in a canvas pouch, before shoving them in her silver case. 'My brother bought me them when I was little and he came to visit me.'

I wonder what she means by 'visit me'.

'You're a natural,' she adds. 'Miss Phoenix, with the devil

sticks – here.' Suz tips out what's in the top hat.

She counts it out. Eleven pounds and eighty pence. 'A fortune! You can stay longer, Frog. You bring me luck.'

She grabs the chalk and draws vigorously, kneeling down on the sun-dried pavement. Soon there's a picture of me, spinning and flying in flames. My hair is tongues of fire tipping upwards, topsy-turvy. My eyes, spirals like Catherine Wheels.

As she tries to lever herself back up, I notice she has something wrong with her left leg. Compared to the right, it's withered and not as well muscled. She has to use an arm to straighten up.

'Worse on a rainy day,' she laughs, when she sees me looking. But there is pain through the laughter.

She holds out her hand for the twenty pounds I owe her. I watch her tuck it inside her baccy tin.

'So now, what about that drink?' she says.

The Mermaid

I order a glass of white wine. Suz orders a double vodka.

'Crisps too.' she says. 'Salt and vinegar. On account of I'm vegan.'

I leave her sitting at a corner bench and go to pay for the drinks, telling myself that this is all part of the grand plan. You have to invest to benefit. You can't reap the rewards without initial outlay. That's what Daddy's always saying.

And it's relationship-building, I think. In order to move forward I need contacts.

But how does that fit with Rule #6?

As I pay for the drinks with our earnings, I think of the long night ahead, the long night I will have to spend alone.

My arms ache wonderfully after all the juggling.

When I get back to Suz, she's crouched on the floor next to an enormous shaggy dog, chatting animatedly to its owners and fondling its ears. Every now and then, she laughs, the sound as sudden as a handful of gravel being thrown at a window.

'I have a special way with dogs,' she says, when she sees me. 'I was just telling this lovely couple here, I just love dogs. Don't I, Dennis?' She smacks a huge kiss on top of the dog's head and holds heavily onto the table to lever herself back up.

I can see the couple want to be rid of her. 'Bye, Dennis,' she shouts, as I lead her away.

Suz drinks the vodka in two seconds flat, and says she wants another one.

'I'll pay,' she says. She shows me a crumpled fiver in the palm of her hand. I have a feeling it was the tip that Dennis's owners left on their table.

'So, what do you do, Frog, when you're not Duke of Edinburgh-ing?'

I feel the white wine warm me. It's cosy in the pub, full of happy holiday-makers. Next round, I order a double vodka too.

I find myself telling Suz about Daddy and the Handbag, and she nods sympathetically.

'Oh, god, yes. It's always the same story, right? Abusive stepmother. Alkie father. Foster care. Sofa-surfing till your mate kicks you out. Yada, yada, yada.'

I think:

Housekeepers, gardeners and grooms.

Daddy with his glass of whisky.

Zebra-print fingernails.

'Something like that,' I say.

I tell Suz all about my different ponies.

'Oh yeah? Oh yeah? Nice.'

Suz tells me she used to ride, back in Melbourne.

'On the beaches, galloping through the sand,' she says. 'Best feeling ever.' She's on her third double vodka, and I'm not sure who's paying. She has a face full of listening.

I tell her about my mother and the circus and all of my plans.

'You know what you need, Frog? You need a manager, that's what. You need some luck. You need...You got a cigarette?'

She's shaking her hat upside down on the table. The barman is giving us slanted glances; he's looking Suz up and down like she's something the dog's just rolled in.

Then she leans forward, heavily, on the table, and gets herself to stand up. Her face is screwed up with effort.

'Gotta go now, Frog. S'been lovely meeting you. You keep safe now, d'ya hear me?'

'You could be my manager,' I say. It all seems obvious suddenly. It's the missing link, the thing I need. I am talking faster now, trying to stop her from leaving. 'I could pay you for more lessons. Give you a cut of anything I earn as a performer. You said I brought you luck –'

Suz stares at me, her chalky hand still gripping the edge of the table. Then her face is transformed by a broad smile.

'We should celebrate,' she says. 'I know just the place.'

Tiramisu

'It might take up a little bit more than our earnings, Frog,' she says, as we walk down towards the sea through the lanes. She rises up and down slightly with each step, her hip pushing out. On each downhill step, that wince. She's crammed her top hat over her dreadlocks, and looks like a limping Artful Dodger.

'How much have we spent?' I try to ask her, but my voice is thick and slow. We only had eleven pounds to start, I think. And the five that Suz took from the dog couple. I think we might have spent the twenty I gave her for teaching me devil sticks. And we bought all those drinks. So that would be…a lot.

'You OK to take my arm? I'm not so good on these down bits, since my accident.'

'What did you do to your leg?'

'Aww, this? It's nothing. *Humpty Dumpty sat on the wall, Humpty Dumpty had a great fall,*' she sings. 'Let's just say, I decided I'd have a go at flying, and the ground had other ideas. But they fixed me up good. Put Suz back together again.' She pats her left hip. 'More metal in me than a car scrapyard. You got any more money?'

I pat my bag. 'That's fine,' I say. 'Totally fine.'

Initial outlay, I think.

The restaurant turns out to be Italian. One of those that's all low ceilings and warm pizza smells and candles in wine bottles. A middle-aged couple eating pasta give Suz the once-over and then turn away. This makes me angry. *I could take their heads and slam them down in their bowls of linguine,* I think, *until there are clams in her hair and passata down his face.*

I realise I am very drunk.

Suz surprises me by asking for a table in Italian.

A waiter, small and dark-haired and big-bellied, shows us to one right at the back of the restaurant.

'Doesn't want us to be by the front door when people come in,' Suz hisses. 'But that's OK. Who could blame him?'

I could, I think. *I could blame them, and then I could —*

Suz orders a bottle of wine and two more double vodkas.

'Do you think we should?' I say. 'Honestly, Suz. There's not much money. We only earned eleven pounds, remember?'

Suz leans forward and grabs both of my hands. 'Frog… Frog,' she says gently. 'You need to relax. We're celebrating, remember? Everything has to be nice. And who says I don't have money?'

She winks and draws out two crisp twenties from under the table.

'It's a treat,' she says. 'On me. It's from some…winnings.'

Her eyes are wet now with tears and vodka. 'It makes me feel human, being here. Don't spoil it, Frog.' She clasps my hand in her grubby ones, and I find I don't mind.

'Now for pizza!' She claps her hands.

Suz orders bruschetta and tomato salad to go with her Florentine pizza. 'No meat?' she keeps saying to the waiter. 'You sure you'll hold the egg and mozzarella?

'I don't do animal products,' she tells me, for the hundredth time. Then: 'Olives,' she yells. 'Let's have plenty of olives. They're totally vegan.'

I'm not sure I can eat anything, but when my pizza comes, it makes me feel better. It's herby and handmade and totally delicious. Out of deference to Suz's passionate animal rights stance, I have chosen one with aubergines and artichokes, and it's been so long since I had delicious food that Suz is right: it does make me feel human.

The waiter pours in some wine to taste, and Suz snatches the glass and bends her face to it, sniffing deeply, like a dog.

'Divine,' she declares, mimicking my accent. 'Quite simply divine.'

When he refills her glass, she drinks it straight down without tasting a drop.

I find myself showing Suz my mother's photograph, and she pores over it, sighing. 'She's beautiful, Frog. She has your eyes.'

She wipes off a smear of sauce that has got onto the corner of the photo. Gazes at it with those understanding, sea-glass eyes. 'You gotta do as she wants, Frog. Make her proud. She's riding the back of a giant bird right now, looking down on you.'

'A bird?' I say. Our voices are loud and I know there are people watching: that lady with the sunburned shoulders; the man with the long face with his long-faced son.

Suz is breathing all over the picture. 'She'll be on a starling, Frog, or a kestrel. Or a red kite. No doubt about it. I have the Gift.'

'The Gift?'

Suz lowers her voice to a whisper. Heads turn back to their meals. 'The gift of talking to birds. They tell me things. When I go, Frog, I'll be sitting on the back of a seagull, riding high over the ocean...Dessert, please!' she bawls.

The waiter comes, his mouth a tighter line than when he started his shift.

Suz orders a sundae and an Irish coffee and I order tiramisu. I feel a little sick.

I watch as Suz drags her hip over to the glass counter and points out all of the flavours of ice cream she wants in her sundae. I can see her waving her arms and explaining in Italian which sprinkles she needs. From the back, she doesn't look world-worn. She looks like a little girl.

When she's slurped her way through her mound of *pistachio -fragola-limone*, Suz leans forward heavily. Her eyes are bright and brimmed with friendship.

'Listen, Frog, I gotta go to the little girl's room. You enjoy your coffee, won't you? S'been nice.'

She takes my hand then, and clasps it, trailing it across the table as she gets up and hobbles away.

I watch her make her way to the washroom, dipping her head at the other guests as she goes. Even through my drunk haze, I can tell the waiters want us to leave. There are hardly any other diners left.

A manager, I think. That's what I need.

Although Suz has only gone to the toilets, the pool of warmth that's wrapped me since I met her ebbs away.

'*Signora?*'

The waiter is hovering. He has our bill on a little tray, and there are two sweets on it, one for me, one for Suz.

'Thank you,' I smile. My voice comes out all thick.

The amount is ludicrous, far more than Suz's twenties, or our earnings, even if we still had them. I will have to dig once more into my savings.

But it's all right, I think. Totally fine. It'll all be made back once I'm earning, won't it? And I try to remember all of the plans Suz talked about; they sounded so extravagant and wonderful and hopeful when she outlined them. I can't think of even one of them now.

'You pay by card?'

'Oh, cash, please.'

Suz is being a long time. I wonder if she feels ill, like me. I wonder if I should go in and see if she's all right in there. Offer to hold her hair back if she's throwing up. But the thought of holding those filthy dreadlocks is a little too much. Suz isn't Beanie.

I realise Suz hasn't left me her twenties.

I reach into my rucksack, feeling the waiter's eyes on me, and draw out my brown envelope. To my relief, it's still there, fat and full with cash. Just for a moment I thought…

I smile at the waiter as I ease out some notes and start to count them.

But then I begin to feel very cold and hot at the same time.

In my hands are pieces of torn-up paper, scribbled and doodled with chalk drawings, birds and ladybirds and giant eggs. I let out a sort of a whimper and pull out more of the papers, fistfuls of them, while the waiter looks on. Only more and more pieces of paper.

No money. No notes.

Suz has taken it all.

Helter Skelter

And now I know that when I go into the ladies, she won't be there.

There's an open door, just by the kitchens, leading out onto a backyard with bins and crates, and an open gate to the street.

She must have known this would be the best restaurant to choose, to make an easy exit.

'*Signora*, you must pay. We call the police!'

I hardly hear him. I am breathing too fast, too fast, but I must focus.

A thought flashes into my head. Her leg. Her hip. She can't be far away. Ignoring the shouting waiter behind me, I scramble past the bins and head out into the street.

I'm going to find her.

And when I do, I'm going to kill her.

Swing Seat

Suz is gone. And so are her chalks, and her bags of friendship bracelets and her devil sticks.

She has left me my picture, drawn on the pavement just outside the ghost train. No words, just a yellow-headed girl, spinning endlessly in the spilling sunlight, fire batons and fireworks and shooting stars.

So long, Frog.

I want to scribble it out viciously. I force myself to take calming breaths and scan the plaza. Only a row of silver-haired ladies, nodding off in the evening sun.

She can't have gone far – please make her not have gone far.

I run up and down the narrow lanes, asking inside restaurants, peering over walls into gardens, even though I know she couldn't have climbed them, not with her hip. I race along the streets of the Old Town, back through the fairground, back past the ghost train. People's faces, bemused, open-mouthed. Pushing past elbows, bags, bodies. Take a right, and then another, and I am back at the funicular. Still full of holiday makers, eating and drinking. I run past the fish stalls and past the miniature railway to the fishermen's beach.

Here are only boats, gape-sided wrecks, forgotten hulls, broken and cast-off. Once alone, I stumble and almost faint. Slide down to sit on the shingle and weed. Collapse on my hands and knees to try to breathe.

Breathe.

Breathe.

I fumble in my bag for my pills but there are none. Suz has taken those too.

I have searched every street.

She has taken everything.

I have nothing.

The clouds are knitting together as I emerge onto the common on West Hill, following the path to the top. There are no stars tonight, only the smudged clouds, purple-bruised and sullen. A group of men shout, 'All right, love?' and I ignore them, fix my eyes forward, try to focus on walking purposefully.

And all the time, a voice throbs and sneers:

No money. You have no money.

What are you going to do now, Willow? How are you going to live, Circus Girl?

At the top of the hill there's a children's playground, and inside I sit on a swing and pull out the Happiness Kit and hold it to my cheek. I think of Daddy's card which I gave to the homeless girl at Paddington, think of the smooth, crisp notes of my gap year money. With trembling hands, I line up the objects on the swing seat next to me, realign them, reorder them, one by one.

A plaster to heal you when you hurt.

A diamond to bring a sparkle to your eye.

A Love Heart sweet so you know that someone loves you.

I whisper the words over and over, like a mantra. Like all of these random things will somehow hold me together.

On my wrist is the grubby string of the friendship bracelet that Suz wrapped around me, the first time we met. I yank it off viciously, stare at the orange and black threads. Then I place it in line on the swing.

A friendship band, to remind you of things broken.

I take Beanie's head girl badge and pin it to my coat. Wonder when I stopped talking to her in my head. At the bottom of my bag are the two photographs: my mother and the folded newspaper clipping of me and Spook. I unfold it and stroke his nose. At the bottom, there is the caption: *Miss Stephens and Spook, all smiles after their big win.*

Miss Stephens.

Mrs Fox had been going through my things in my room.

It wasn't because she knew I was a runaway. She hadn't read about me in the paper, after all. Which means…

Which means I could still be in my room right now. I might never have met Suz. Might never have lost my money.

I left too soon.

Somewhere, a dog howls.

Not since those first days at St Jerome's have I felt so alone.

Willow, Aged Six

It is fun at first.

I sit at a scratched wooden desk, and I try to keep my legs still as the lady asks me lots of questions. 'Just to see what we're dealing with, you understand.' I have to sit a numbers test and an English test and a science test, and she sighs at my answers. 'Very good at storytelling,' she tells Daddy. 'Your daughter's a very imaginative little girl.'

Daddy says something to her in a low voice, and she smiles and takes firm hold of my arm. 'We'll make sure she's safe here, Mr Stephens, don't worry.' She's wearing a man's tweed jacket, and gold glasses hang from a chain over her large chest.

She steers me through a doorway and makes me sit on a polished chair in a room that smells funny. Later I will learn that the smell is beeswax. Beanie's house smells like this, and Miffy's and Lexy's. Opposite hang rows of photographs of stern women in Victorian clothes, their eyes sliding over me as I drum my feet on the shiny floor.

Words drift: 'Not had much of a firm hand…au pairs…' and 'Work commitments…new business venture…'

I look to see where I can escape, but this room is high up; the school brochure said that you can see three counties from here. Daddy comes out at last, followed by the lady.

He's smiling, like he is about to give me a huge present.

Instead, he rips my world away.

'Mrs Threshbold says she'll be happy for St Jerome's to be your new home,' he says. 'You'll be a weekly boarder.'

He squats down beside me, but I can tell his eyes want to slide to his watch. 'That means you get to come home each weekend and we'll go out for treats. Would you like that?'

He turns to the lady again, who is looking at me kindly-but-firmly, as if she likes a challenge.

'We keep a very close eye on our girls, don't you worry. She'll be safe and sound with us.'

Daddy shakes her hand, and inside I scream and scream.

Transcript of Telephone Conversation between DS Tracy Scallion and Willow Stephens, Saturday 21 May 2016 at 10.23 A.M.

Scallion: Willow? [pause] Where are you, love? You need to tell me where you are.

Willow: [pause] Is it just you?

Scallion: Willow Stephens?

Willow: I need to know if it is just you.

Scallion: Yes, it's just you and me, love. How are you? Tell me how you're doing. Where are you staying, lovey?

Willow: I'm not telling you. I'm not coming back.

Scallion: No one's making you come back. We just want to know if you're safe.

Willow: You can't make me come back.

Call ends.

Dear Beanie,

So I'm a street performer now, just until I get my big break. It's a real haven for creative types, Hastings. I wish you could see me. I can juggle fire!

I get crowds, Beanie, watching me as I do my routine. Of course it's not exactly the Cirque du Soleil, but it's amazing experience and keeps me practising my skills for when I'm in the ring. Sawdust and fire and dancing, Beanie. I wonder what name I shall call my act. I wonder what I should call myself, I wonder —

Cliff Hanger

There are caves inside this cliff, hundreds of them, pressing deep beneath me, wormholes, secret places where smugglers and wreckers would push French brandy and tobacco and tins of tea into crevices.

The information sheet is splattered with rain. I climb over the thin railing, and pick my way past the danger sign to a rock. Below me, the sea is grey froth at the bottom of a deep ravine.

A seagull, sleek as a king, lifts itself into the sky. Opens its red mouth and jeers at me, juddering in mid-air.

I lean over, and rip all of my letters to Beanie into tiny shreds. Feed them one by one into the hungry sea.

Watch them fly.

Act II

Money in	Money out	
£4.17 (total of cash in pocket)	Rest of gap year savings	£653.76
	Total spent:	£-
New total: £4.17		

Night Cradle

I pull my hat down, far below my ears, to keep out the wind, which is picking up now that the night's coming. I choose the bus shelter on the seafront in the end. It's the fourth place I've tried. There's someone else fast asleep, curled up in the corner, bundled in their sleeping bag.

I lie down on the slatted bench, tug my sleeping bag hood over my head and under my chin. I am fading away, a stray dog, an animal. Snakelike, I shed skins, creep inside others to try them on for size. To try to find out who and what I really am.

The ridges are hard under my hip. Drunken noises rise from the bar opposite the beach. A group of men stagger, shout and swear. A can is kicked, strikes the iron leg of my bench with violence. One of the men lurches, his hand splayed psycho-like against the glass of the shelter. Then it's gone, and there's only the sound of retching, and laughing.

Shredded voices in the sea-slapped night. Somewhere, the fairground screams.

A sound, slow and hard and endless. The men are back. One of them is pissing up against the side of the shelter. I clench my hands inside my sleeping bag. Take the first object I can find out of my Kit of Happiness and squeeze it tight. Try not to breathe. Pray that they will not come inside and discover that I am a girl.

A hand, splayed briefly. A face, beery and full. The glint of a street-lit eye. I squeeze my eyes shut. The feel of breath, warm and faecal. Then he's called back, lets his friends pull him away, back to their lives, back to their homes. I hear him call me something vile and ugly, but I don't care. They're gone, and when I open my hand, I see that I am clenching a button.

Is this what going mad is like?

The noise retreats. And I lie awake, in the slow ticking hours, watching the stars prick out one by one, listening to the slow sad slop of the sea and the birds and the fussing wind.

The sea's getting restless. It heaves itself in great sloshes, thick as paint.

You can never sleep properly out in a public place.

If I thought my room at Mrs Fox's was bad, with its spidery bath and staring dolls, this is a thousand times worse. I think of my bedroom at home, my banks of books and clothes and cuddly toys that I can't bear to give away. My desk with the vintage typewriter that I asked for and never used. My horses, scratching their chins on the stable doors. The stables, top of the range, deluxe, with private shower and tack room.

I would kill for that now.

Loose Change

When it's light, I follow the promenade along the seafront, towards the fairground. A sleeping fairground: all empty Waltzers and trodden-on chip papers. My stomach growls. My hip aches where I've slept on it.

I slump against the sea wall. Huddle into my hoodie. I'm still cold after my night on the bench. A thin, bitter wind knifes me. I pull out my sleeping bag and tuck it over my knees, trying to think what to do. First I'll get a coffee, and then I'll resume my efforts to find Suz. And then –

Something chinks at my feet and I look down.

A pound coin.

A little girl darts away to her smiling mummy. They're already walking away, the little girl clutching tight to her mother's hand. They're pushing a buggy too; I can just make out the soft furl of the child's hair.

Oh god. They think I really am homeless.

But you are homeless now.

Night Music

Do you miss me, Daddy? Do you?

I want you to miss me.

The bundle beside me sighs in its sleep, something between a groan and a whimper. It kills me, that sigh, because I think about how it's a sound that, normally, no one would ever hear. A little lost sigh amongst the wind and the waves and the sea. I pull my sleeping bag over my face and lie awake for a long time, thinking about it.

Can you hear me, Daddy? Will you ever –
will you
ever read
this?

Scarecrow

I clean my teeth at the public lavatories on the seafront, wash my face and spit. I unwind the plastic bag and stare at my hair in the speckled mirror.

I am not me. I am completely transformed. My hair is short and bleached, the colour of straw. It is a nasty yellow, but at least I no longer look like Willow Stephens, Runaway Schoolgirl. I wash it with liquid soap in the freezing cold water, and dry my hair as best as I can with paper towels.

I wonder if my hair will fall out with all of the bleach I took from the cleaner's cupboard. I wonder if I'll ever be able to afford conditioner again.

The face in the mirror is a pale, frowning thing. I lean forward and stare deep, ignoring the sidelong looks of the mother at the basin beside me. Her child hollers for more loo roll and still I stare, trying to find who I am. I feel like I have shed my skin; as though worlds and words and fragments have blown it away, like torn-up photographs. I don't know who I've become.

Inside a cubicle, I get changed, ignoring the wails of a child outside my door – 'But I need a wee, Mummy!' I have no clean underwear, no clean socks or tights. I use roll-on under my arms, and wear my cleanest-looking leggings. Turn yesterday's socks inside out.

When I emerge, I see that the woman has left her hand-bag next to the basin as she crouches in front of her child in the cubicle. There's a lipstick on the basin, on its side. I take it. A credit card poking out of an overstuffed purse. Quick as a whip, I reach inside and slide it out, between thumb and forefinger. The girl in the mirror looks grim-faced; she is not someone I know.

I put the card inside the pocket of my yellow coat. Walk straight out, shoulders back, head high. Inside I have shrunk smaller than a child.

Using the wing mirror of a parked car, I pull the lipstick over my lips until it is a bright, bold slash. Belt up my coat against the wind. Feel the rounded edges of the woman's bank card inside my coat pocket. I go into the budget super-market and fill my basket with bananas, crisps, white sliced bread and chocolate. Pot noodles. Things we'd buy and share at St Jerome's. Black market, boarding-school fare.

At the till, I wait behind a bearded boy and a girl in a hijab. They have a trolley full of squirty cream, and are trying to pay with vouchers. I reach automatically for my pills, and then remember that I don't have any, not now. I try to visu-alise something calming, like snow falling or lapping waves, and all the time my breath comes dry and rapid.

The till drawer rings. The woman at the till laughs. Passes them their receipt, and then looks at me enquiringly.

'Any bags?' she says. I shake my head. Zip open my rucksack.

The items are rung through quickly, and I stuff them into my bag, trying to control my shaking hands.

'Getting colder,' says the woman, whose name badge says

Pleased to meet you. She is called Margaret.

'I'm sorry?'

The last item is scanned. Two bars of fruit and almond chocolate. I force myself not to tear open the wrapper there and then, and cram the whole thing into my mouth. Place it neatly inside my bag instead.

'Ever so cold. You should have come down last week, love. Had a heatwave, we did.'

She laughs comfortably and presses a button.

'Do you have a Save 'n' Spend card?'

I shake my head. Force myself to take out the cash card of Ms Christine Jones and hand it over.

'Contactless, please,' I say.

She looks pleased. Waves the card over the sensor. 'There, done. You enjoy the rest of your day now.'

And she passes me my receipt.

Easy as that.

Exposure

Only eight hours to kill until it's dark again.

Eight hours till I have to clench my teeth against another night.

I shiver, and take my sandwich, press a handful of crisps over the squashed banana with filthy hands that don't belong to me. I sit on the edge of the sea wall, hunched up, watching a gull peck the life out of a ham sandwich. It's warmer in my coat, but I feel too exposed, like a blob of bright paint. I wanted to reinvent myself, to turn myself into someone different, uncrumple myself like a newly emerged bright butterfly. But instead I am a grub that must burrow itself into the shadows.

I eat my sandwich mindlessly, as the seagull fixes me with one red beady eye. I read a newspaper left behind by a holidaymaker.

I turn from the gull as it is ripped away by the wind, and start to fold up the newspaper. As I do, the wind lifts the top page and ruffles it as if to get my attention.

And there I am.

Daddy's used my school photograph – the awful one where I was trying to copy Beanie and her friends' fishtail plait and it hasn't quite worked and I look shy and stupid.

Trust him to get it wrong.

Has he even got any photos of me that he took himself? Has he? Martyna and Sonia and the others were always taking pictures: me on the swing, me on my pony. *Ask Martyna!* I want to scream at him. She'll have plenty of pictures of me on her phone. If she hasn't deleted them all because I was such a bitch to her.

I get such a pang then that I have to stop and do slow breathing for a while before I read on. Martyna, who was always baking with me, when she was just the au pair, not our housekeeper. She would try to show me how to make *paczki* – those Polish doughnuts she loved so much – getting me to sprinkle them with orange peel and chocolate and powdered sugar. Afterwards, when the kitchen smelled of the wild rosehip jam she'd make to fill the doughnuts, we would sit eating them with cups of sweet coffee.

But I could never finish mine. I would eat one to please her, but I didn't like it much; it tasted of homesickness and tears.

I turn my attention to the article.

MISSING: MULTIMILLIONAIRE'S DAUGHTER
VANISHES ON HER FATHER'S WEDDING DAY
Schoolgirl Willow Stephens, 17, disappeared during the
wedding preparations for her father's big day. Gary Stephens,
54, is a wealthy businessman who made his fortune buying
and selling amusement arcades.

My nails dig into the paper as I read. I feel my breath coming hot and quick. Amusement arcades! Daddy with his wonderful businesses. Our oh-so-*nouveau* house with its monstrous fake Roman pillars and its pretend-ancient wisteria that Daddy had three gardeners transplant to make us seem authentic. Our mini ha-ha, which took the gardener three days to mow, and our manmade lake with its pissing cupid in brand-new stone. And now everyone will know how he made his money.

I look up, and there's an old man, snowy hair ruffled by the breeze, reading the same newspaper. His head lifts and he meets my eyes. I flinch away. *Will they know? Will they all recognise me now, the people in shops, passing me on the street? Do they know who I really am?*

SIGHTING
Oh god.

Brian Pickles, a lorry driver from Essex, claims that he picked up a young hitchhiker resembling Willow on the day of the wedding. 'She seemed edgy,' he told us, 'like she was running away from something. I was worried for her wellbeing as she is the same age as my granddaughter.'

*   CCTV footage shows a young girl entering train toilets and coming out with shortened hair. Police want to hear from anyone on the London Paddington train from Oxford on*

Saturday lunchtime.

BIZARRE

In a bizarre twist, a homeless girl is being charged with fraud after over two thousand pounds was found taken out of Mr Stephens' gold bank account. It is believed that Willow set up the homeless girl, known only as Nat, in an attempt to establish a decoy for the police. Willow Stephens, a high-performing boarder at St Jerome's School for Girls, suffers from anxiety and depression. It is believed that her disappearance is linked to her father's marriage to twenty-seven-year-old Kayleigh-Ann Evans, his personal assistant.

There are concerns for her safety.

If you have information about Willow's whereabouts, please phone 0800 229431.

Mr Stephens is offering a cash reward for information leading to his daughter's safe return.

So Daddy and the Handbag still went through with the wedding, then. It didn't stop them. Didn't make them think that, actually, it may not be such a great idea to get married when their daughter and soon-to-be stepdaughter is actually missing.

They didn't think that she'd packed her bag and stuffed her dress inside a tree and placed herself in obvious danger by hitching a lift with a totally random stranger and had withdrawn all her savings out of her account, so was obviously not thinking of coming back any time soon!

Oh, I know, I know, it's like *The Boy Who Cried Wolf*, isn't it? But running away for the first time when you are seven is very different from a spoilt seventeen-year-old getting into a strop because she doesn't like the idea of her rich Daddy getting married. Is that what Scally really thinks of me?

But I'm not that girl anymore, am I? Isn't she who I'm running away from?

I think of the homeless girl at Paddington, in her grubby too-big coat; the look of fear as I leaned forward to slip Daddy's card into her cup. I didn't care at all about her, did I? Not really. I was only out for myself. I thought that I would get one over the police and my father by setting her up. I wasn't giving her money; I was placing her in a trap.

I hope that she's all right, that she's been fed, and that people are being kind to her. Maybe it'll be a blessing in disguise, going to prison. At least it'll be warm. I think of my night on the seafront and shiver. At least she'll be safe now.

Won't she?

I stare at the picture of Willow Stephens looking back at me, and our eyes lock, and I think, I really think, that I –

don't know

who

I am

any more.

Transcript of Telephone Conversation between DS

Tracy Scallion and Willow Stephens, Friday 27 May 2016 at

10.11 A.M.

Willow: Where's Daddy? I want to talk to Daddy.

Scallion: Your father's not able to speak right now. We're

looking for you, Willow. We are coming to find you.

Willow: You don't know where I am.

Scallion. Lovey, you can't hide forever. I know that you'll have run out of money. You'll be lonely, even if you have found someone to hook up with. The days are long, aren't they, Willow? And the nights are even longer. Where do you go, Willow? Do you hang out with the other lonely people, on the streets? On benches? In bus shelters? Are you cold at night, Willow? Your money's getting low now, isn't it, love? You've made your point now. Don't you think you should come home?

Willow: I'm never coming home. No one can make me.

Scallion: You're right, Willow. You're your own person. Nobody can make you do anything. But you can't live like this. Someday soon, you're going to run out of money and luck. It's dangerous out there alone, lovey.

Willow: Is she gone? Is she still there?

Scallion: [sighs] Who, lovey?

Willow: The Handbag – Kayleigh-Ann.

Scallion: Your dad and his wife are still together, if that's what you mean. Where are you staying, Willow? Give us your location so that we can come to get you.

Willow: How much is he paying you this time?

Scallion: [pause] Your father doesn't pay me, Willow.

Willow: Did they still go?

Scallion: Go where, love?

Willow: Did they still go? To the Maldives? On their honey-moon? They still went, didn't they? Didn't they?

[pause]

Call ends.

Balancing Act

Posh Pawn has a plasma television for sale in the window.

On the screen, it's all set up for a press conference, and my heart flips as I see him.

Daddy.

It's been three days since Suz stole my money. Two nights

sleeping rough. One hour since I made that phone call. The lady with the baby was more than happy to let me use her phone when I said that my sister was ill; I desperately needed to contact her. It was easy to lie, but harder to ignore the flinch of fear and sympathy in her eyes. Did she know that I was lying? I don't know.

There's Daddy on TV, in a crumpled shirt and crooked tie, his hair ungelled, his eyes shadowed. He looks tired and old, as if he's not been sleeping.

This is all because of me, I think. He's here because he's afraid for me. He's worried I could be dead. Or kidnapped. Or in danger. I've caused this. I've made his nights long and sleepless, and worry for me has raddled his face with extra lines, and made him look suddenly older than his fifty-five years, rather than much younger, like on his wedding day.

I try to feel happy about this.

It shows he cares, I think. He's terrified I won't ever be found. I might be dead. His only child could be lying in a shallow grave, in some wood or wasteland or ditch, and he wouldn't know. He's terrified about that.

I try to feel happy that I have caused Daddy this fear.

He's sitting next to Scally, and there's no sign of *her*, none at all. Scally leans close to him and mutters something, and Daddy nods, turns to face the camera.

I lean forward. I want so much to hear what Daddy's got to say about me; to hear how much he's missing me, that he wants me to come home.

The camera zooms in a little. Daddy clears his throat, looks straight at me.

'Willow,' he says.

Time stops and slows. I drink in Daddy with my eyes. Now it's going to happen, I think. He's going to say that he loves me, that he's going to come and find me, that he's going to bring me home.

There is no sign of Kayleigh-Ann. He's left her to come here, to this crowded room, to talk to me. To plead for my safe return. For me to come back.

'Willow, please come home. I want you to come home. I believe –'

My heart's skittering so much I can hardly breathe.

'I believe that we can work things out, I believe –'

But what Daddy believes, I don't hear. Because at that moment, there's a ripple through the row of seated people. Daddy's eyes flicker to the right, and there's the twitch of a smile.

And now Scally's standing up, and other people are pressing themselves back, like at a cinema, to let someone pass, to get to their seat next to Daddy. And that someone, of course, is Kayleigh-Ann.

The reason that they need to give her a lot of space is evident immediately. Because she has really put on an awful lot of weight since I last saw her on her wedding day. This Kayleigh-Ann is looking rounded and glowing, and her serious face and Daddy's can't disguise the happiness they feel, and nothing can hide the way he places his hand briefly over her hand on her rounded belly, swelling under her stretchy plunge-necked top.

Daddy is still saying words, and I'm aware of his mouth moving and rounding and unrounding but I can't hear, I can't hear any of them, because, because –

he's not really thinking of me at all, is he? He can't be, not if
not if
her hand, his hand
is placed on that bump, that belly, that

that thing
that he's already replaced me with.

Willow, Aged Fifteen

'Open your eyes – surprise!' Daddy says.

I unpeel my eyes, and squeal with delight. 'Oh, Daddy, you got him, you got him!'

He's beautiful, just like the ones you see in the circus. He's Appaloosa, with a white muzzle mottled with black spots. I reach forward and he comes trotting over at once, nudging my hand for food.

'He needs a lot of work,' Daddy smiles. 'You'll have to break him in. Think you can manage?'

I blow gently into Spook's muzzle, let him kiss me back. He is so striking, I can already imagine us together at the school gymkhana. He'll be instantly recognisable, the only spotted horse, and of course with me as his rider.

I can't wait to take him to school to show Beanie. I'll even let her ride him sometimes.

I fling my arms around my father. I snatch a glance in *her* direction, to see if she's put out about my beautiful new horse, but she's looking across at the field with such a look of wonder on her face that I have to look too.

'I couldn't resist,' Daddy laughs. 'I know that Ted Bailey must have thought I was a walkover, but they came as a pair really. Couldn't separate them.'

The Handbag presses her hand over her mouth, speechless for once.

I feel my heart racing, and force my breathing to stay at normal level.

It's *my* birthday, I'm thinking. It's my birthday, not hers.

The Handbag clutches me, starry-eyed. 'Isn't it brilliant?' she says. 'Isn't it amazing that we've both got spotty horses, Wills! We can train them together, get them to perform tricks like at the shows. Oh, Gazza, you're amazing – thank you, thank you!'

Her horse is very like mine. I have to listen as she runs through hundreds of ridiculous names for him, finally settling on Spotty.

I want to spit and bite. Instead I pose as Daddy takes a photo of the four of us, and make myself smile as the Handbag takes a horse-and-rider selfie to post to her friends.

Then I watch as she leaps onto Daddy to hug him, wrapping her legs around him as if she's ten years old, not fucking twenty-four.

Lucky Dip

'Come on then, girls. Scream louder – you know you want to!'

A man's voice, twangy vowels and smirky through the loudspeaker. A clutch of girls on the Scream Machine kick their legs and squeal. One of them leans forward and looks down as the gondola is slowly ratcheted upwards. Above them, the drop tower blinks with a thousand lights.

I keep thinking I see her, on the carousel, on the dodgems.

'She has my money!' I want to shout. 'She took all of it.'

I go up to the man in the ticket booth of the Scream Machine. He's swiping at his phone, all the time keeping up his patter – 'Scream, girls, screaaaaaaaaaammmmmm!'

'I wonder if you'll send out a message?' I say.

His eyes slide over to me. 'What's that, darlin'?'

Now he's looking at me properly, and I force myself to smile. Bright as glass. He smiles too, but it is slow and creeping. I remember that I am wearing red lipstick. Dig my nails into my hands.

'I need to find my friend,' I say. 'She's got blonde dreadlocks' Speaks with an Australian accent.'

He flaps his hand at me. 'Gotta just do this one,' he says. 'Aaaaannnnnnnd, screammmmmmm!' He drops a lever, and the gondola, which is perched high at the top of the tower, plunges rapidly in a shriek of cries and kicking legs.

'Well?' I say. 'Have you seen her? Will you help me?'

He laughs silently, watching. 'And why would I help you?' he says, without taking his eyes off the girls as they scramble off, brushing their skinny jeans and denim miniskirts down.

'Well,' I say, leaning closer to his booth. 'Maybe you could buy me a drink…'

He smirks. 'Now you're talking.'

I fidget, scanning the crowds of kids and couples, as he speaks into the Tannoy.

'And now a message for anyone who's seen a blonde-haired girl with dreadlocks, usually seen playing with fire, please come to the ticket booth. Her friend desperately needs to talk to her.' He turns to me. 'That all right, darlin'?'

I snap on my smile. 'Oh, yes, thank you,' I say.

I hover beside the ticket booth for the Scream Machine for over an hour, all the time thinking I can see her. I'm also waiting for a hand on my shoulder, for someone to recognise my face. *But I don't look like Willow Stephens,* a voice inside me says. *Not any more.*

You are the girl named Frog. The girl in the yellow coat.

'I am no one,' I whisper. Suz, of course, doesn't come. Neither does anyone claiming to know her whereabouts. She is as invisible as me.

'Clocking off now, darlin'.' A voice at my shoulder. It's Ticket Booth Man, come to claim his reward. He lays his hand casually on the base of my back. 'How about a little drink at The Mermaid for starters?' he says, and his voice slides down my spine like engine oil.

I wriggle away. 'I don't think so,' I say. 'But thank you anyway.' I don't stay to hear the name he calls me as I slip off through the crowds, dodging around a man carrying a child on his shoulders and a woman pushing a double buggy. Instead, I spend my last coins on a hot chocolate and a bag of doughnuts, eating them sitting on the steps of the ghost train.

There's someone following me along the boardwalk. It's raining now; I can hear it falling in great splatters, but through it, a sound: panting, breathing.

I swing round.

It's the fairground man. He's hunched against the rain, in a black jacket, but I can see the whites of his eyes. He bares his teeth at me. I look above him, at the promenade, and wish I had chosen to walk along the road, where there's traffic and chip shops and people. Here, beside the beach, there's nothing but bristling sea on one side, and the dark arches on the other. A few fishing boats, rotten and dead, tilt in chains halfway along the beach.

'You up for a good time, sweetie?'

'Go away. I've changed my mind. I don't want to go to the pub with you.'

I try to push past him, to where the steps are.

He stands in front of me, and the boardwalk shudders. In the light of the lamps above, his eyes glint like granite. For a small man, he fills up a lot of space.

'I need to go now, please.'

The air is thick with menace, dark as a threat.

Fairground Man laughs. Then he whistles.

Another figure sidles up from nowhere, from the shadows of late evening, when day sinks into dark.

A boy, nineteen or so. Blurry tattoo on the side of his neck, skinny hands like a lady's. He would be beautiful, if it weren't for his eyes, which are bright and mad.

'Piss off,' I say.

An outbreath, forced through laughter. The boardwalk rocks as he jiggles on the soles of his trainers.

'I don't like people who change their mind,' says Fairground Man. 'It's not fair, is it, Hash?' Teeth flash silver. His eyes are cold and dead.

'Not fair...' echoes Hash, in a high, soft voice. He moves forward, and places his hand on the wall of the arches. The hairs on the back of his hand are pale. He is holding something.

I look for somewhere to run. I am fit and strong. I can get out of this.

Turns out I can't.

I always knew this was coming. You can't keep running without expecting one day to get caught.

There's danger in men's smiles. Who was it said that? Lady Macbeth? Or was it daggers? Hash has a knife, I see that now. He has a little knife hidden in his fist, and the mean edge of it glints, just enough for me to see. He wants me to see, I realise.

'Want me to keep you warm?' Fairground Man says, smiling. 'I know a place.'

I need to find somewhere to hide. I need to run –

But it's too late for that. Two men and one girl is no

match. Sudden as a shriek, they're onto me, pushing, pressing me against the wall of the arches. Above, traffic hums and roars. Somewhere, an engine throbs.

I writhe and kick and fight – try to bite the hand that clamps me. For some reason I think of the Haunted House. *Three tokens per person!* it says, in letters which drip blood. There's a picture of the Grim Reaper with his scythe. The rain streams, and there is nobody to see me. My only weapon, my scream, is trapped like a bird behind a rough hand. Fairground Man's signet ring digs into my cheekbone.

I can't let them push me down.

There's a bizarre dance shuffle and gasp as they try to move me into the shadows where we can't be seen. Beneath us, the boardwalk shudders.

I can't fall, mustn't let them push me into there, where the day's been sucked into night; I must stay out, near the sea. Can't let them push me over.

Scuffling shoes. Breathing. The sour bite of a fleshy hand.

'Bitch bit me –'

Can't hold, can't hold them away much longer.

'What the–?'

A whoosh of something bright and hot and flaring. The smell of Kerosene and smoke.

Another dark figure, small and wild. Hair dancing like snakes.

'Ouch – get it away from me –'

A whirligig of flames, ribboning great arcs through the ripped darkness.

Howls and sparks and madness. A burning brand is pushed up under Hash's chin. Through the flames, a pair of glinting eyes, smoke-maddened. Dancing crazy patterns. Broken tooth, black mouth, swinging dreads.

A voice. 'Get off her.'

That voice. I'd know it anywhere.

Suz.

She's back.

One of the men laughs, but uncertainly. The flames zither over his skin.

'Get off her or I kill you.'

Now they stop. Just to snigger.

'It's a little lady.'

'Hello, laaadyyy.'

There is a swooshing sound, and something lands by our heads. The man twists round to see, and splutters, swears.

'What the –'

Another missile flies, bounces against the boarding, and lands in a thud of sparks. I wrench myself free from Hash's hand, and back away. Wooden slats bounce as I stumble to the ground. My hands find wood, not flesh. I stay there for a moment, on my hands and knees, breath screaming.

Free.

Suz is letting her devil sticks fly at all angles. They land, a burning circle around the men, a pigeon's breath away from their eyes, their ears, their hair. Fairground Man takes a step towards Suz, hands outstretched, and she is onto him instantly, letting another of those batons fly. It loops over his head and narrowly misses his right eye. And now he's on the ground. Did a baton hit him after all? He's clutching his head and is moaning.

Suz is hunkered down, fists clenched, in her mad woollen coat, a dark figure, eyes blazing. With her dreadlocks high and wild around her head, she looks like Medusa.

'She's crazy.'

'Mad bitch. Let's go.'

I get my own fire back. Grab Hash and grapple with him, punch his shoulders, stomach, face.

Feels good. I feel strong.

He can't take it. The thump and shudder of the boards as he runs off.

'Bind the other one! Tie him up!'

Suz throws me lengths of something hot and spiky. Fairy lights. They're lit by battery, metres and metres of them. She helps me bundle the lights round Fairground Man, her knee on his chest. I can tell she's in pain with her leg by the way she's gasping, but she doesn't stop, and for a moment I think she's going to kill him; his eyes are bulging in the orange lights, like there's still fire in them. Like there's hell in them.

'Wind it round the bastard. Let's dig a hole. Drown him.'

I force the lights over and under and around him until he's trussed like a Christmas turkey.

'Help me move him.'

Somehow we're pushing him, shoving him onto a boat. It's rotten, like him. There's a stench of dead birds and guano and ancient fish, long caught and decayed.

'Leave him there. Just leave him.'

Suz kicks open the door of the cabin as I wrestle him inside. Lobster pots and coils of rope and things half-rotten. A horror show.

'Get him inside.'

We ram rotting planks of wood against the door. He's not going anywhere soon. Leave him to stew in his own stench.

He's trying to plead, to beg.

'Should have thought of that, shouldn't you?'

Suz shoves him with her good knee. Hard. Winds him.

I want to punch and throttle him. I restrain myself.

When we look back, we can still see him through the window, twinkling orange: on-off, on-off. If he's shouting, we can't hear him.

110

Barbie Dolls

Suz starts to walk away. I stare. Rain drums, harder than ever. She's shrinking, a dark figure in the hissing street lights.

I hurry after her. Take her by one wet woollen sleeve and force her round to look at me.

'You!' I say. 'You. You took everything, all my money. Everything I had.'

I press my face up to hers, and I am screaming now, into that wet, shiny, rain-run face. I note with satisfaction the flash of fear that she replaces, quick as a whip, with a careful blankness.

'You conned me. You made me think you were my friend —'

'I needed to survive. It's what I do... it's what I know —'

'Where is it, I'll —'

I'm searching through her stuff now; I've grabbed the handle of her case, and we're playing tug-of-war with her devil-sticks.

'I'll have them!' I scream — somewhere I hear my voice scream. 'Give them to me. I'll have these instead, you thiev-ing, awful *cow* —'

She's breathing hard; I can smell the hot, sour stink of her breath. She yanks the case from me and staggers back, almost falls, but gets her balance. I'm just left with her binbag of crap. Under the street lamp, I pull handfuls of useless, smelly stuff out, all over the shining pavement, and she's on her hands and knees, just as quickly scooping them up and trying to shove them back.

And I'm still shouting, my voice raw and wet and vicious: 'Where is it? Where's my money, you *tramp*?' I call her worse names, vile names that I've dug deep to find. Words with

111

spitting consonants and short, harsh vowels. And all the time I'm pulling out holey tights and crumpled clothes and unwashed socks and filthy towels and strange, stupid things: tiny ballet shoes with grubby ribbons; a bent and naked Barbie doll with dog-chewed hair; a carrier bag stuffed with pigeon feathers; a glue gun; a packet of pumpkin seeds; fistfuls of paper origami birds; a splay of sherbet-filled plastic straws; a pocket guide to Paris.

'Stop it!' she's saying. 'Leave my stuff. Leave –'

She kicks me, hard, in my shin, and I yelp and groan, watch through the rain as she scrabbles to pick up her stuff, then grabs her bags and limps away.

'You're mad,' she shouts over her shoulder. 'Crazy – off your tree.' She loops through the streets, criss-crossing over the plaza, zig-zagging across the road. A lone paper bird sinks into a puddle.

'You come back!' I bawl.

I need to let it all out – I can't focus for the moment, for rage. Around me, the fatty fug of chips, doughnuts, popcorn.

Suz is running up the steps now – I can just make out her form, moving towards the top of West Hill.

She's not getting away with this.

I give chase, and I am faster. Even with the lack of food, without training, all those years of riding and gymnastics and dance classes have paid off.

I find her, panting, by the bench beneath the sycamore trees. She's bending over, coughing.

'Please don't...take...my kit,' she says. It's there on the steps, streaming lamp-lit rain, golden against its silver sides.

'You can stick your fire kit. Where's my money? I want my money. It was my savings – everything I had.' Each sentence brought out, forced out, as I'm gripping her shoulders, and she's surprisingly thin under all that wool. Her clothes smell sour: rank, wet wool and something old and savoury and unwashed. She gives in, very suddenly. The rain over us streams through shiny laurel leaves, on the greasy path.

'I don't have it,' she says, and it's like she's waiting for me to hit her. She's closed her eyes, and her face looks otherworldly, as if she's a pixie or a sprite. Her cheekbones harsh-shadowed under her hood. I let her go in disgust.

'Take your stupid fire sticks,' I say. I sink down onto the bench. *In loving memory of Edith, who liked to sit here.* Dimly, I wonder who Edith was, and why she liked to sit here; it's a terrible place to sit, a dark, dog-walker's alley. I put my head in my hands. My mind, which was jumping and fizzing, is now simply numb.

There's a creak as Suz sits down too.

'It's gone,' she says, when she can speak again.

I look up.

'All right?' Her chin is defiant. 'It's all gone. I needed to pay some people what I owed, and there's nothing left.'

I give up. We sit, clawing for breath, on the slimed bench. Down below, the sea snakes and ripples with red and yellow street lights.

'And my pills?'

She shakes her head.

'So, that's it then,' I say.

'That's it,' she agrees.

I don't know what to do. I have nothing.

I think of how I can pull myself out of this mess.

No 1: Find a phone. Ring Daddy.

No 2: Speak to Daddy.

No 3: Wait for a while, not for long; it may be only a matter of hours. Get in his car. It will be big and sleek and valeted, and it will smell of new leather and newer money. It will be driven by his chauffeur, the one who likes to watch French movies late at night and pace around the lake smoking his strong cigarettes. When I was younger, I would pick them up and smell them. Once, I tried to light one and smoke it. It tasted of loneliness and the time before dawn when the sky is still violet.

No 4: Be driven all the way back to Oxfordshire. Enter the house. Up our driveway. Shoes off. Hot bath. Food, prepared by Martyna and served with a scowl. A pair of shoes, in the hall, silly-high, alien. A house drenched in perfume, heavy and sweet and strong. There may still be confetti caught up in the lawn; a paper lantern in hot pink tugging at the willows or in the lake amongst the reeds.

There'll be the ping of the microwave, laughter in the kitchen and the clink of glasses.

For me, a hurried telephone call, smooth promises and a determined smile.

A uniform, freshly cleaned and pressed, laid out; a trunk, freshly packed.

Another long car journey. Girls' stares. Whispers.

Counselling. Counselling. Counselling.

I can't do it.

I can never go home.

I stand up. Begin to walk. I am no one. I have nowhere to go. No one wants me.

'Wait.'

Suz is back, coughing still, limping after me.

'Go away.'

'I can help you.'

'I don't need your help. Leave me alone.'

'I've got somewhere to stay.'

I shake her off, and head towards the seafront, towards St Leonards. I don't know where I'm going, and I can tell she knows that I don't know. It makes me angry again.

'It isn't much,' she calls. 'I can help you.'

'Are you mad? Why would I need your help?'

'You don't have anywhere. I saved you. From those fellers. I have skills I could teach you, remember?'

The rain streams. My bag is sodden against my back. I slow down.

'It's not far,' she shouts. 'I've got tea.'

I stop.

A cup of hot tea sounds good. *Tomorrow*, I think, *I will get sorted out tomorrow. I will make decisions, make a list. I will ask at the café if they can put me up, let me work for them –*

I –

I can't go back.

I turn to Suz.

'Just for the night,' I say. 'You owe me.'

We reach the place by climbing a fire escape. It's rusted and peeling, and has seen better days. The house is one of those big Edwardian ones with a sea view if you crane your neck far enough. It looks like it's in the process of being done up; scaffolding cages the front.

'Look,' says Suz. 'You can just see the pier – see that?'

She hangs right off the ladder, craning her neck. It's still hissing rain, but she doesn't move. She's staring out to the small patch of sea, biting her lip. 'I effing love that place,' she says. 'Cried my eyes out when it burnt down.' Then she seems to collect herself.

'Quiet for this part,' she hisses. I watch as she swings herself up off the steps and onto the roof. It's broad and wide and someone's made an effort with a tiny roof garden: a hammock and a bit of trellising and a plastic sack of soil with a few straggling tomato plants.

'Quick, they're home,' she mouths. She treads softly over

115

the roof and past a skylight. Below, steam rises, curry-scented. Someone's cooking.

Over this side of the roof it's much scruffier. Lumps of broken concrete, and a child's bicycle. A rusted barbecue bucket. A pile of baskets. And everywhere, chalked drawings: overlapping flowers and strange animals and cities with melted skylines and Kafka-esque dead-ends and Escher-esque alleyways. It's like some monstrous and beautiful tattoo.

Except the rain is melting it.

Suz slushes through the chalk-slime, and pushes aside a stack of plastic, weather-warped tubs and crates. There are sticks and branches and metal poles and toy dinosaurs and mirrors and odd shoes and wellies with flowers and checks and squiggles and footballs and tennis balls.

A broken ironing board.

An old-style TV set with a smashed screen.

A table with no legs.

A hula hoop.

A lampshade, mustard yellow.

A leather Chesterfield sofa, with a ripped and ruined seat.

Pinned-up feathers on a washing line.

'They can't see us here,' Suz says.

I don't ask who 'they' are. I am shivering violently. All of a sudden, I feel tired and ill.

The skylight on this side is covered by a rug that once must have been lovely. Now it is beaten and old and rat-tugged.

'There's no light,' Suz whispers. 'You have to feel your way. Just follow me.'

I watch Suz reach down the matching skylight on this side, and fiddle with something until she's satisfied.

'You have to be careful – there's a drop before you reach the ladder. But it's totally safe, if you know what you're do-

116

ing.' She gives me a quick smile, and vanishes down the hatch, hands gripping the frame for a moment, and then they too disappear.

I shuffle my way forward on my bottom. I don't know if I can ever stand up again. Maybe it was all the running, or I'm suffering from delayed shock from what happened at the beach, but I can't seem to stop shaking. I slide my legs down the hole and try to feel for the top of the ladder; feel Suz's hand grip my ankle and guide me. Close my eyes for a moment, and then half-slide, half-fall onto the ladder, and down it to the passage below.

It's a house of horror.

Abandoned. Dark. Musty.

'Used to be a shop. A department store,' Suz says. She busies herself, removing her cardigan, hanging it on a shop dummy with an afro wig and yellow John Lennon glasses. One of its arms is raised and holding a plastic wand. Suz pauses to examine a tooth in the blade of a vintage-looking ice skate with no laces. She sees me watching, and beams her crooked, broken smile; gestures vaguely around with the ice skate.

'Wonderful, don't you think?'

It isn't wonderful. It smells, and it's horrid.

A counter in fifties' laminate looms ghostlike. Everything smells sour, like old garlic, potatoes, things left in the dark to fester and push out invisible threads. We pass a cubbyhole with a blackened toilet.

'Watch your footing. We have to climb over rafters to get to my kitchen.'

I nod, and wish I could stop shivering.

'There's no floor on this bit. It's my mezzanine,' Suz says. Her eyes are watching me closely. I realise that she is proud of this place, that it's her home, and she's desperate for me to like it.

I swallow. 'It's lovely,' I say.

She looks gratified. 'Come on, I'll make you tea. And sausages,' she says 'I'm totally vegan, but I do eat sausages.'

Balanced on the rafters are jars of lentils and pulses and beans and flour, peanut butter and jam and chocolate spread. Strung around the beams are fairy lights and strings of paper birds.

'I can't eat animals,' she says. 'I feel their pain. Like a tight band. Makes me stop breathing. These are my Suz sausages. Sit down, come on. I'll cook some for you.'

I look around, but there's nowhere to sit: only the rafters and a filthy-looking pile of cushions and mattresses pushed under the roof.

Suz laughs. 'Just don't look down,' she says. She takes her boots off and walks straight across the beam and back without looking, stoops to pick up a plastic bowl with a cloth over it. There's a little camping stove in the corner and she sits cross-legged in front of it and starts frying whatever's in the bowl until it starts to throw out acrid smoke, all the time casting me sidelong glances.

I sit on a beam, and try to take off my damp coat, give up, sit staring down to the dusty sheeted floor below and wondering how much courage it would take just to slide off and drop.

'Ta-da!' she says. 'Suz's sausages. Made of lentils, flour and peanut butter.' She passes me the pan and a fork.

They are truly awful. Dusty and old-tasting. I try to eat, but all I want to do is to lie down somewhere and maybe never wake up.

Suz is passing me something hot and steaming. I take the chipped mug. The Cadbury's Easter bunny leers up at me and winks. I hope it's tea. It isn't.

It tastes…hot. There are things floating, which look like husks of bugs.

'Cardamom tea,' she says. 'From the market. They have spices…on offer, kind of.'

I imagine her filling her pockets. I sip, and try not to mind that the mug is deeply stained. Like the bottom of a pen pot, scribbled round and round with biro. The tea tastes of perfume.

I shiver again.

'Hey, you're cold,' she says. 'And still wet. Here –'

She helps me take off my soaking coat, and I just let her; I don't care any more. I let myself lean forward as she peels away my damp top and rubs me vigorously with a gross-looking, evil-smelling tea towel.

'Come on, you can have my bed to lie down on, it's totally fine.'

I let her lead me to the stinking sheets on the stained and awful mattress, and I lie down, and close my eyes. When I open them, Suz is hovering over me like a mother hen, and behind her is a row of naked Barbie dolls.

'There,' Suz says. 'There you go. That's better.' I feel like she's rubbing away yet another layer of myself.

Soon, there will nothing of me left.

Dream-dancer

My mother's face turns to me, smiles, as she pats her hair. 'Come,' she says, beckoning me to sit on her lap. Her hair smells of rose oil and magic.

'I will teach you to fly,' she whispers. 'Close your eyes now.'

And I climb onto her lap and I close my eyes as she wets her finger and smooths cool powder over each eyelid, applies kohl with a thin brush.

'Now stand against the wall,' she smiles. 'Go on, pretty one.'

I run to where she is pointing; it is a round board and I am to stretch out my arms like a star.

'And your feet too,' my mother's voice says. 'Keep your eyes closed.'

So I stand with my arms and feet outstretched and my butterfly eyes, and I laugh as my mother sends something whistling past my ear. It digs with a thwack into the board. There's another, by the right side of my head, and all around my legs, pinpointing me like a dot-to-dot picture.

But I am scared.

I do open my eyes. And this is when I begin to cry, because Mother is smiling and laughing with her curved red lips, hurling knives at me, one after another, and now she's coming closer; her face is that of a giant, like the troll in my fairy tale book who frightened me with his big red lips and huge globe eyes.

'Stop it,' I say. 'I want to fly.'

But she's still throwing the knives, and they sing as they land. Soon she will chop tiny pieces of me and I will be nothing.

Bed of Nails

When I wake up, Suz's face looms close. She's holding another mug of the cardamom tea, and something that steams in a tin.

'Chocolate porridge,' she says. 'I let you sleep. You were crying out a lot.'

I breathe in with a shudder. I am still here, in Suz's terrible house and her terrible sheets. I look down beside me and there are the rafters, with the yawning space below.

Then I look around frantically.

'My bag,' I say. 'My Kit of Happiness. What have you done with it? You've stolen it. You –'

She puts the tin and mug down. Nods towards the corner. 'It's here. It's here. Your stuff's here. Jeez. Why would I want that bag of crap, anyway?'

My heart slows. There's my bag, as she says, hanging from a nail on the rafter.

'I need the loo,' I say.

Suz shrugs. 'There's the backyard. Anything else, you have to use the public toilets. I wash in the ones by the beach.'

I look at Suz's dirt-ingrained face, and doubt that she bothers to make the journey that often. Then feel bad. Then don't, because it was her, after all, who stole from *me*. So she's just paying something back.

I curl my hands around the tin of porridge and sniff it. It does smell of chocolate, although it looks like something a child would make out of mud and wood chippings.

'Cacao nibs,' says Suz.

'From the market,' I say.

She laughs and coughs. Her fingers shake a little as she fumbles around for her Rizla papers and her tin. She leaves me to my porridge and walks across the rafters to the counter, ducks down behind it, and there's silence. I wonder what she's doing behind there. I taste the porridge with the fork she has given me. Apart from the fact that it's made with water instead of milk, it's not so bad, the cacao nibs crunching into the oats. I eat it between sips of scalding, perfumed tea, and start to feel the warmth back in my bones. Later, I will find somewhere to wash and go to the loo, and maybe look for my toothbrush, and then I'll start to make plans.

I get up cautiously, testing out my shaky legs and keeping well away from the drop between the rafters. Apart from my still-damp socks, and the faint memories of my dream, I feel all right. As all right as it's possible to feel in a squat with no floors or ceilings, which stinks of stale garlic and staler weed.

Suz has risen from behind the counter. She's picking her way carefully towards me, and she's a little unsteady on her legs. I look at the can in her hand. It's black coloured and looks like it's strong, whatever it is. She looks down at it and laughs.

'Don't worry, it's totally vegan,' she says, but her voice sounds sort of thick and distant.

'I'm not staying,' I say, but even to my ears my words don't ring true. I have nowhere else to go.

Suz's breath has the sweet-sour reek of cider, and her hair looks like it could do with a good wash. But I suppose that goes for me too. I step away from her, nearly losing my balance as I forget about the lack of floor.

She grips me in her strong hands. 'Careful,' she says, only slurring a little. She shakes her can and places it carefully next to a jar of something brown and lumpy that says it is almond butter. The paper birds flutter, and she sees me looking.

'Make them out of scraps of paper I find,' she says. 'I'd sell 'em, but they take too long to make. Gotta measure your input against output, right? The bracelets, though – now you're talking.'

I have no idea what she's talking about.

'We'll make beautiful art first,' she says, 'to earn our living.' She pulls her satchel from a Barbie-doll hook, and stoops to lace her boots. Then she beams a wide, huge smile at me. 'And then,' she says, 'I'm going to teach you to walk on air.'

Chalkdust

We climb back down the fire escape until we are in the tiny backyard. From this level, in the bright, cool morning light, the contrast between the two sides of the building are even more apparent. On Suz's side, it's all gaping broken- and boarded-up windows. Graffiti tags are sprayed hurriedly over the back walls. Suz scowls when she sees them.

'Absolute garbage,' she sniffs. 'Where's the beauty in that? Where's the art?' I watch her as she chalks on the wall: *3/10 Could do better.*

'What *is* this place?' I ask.

'It used to be a hotel before it became a department store. Then druggie squats. Then it won lottery funding to get turned into an artists' residence for the whole community, then it was bought for uni accommodation.' She shrugs. 'But that fell through. So it's back to squats, I guess.' She winks. 'On my side anyway, but that won't be for long. The other side's already been turned into posh apartments. They'll come for this side soon.'

She points to a *For Sale* sign poking out of a straggling hedge. I wonder what she'll do once it gets sold. I shiver. What *I'll* do.

Out on the pavement, Suz darts forward to grab a paper bag that's caught in a hedge, folds it carefully and puts it into her pocket. 'Needed some more blue,' she says.

After we wash in the public toilet block – well, I wash, using what's left in my little plastic travel bottles, and she just ducks her whole head under the taps, then shakes her hair like a dog and sighs – we make our way past the pier to the promenade. Suz chatters on about her absurd scheme, which she 'dreamt', she said, 'like it was effing fate or something…I can totally be your manager. It was my dream that gave me the idea, and then waking up and seeing you there, asleep and moany and sweaty. Then I looked out of the skylight this morning, and saw two pigeons sitting, just looking at me. *Two* pigeons, Frog! You know what that means?'

I don't know what that means.

Suz surveys me with her blue-green eyes. They're not sea-glass today, more the colour of a storm-darkened sky. 'It means LUCK, Frog. We're going to be successful, and have our heart's desire!'

The sky seems to shiver then, and the sun comes out. Suz laughs delightedly.

'Draw!' she commands. We kneel down on the pavement, and she gives me chalk.

We sit all day, absorbed in creating strange worlds. Hers are of mad, monstrous flowers, with tiny rooms in their stamen and eyes in their buds. Insect people crawl up the stems, hairy human legs on grasshoppers' abdomens.

'It means nothing,' she laughs, when I ask her. She switches to drawing her dream: pictures of a dark-eyed girl with a smudge of yellow hair, flying through the air and back-flipping on a tightrope. The girl has thick wrists and ankles, and I don't need to ask to know that it is me.

'It'll be you, when I've stage-managed you,' she laughs. 'When I've taught you all I know, and made your costume and done all of your promo. You'll make our fortune, Frog.' She leans over her drawings, careless of the chalk dust over her knees and feet and Aladdin pants. She starts to hum. She is utterly absorbed.

I draw buildings with small, tightly shut windows and great creeping ivy and wisteria bursting out of the bricks and tiles. I draw flying pigs in white ruffs, and flying babies with wings.

I don't tell her what it means either. I don't draw my dream.

Sometimes, we make money. Mostly we don't.

Suz's Vegan Curry
To feed two

2 onions
1 tin of tomatoes – *valu* range
1 tin mixed veg ('or real if you can get them')
1 beetroot★ (Don't ask. This is Suz's special ingredient and is 'good for the brain'.)
Curry powder/spices
1 banana/desiccated coconut (optional, but both highly recommended by Suz)

1. Fry the onions and spices together, taking care not to burn them. (Suz always does.)
2. Chop the beetroot. It will stain your fingers, and everything else it touches. This does not matter. It is a vital ingredient, according to Suz.
3. Throw into the pan, along with the mixed veg. What they are is irrelevant. They'll all turn purple by the end anyway.
4. Pour in the tomatoes and an extra can of water, taking care not to step backwards into the gaping cavern that is the missing floor as you do so.
5. Leave to burp and splatter (for at least an hour.)

Optional: If you're feeling decadent, serve with chopped banana and sprinkles of desiccated coconut. This is not advised as it tastes absolutely disgusting, but according to Suz, makes it 'even more vegan'.

★ If you visit the loo the next day and happen to look down, do not think you are bleeding to death. This will be the beetroot making its way through your system.

Walking on Air

'This is the perfect spot,' says Suz.

I make a face. 'Are you sure?'

'Sure I'm sure! Just look at it. You'll be like the Karate Kid. I'm like your guru, mentor, whatever.'

'Except you're not Chinese.'

'Except I'm not Chinese,' Suz agrees. She squats down and draws a line on the floor with chalk. 'This here's your tight rope. All you have to do is walk the line.'

'But it's on the floor,' I point out.

'Well of course it's on the floor, dumb-ass! What do you think I'm trying to do – kill you? She finishes drawing the line and straightens up. 'That comes later,' she grins.

We are up on the rooftop. We can see for miles, towards West Hill to the left and Beachy Head to the right. Somewhere are the twin funiculars, caterpillar-crawling their way endlessly up and down the cliffside. And the new shopping centre, with its brand names and plazas and retail outlets. There's the station. There, Old Hastings, with its twisty, twiny streets and fishing shacks.

And always the sea, endlessly moving. It's behaving itself today, all pink and gold shimmer.

'Are we safe?' I ask, nodding towards the neighbours' skylight. There's no smell of cooking today, and it's firmly shut.

Suz nods. 'They'll be at work. Only their cat's at home. A ginger monster. He'll crush you in his maw like a spider if he ever sees you.'

She says this carelessly, as if it's a perfectly normal thing to say. I watch her move the broken trellises on our side, defeated by the relentless sea gales. There are a couple of chairs, orange plastic and losing their springs. We have some like them in our prefects' common room, but ours are covered in pillows and cushions and throws. *Had*, I remind myself. I am not part of that world any more.

'Ready?'

I shrug and walk the chalk line rapidly. 'It's not exactly difficult,' I say. I turn and do it again.

Suz doesn't answer straight away. She's sitting cross-legged under a huge, holey sun parasol, which is all horrible seventies brown and orange flowers. Beneath it, the shadows make her seem unworldly, Puckish.

'Hmmm,' she says. 'I'm not sure...'

I begin to get impatient. 'What aren't you sure about?' She frowns a little, like an *X Factor* judge about to give her verdict.

'Fair,' she says.

I scowl. 'So what do you suggest, to make it *better*?'

She jumps up. 'Feathers,' she says, 'and fire.'

She disappears down the skylight, and returns, huffing and gasping, trying to push her precious silver case through.

I help her.

'You want me to carry fire?'

She takes out her lighter. Flicks it with a chalky thumb. 'I want you to *eat* fire.'

Suz keeps calling out commands while I struggle, swear, sob and hiss with pain.

She keeps yelling as my throat rasps, the skin around my lips blisters and the inside of my mouth burns when I get it wrong. My mouth aches from stretching it around the cotton. My eyes stream and I am high with breathing in the fumes.

But I don't stop.

Days and days later, I still don't stop.

'Keep ya hair tied back, ya nonce.'

'Hold your breath. *Hold* your breath! Jeez, are you trying to kill yourself?'

'Tip your head back far enough that the fire goes straight up toward your hand.'

'Close your lips. Close your lips *now* – mind the torch.'

'I have a headache,' I say.

'That's totally normal. Keep going.'

'I'm going to be sick.'

'Have some water. Again.'

Until finally: 'Not bad, Frog. Not bad.'

After I've swallowed enough fire to fill a thousand dragons, I try it while walking the chalk line. Suz sits beneath her parasol like a queen. A queen who drinks extra strong cider and has a liking for subversive art.

'You've got to let yourself go more, Frog. Be really wild, release your inner fire demons. Like this.' And she capers around the roof in her broad bare feet, shaking her dreadlocks, rolling her eyes. In her hands, the fire sticks become magical weapons, brands forged from a nest of dragons.

When she tires, which is soon, her breath rasping like a hacksaw, she tosses them to me, one after another, panting. 'OK, now your turn, Fire Girl.'

And she whoops and she hollers as she watches, drumming her beaded feet on the ground as I dance and whirl, clapping her hands at my fire-eating finale.

'OK,' she says after a while. 'Time to raise the stakes.'

I shake my head, peering out to sea. 'It's getting dark.' I say.

She shoves her parasol into a plant pot full of desiccated soil and begins to climb down the ladder. I hear her coughing as I pack the devil sticks carefully into their case.

I am tired. I keep burping petroleum. Even a pan of slimy vegan sausages might be welcome.

Suz's Vegan Sausages

1 handful of flour ('S'posed to be chickpea flour, Frog, but what the hell is that, anyway?')
2 tins of beans 'Any type will do.' (But not baked. Suz tried that once, and even she said it was a mistake.)
Mixed herbs (If you have them. We don't.)
Something to mash it all up with (Suz sometimes uses the edge of a brick. So it was real dust I tasted the first and only time I tried these.)
A little oil ('Not too much though, or it'll get on the candles and set the whole place alight.')

1. First, use the facilities at the beach toilets to wash your hands.
2. Mash everything up together and mould the sticky mess into sausage shapes with your hands.
3. Wash out your only pan and fry the sasusages in the oil. They will totally stick to the bottom, but apparently 'the burnt bits are the best'.
    Which doesn't say a lot for the rest of it.

Crescendo

'I'm not doing that,' I say.

Suz rolls her eyes. 'You're ready. I *feel* that you're ready.'

'But I can't see anything. It's almost dark.'

She sighs. I hear her suck in a lungful of cheap shag tobacco. 'That's the whole point. We're building you up to doing it blindfolded.'

'Blindfolded?'

'Of course. It's called crescendo. When you build up the excitement and tension to an effing amazing all-out climax.'

'I know what crescendo means,' I snap. 'I did violin and cello.'

I try to peer through the gathering shadows at the beam. Suz has picked the longest one, which joins both sides of the house. It's not exactly narrow, not like a real tightrope would be, but then it's not exactly wide either. And I'll be stopping halfway to swallow fire.

'Just do it, Frog, you know, like the Nike ads.' Suz's voice is slurring again. She's cuddling up to the can of cider that she's rescued from its perch next to the organic almond butter.

'Fine,' I say.

I move the flickering candle closer to the beam and try to focus on what I can make out of the far side of the wall. If I slip, I'll die, there's no other way of saying it.

I push down the sneaking voice, and try to slow my breathing. I have no more pills and no way of getting any more, so I can't afford a panic attack right now – not ever.

'In your own time,' drones Suz. It's difficult to sound sarcastic when you're cider-soaked. I decide to ignore her.

I place my right foot onto the beam and squeeze my abdominals, try to imagine a heavy sphere settling in the core of my belly, which was what we had to do when I did gymnastics.

It's the same as you've always done, I think. *Up on the roof, back home. It's just that, this time, there's a half-drunk homeless girl egging you on, and a mile of black empty space below you.*

I take another step. I am committed now; I may as well go forwards. I keep my eyes trained on where I think the far wall may be, and, all too soon, I am in the middle of the beam, the very centre of this huge, gaping, cavernous house, balanced like a dancer.

If I should fall...

Somewhere, I can hear Suz humming under her breath, and it's the same tune that the Romanian musicians were playing at the Art Café, days or weeks ago.

'Fire!' Suz shouts suddenly, and I wobble. Curse her under my breath. I reach for my devil sticks and light them. The room burns into brightness. Shadows swoop and dance and lunge. I am in the very belly of hell.

'Eat the bloody fire!'

And I do. Teetering in the middle of an ancient beam in a crumbling house, I perform and swirl the sticks and dip my head. I am dancing with the devil and playing with fire.

I have cast off Willow like a burning snakeskin.

Pavement Art

'Paris is a city of dreams,' says Suz. 'You go down the Champs Élysées and every shop's a work of art, every cake a miniature sculpture, every window a giant canvas. I could sit myself at the Place du Tertre in Montmartre and set up my easel and draw and paint all day long. A bit like what I do now, Frog, but earning heaps more money. I'd draw the passers-by, sketch them sitting on giant birds,' she sighs. 'I'd look at their faces, and hold up their chins, and tell them what sort of bird they are. I'd be appreciated there, Frog. You can charge over twenty Euros just for one drawing. Instead of waiting for some tosser to chuck in twenty pence. Know what I'm saying?

'And the galleries. Don't get me started on them When I've sold a couple of portraits, that'll be me done for the day, so I can just stroll around the galleries, maybe soak up some Impressionists at the Musée d'Orsay, or peruse the Neoclassicals at the Louvre or gaze at Monet's lilies at the Musée de l'Orangerie, before getting hungry and hitting the Marche Mouffetard for some really cheap fruit and vegetables and bread. If I get tired walking, Frog, there's even a little white train that'll pull me to all the best places. Waddaya reckon, Frog? Waddaya reckon? That's what I'm going to do, Frog, when I save the money and get myself a passport...'

And she sighs and hunches over her *Pocket Guide to Paris 2006*, the only book she ever reads. I hear her through the night, thumbing pages in the candlelight.

Pigeon Drop

The wind's up.

I struggle along the promenade, buffeted as if by an invisible force. I have two shopping bags stuffed with purchases. I hung around the market as they shut up, watching the stall-holders wrestling with the canvas awnings and poles and shouting for their helpers, their children, their dogs. It was like watching a circus big top being dismantled. One minute, a little village of huddled tents and canopies, the next, a few boxes and crates shoved neatly into white vans.

'Want them, love? Three for a pound.'

A florid-faced woman, struggling with a crate of cauliflowers, nods towards a box of aubergines. I am not sure how to cook them. But I remember Martyna – or was it one of my au pairs, the sad one, with dirty blonde hair? – cooking up something she called *lecsó*, chopping aubergines and frying them meltingly with peppers and onion and paprika. Suz would love it.

'I'll take all of them,' I say. 'And the mixed veg too.' I point to a box of browning cabbages and carrots and onions, all tumbled together in the rush to get out before the storm.

She laughs and nods. 'Awright, love. You drive a hard bargain, don't ya?' She watches me as I scoop the vegetables into Suz's satchel, along with the aubergines.

'One pound,' I say firmly. She's not to know that I found the coin on the pavement by her stall.

She shrugs and tucks it into her money belt. Then one of the awnings is ripped away and takes off like a giant mushroom.

'Hey!' she shouts, and runs to join the men who are trying to rescue it.

I grab cloves of garlic and handfuls of bunched thyme, and pick up several apples that are rolling around on the ground.

'Hey, you –'

More shouts – at me this time. But I'm gone already. I have perfected the art of melting away. How to disappear. Watch the Wonder of Willow! See How She Vanishes! You Will Not Believe Your Own Eyes!

So I'm battling along the path, lowering my head and bracing myself against the wind, bags cutting into my palms. But I'm excited, too. Suz will be so happy when I make us this vegan feast. I am even going to risk using her flour to make flatbreads. If I close my eyes, I am sure that I can remember how. I think of Martyna's big red hands kneading and pummelling at the dough, and slapping it against our wooden worktop. Daddy got a bespoke carpenter to make the butcher's block central island. It is almost the same size as a football pitch and used to take Martyna most of the day to keep the wood oiled. There was rage in her flatbreads, but sorrow too.

I remember that now.

A sudden gust pushes me sideways, and I gasp. It is almost frightening, but exhilarating too. I reach down to grab an onion which has rolled out of the bag, and push forwards, laughing and gasping. There is no one about. Wisely, they have stayed indoors. Gulls are ripped through the sky, which is sullen grey and apricot. The little kiosk at the entrance of the pier is empty, the ice cream van outside gone.

It takes me forever to cross the road and climb the fire escape with my bags. I crawl across the roof because I am afraid I will get blown away. Or struck by lightning. Or both.

There is a flash, which lights up the whole world and makes me scream. I can't remember the rules for being in a lightning storm, but I do know that you are not supposed to be alone on top of a roof.

Inside, the house is silent, and too warm. It is as if all the electricity in the air has bunched up and collected in this space. My nerves jangle. A crackle, and the house fills with white light, like the after-flash of a nuclear bomb. Rafters, windows, beams, corners: all of the hard edges and lines are outlined like knife cuts, like the skeleton of the house has been X-rayed and exposed.

'Suz?' I call.

The heat pushes upwards, like a physical mass.

I place the food bags carefully on the Barbie hooks, and edge along the planks to find Suz. She's not in bed, and she's not on her usual perch, swinging her legs in the middle of the central beam, singing. She's not in her favourite corner, cross-legged over her latest creation, busily stitching or painting or drawing. And she isn't engaged in her one-girl chalk battle against the crap graffiti-ist out in the yard.

Then I hear it: the keening.

It is a sound that lifts and lowers, sends shivers in my bones. A constant moaning that rises into whimpers of terror as the storm flashes and rumbles. We are in the very eye of the storm.

'Suz?'

I search the whole house, climbing down the ropes on the walls, circumnavigating across to the different levels and floors. I follow the sound as it pines until, at last, I find her.

Suz.

She is hidden underneath a three-legged table, right on the bottom floor amongst the rubble of previous squatters. She has pushed mattresses and boards and planks up against the table, as if she's in a nuclear bunker, or an air-raid shelter. I pull aside a piece of wood just as there's another flash. There's an immediate rise in the wail.

'Suz? It's me, Frog.'

At first I don't recognise her. She's sitting in a filthy nest, hair hanging down instead of in its usual bright hat, her eyes closed, shivering violently. An unwashed fug rises from her. She's closed her arms around her chest, and is panting, teeth chattering, all the time making that horrible, unearthly keening noise.

'Suz, what's wrong?' I climb inside, not minding the reek of fear and dread, and try to cuddle her, but it is like hugging stone. She is in some other place, experiencing some other terror.

In the end, I just sit with her, and all the time she is rocking, and keening, and chattering, eyes closed, or staring like a blind person at some horror that only she can see.

'I don't like storms.'

It's a whisper, a butterfly breath.

I wait.

'They remind me…of when it happened.'

I squeeze her hand, cuddle her, and this time she lays her head against my shoulder, her body softens.

'It was when I was travelling around Europe, and there was a beach party in Turkey. Fireworks, plenty of booze, plenty of guys there. We drank and we smoked a lot of weed, and there was all kinds of other stuff being passed around. I took it all. I was fifteen and I'd had enough.

'I'd run away from my third set of foster carers, and just taken off. It was wonderful. At first. Then there were some things that happened…'

She takes a shuddering breath. The house is quiet now. I light a candle in a jar and bring some cushions into our nest. I manage to roll her a cigarette, and light it, and put it into her mouth. Stroke her cold hand.

'So, we'd been skinny-dipping and all of a sudden I was alone with the boys. There were six of them, and me. They were in their twenties…I guess I was wanting to show off, but also I was kind of lonely.' She breathes out a huff of bitter-scented smoke. 'I ended up with this one guy, and all the time we were doing it, I was looking over my shoulder at the fireworks, and never have I felt more lonely. And after, he just kind of laughed, and that's when I saw his eyes, with the fireworks dancing in them, and they were mean eyes. They were dead as stone.

'He called something over his shoulder, and I was wandering about, drunk and high, trying to find my clothes, trying to pull on my bikini over the sand, and then he pushed me back down, and said something in Turkish or Greek, and I felt cold, all of a sudden…and still the banging of the fireworks.

'When I looked behind him, they were all there, his mates, the ones I'd been flirting with, in the sea.'

Suz is fumbling in her bag, lifting cushions, and I know what she's looking for. It's what she always needs when the darkness comes over her. She finds her tin, takes out a little plastic bag of the stuff she calls 'spice', and opens it with shaking hands. I look away. I can't bear to be with her when she takes it. I can't bear that version of Suz.

'Please don't,' I say. But I know that, for her, it is the only thing that will help.

Suz takes a huge hit, I can hear the gasp of it as it fills her lungs and blanks out her mind. Soon, there will be peace. Before the hell of it.

'There were six of them, Frog. And all the time, there were the fireworks. I tried shouting, but nobody could hear me. Every time there's a storm...I'm reminded...I'm reminded of the fireworks...'

Suz stops talking now. She's in that zombie state, eyes dark and blank as a blind man's.

I leave her sitting and staring, taking the rollie away and the candle, so that she doesn't hurt herself. Then I climb slowly back up to the crow's nest. There, where I left them, are the carrier bags of vegetables. I leave them hanging up, and crawl along the rafter for the peanut butter. Eat it, huddled in my yellow coat, in the storm-cooled house, straight from the jar.

Below me, the keening has stopped, but somehow the silence is far worse.

Caged Tiger

It takes Suz two days to recover from the storm.

In that time, I feed her, and I lead her outside to go to the loo, and I roll her cigarettes and try to give her clean bedding. In the day, I fire-juggle and braid bracelets or try to copy her chalk drawings.

Today I am a clown. I have painted my face, all sad-eyed and droopy-mouthed. Rule #8: *If possible, hide in full view.*

I am balancing on my homemade plinth next to a lamp post, chin on one hand, crook-legged like a broken doll, watching the police officer. It is much harder to be a living statue than a pavement artist. A fly has landed on my nose. My knees are trembling, and my lower back aches. But there's little crowd gathered now, and the odd sound of coins being dropped. I can tell without looking what they are. Copper coins. Given to a child who doesn't know any better, to pacify them. If I'm lucky, they'll add up to a pound, and I'll be able to buy a pot of winkles.

The officer's young, in a yellow luminous jacket as if he's scared he'll not be noticed for what he is. He's got a radio in one hand and a bag of crisps in the other. I wonder if he's supposed to be eating on duty. As I watch, he tears the packet open with his teeth. Good teeth, I think. He's got brown skin and eyes that tilt at the corners. Beautiful eyes. As long as they don't notice me.

But they do.

He walks up to me and passes me a flyer. It's a picture of me. *Missing Person*, it says at the top. *Have you seen this girl?*

He glances down at Suz's fire sticks. 'You often in this spot?' he asks.

I nod a tiny fraction. Behind him, a woman is looking on curiously.

It's just procedure, I think. He doesn't know who I am. He can't possibly recognise me. All around me are other living statues, in various poses. As I watch, one of them, dressed as a silver pirate, takes a break. Scratches her leg and accepts a Costa coffee from her friend.

'Have you seen this girl?' he asks. He's watching me closely with those almond eyes. He seems awfully young to be a police officer. Maybe he's just dressing up as one, pretending to be something he isn't, like me.

'Look closely at the picture,' he's saying. So I do. I examine this girl's face and her hair and her prefect badge. Willow Stephens, Missing Schoolgirl, looks absolutely nothing like me.

'I don't know her,' I say, which is true enough. 'Definitely not seen her around here.' I realise he's looking at me strangely. Too late, I hear my public school accent ring out, too loud, too clear, too enunciated. At odds with my clown face and scruffy clothes.

'She went to boarding school,' he says, and his voice is carefully casual. 'Her father's a wealthy man. He's pulling out all the stops, looking for her.'

I shake my head, but my legs are shaking now too. I wish I could make them stop.

'Have you been in Hastings long yourself?' he asks. He doesn't seem young any more, just very keen, thorough, good at his job.

'Why, certainly, officer,' I smile brightly. 'I'm a performer, here with my dance troupe. We're kind of on tour, you know.'

He's nodding, but you can tell those eyes are searching, taking everything in. I am just thinking that he's going, I've got away with it, when his eyes shift to my lapel. We both look down, and my stomach drops.

He's looking straight at Beanie's head girl badge, pinned like a trophy.

'May I ask where you got that, miss?' he says. His hand is reaching for his radio.

I gabble. 'What? That? It's mine. I mean, someone gave it to me —'

His other hand reaches for it, palm upwards. 'It's really important that you tell us. We have reason to believe —'

But what he has reason to believe, I don't know. Because at that point, I get up, jump off my plinth and run.

'Look at that clown, Mummy!'

Faster and faster. He's still following me.

I can outrun him.

I forget all about Rule #6: *Do not draw attention to yourself*, and instead focus on Rules #1, #5 and #7. It seems for the best.

I pick up pace until I am at full sprint. People are cheering us on. They probably think it's all some kind of living art performance.

Pretty Eyes is fast and fit. He has pumped-up arms, under his regulation shirt, a gym regular. The pavement pounds. I don't want to go down on the boardwalk, not after the incident with Fairground Man, so I take a right and veer along past the miniature railway, the fish shacks and dab sandwich stalls. Ahead, the funicular.

I duck in front of a group of silver-topped tourists, heads bent over maps and leaflets.

I think that I have lost him, but he's still running, rhythmically, easily, relaxed in his stride.

Ignoring the shouts from the irate ticket seller, I vault the funicular barrier and hurl myself onto a wooden bench in the little carriage just as the glass doors slide shut. On the other side, Pretty Eyes is a fraction too late. He presses his hands briefly against the glass and stares. The passengers inside my car stare too. And then it judders and starts to glide upwards, almost vertical, like the tamest theme park ride never invented. People in the carriage close their open mouths. One little boy is halfway through licking his ice cream; there is a slow drip of blueberry from his chin. A pair of twins, swollen-cheeked and eating double cones, can't keep their eyes off me. Their grandparents glance at each other and pull them away. It is like I'm a wild tiger, and they're all caged in with me.

'Nice weather, we're having, isn't it?' says a mad old lady to no one.

I pant, fighting to get my breath. It wouldn't do to have an attack now. I watch the top of the ride for a glimpse of fluorescent yellow. Would he have climbed up? Taken the steps?

But no, he's climbing into the other carriage, just as I reach the top. He's talking into his radio.

Our doors open. The parents in my carriage drag their children out, away from me. Should I stay inside? Or get out, and head along the cliff path, hide in the National Park, in the woods? I hesitate, but then a group of elderly people get in chattering with excitement. I stay or the descent, gripping the slatted bench with my hands.

Halfway down, the other funicular car passes. Pretty Eyes and I gaze at each other through the glass. He looks furious. I wave, and blow him a kiss. When I reach the bottom, the doors open, and I launch myself out and stumble onto the platform. Scramble up and pelt towards the beach.

I clamber up onto the deck of a boat, panting and heaving. I am safe – aren't I? By the time he comes down again, I will be long gone.

'She went over here...'

A woman's voice. I crane my head to look who it is, trying not to make a sound on the rotting decking.

There are more of them.

Another yellow jacket, and a lady with a Labradoodle.

'Geoffrey,' she calls. Her dog's seen me. It wags its tail and barks.

I will it to ignore me. But it's a stupid, friendly animal. It gambols over to me, tail fanning like a burlesque dancer's plume.

'Go away,' I hiss.

Geoffrey doesn't.

Instead, he rolls on his back, trying to rub something revolting into the back of his neck. It looks like a dead seagull.

I shrink back into the shadow of the cabin, but by then it's too late. The dog's owner is standing below. Behind her, the second police officer is nosing around the hull of the boat, flashing her torch and speaking into her radio. I wonder if Scally's on the other end.

I crouch, praying the dog doesn't give me away.

But Geoffrey's bored with the seagull slime, and looks straight at me.

'Woof!' says Geoffrey.

Both the woman and the police officer see me at the same time. The dog owner screams, and it's only later that I realise I'm still wearing my clown face make-up.

'I'm sorry,' I say.

With a yell, I leap on top of the officer, knocking her off her feet. Geoffrey joins in joyfully. I grab the stinking dead seagull and slap it smack in her face. Both me and the dog are panting. She cries out in disgust, rubbing at her cheek.

The dog owner's holding her phone up to her face, mouth open.

'Sorry,' I keep saying. 'I'm terribly sorry.'

Geoffrey licks seagull off the officer's face, just to be helpful. By the way she's cringing, it looks like the officer's scared of dogs too.

It's really not her day.

I leave Geoffrey's owner trying desperately to drag her dog off, and race across the beach to the toilets. I am clown bright. I grab paper towels and hide in a cubicle, frantically rubbing my face paint off. In the next-door cubicle I can hear a mother trying to get her child to pull up his trousers. I rip off my beautiful yellow coat and stuff it on top of the cistern. I am leaving pieces of me wherever I go. I grab the pushchair which the mother's left by the basins and stroll outside with it, heart hammering, my head held high.

I walk straight through the little crowd of people gathered by the beach. Geoffrey's owner has him under control, and Pretty Eyes has joined the other officer, who's scrubbing at her face with tissues.

Neither of them give me a second glance as I pass.

The moment I am out of sight, I leave the pushchair by a public bench, hoping the owner will find it again. I don't have the fire sticks. I will need to go back to the plaza some time and get them. As my panic shrinks, I start to doubt. How would the police officer even know that I was me? I don't even know who I am any more. I remember how his eyes slid over to Beanie's badge, but maybe he was more interested in taking in my little enterprise: the chalked pictures, the pot of money, the small crowd watching, my fire-eating act.

Was it even about me? Was he just going to book me for not having a street licence?

I jog at a steady pace back home. Back to Suz.

But it can't be home for much longer, can it?

I can't stay in the squat. It's not safe. I've got to find a way to join the circus soon.

Rule #9: *Never give in to paranoia.*
Ha!

The Wrong Side of Clean

There's a house in Old Hastings with a high wall adjoining a tiny, cobbled alleyway. The wall has overhanging trees and ivy, like it's hiding a secret garden. More than ever since the police incident, I have a sudden craving to be alone. I climb up and it's perfect for balancing. No one is in the house; it has the look of empty. *Holiday lettings*, it says, on a sign. *Sleeps ten*. There are stripy blue curtains and a wooden sailing boat in the window.

I stand up, and hold a pose, arms outstretched. I hold my leg up high behind me, reaching out to grasp my foot, and pulling it upwards like an archer. I close my eyes, listen to the birdsong. Then, I take out the devil sticks and begin to juggle morosely. I light the middle one and practise tic-toc, slowly at first, then faster and faster, imagining Suz's face, then imagining leaving her.

Should I stay?

Should I go?

I slow it right down, lobbing the sticks from one hand to the other, until all the tension goes and I am in a half-trance. I blow out the wick and place the devil sticks carefully on the wall to cool down. I climb the willow and lie on my tummy on the strongest branch, letting my head and arms hang through the leaves.

'Don't be sad.'

I scramble up, heart skittering.

A man is hovering over me, casting a shadow. He is quite literally hovering, as he is on stilts. He's a clown, a green man, his face painted in looping ivy, and a pair of giant horns sticking out of his leaf-filled hair. He has crinkly blue eyes and a hipster's beard, full of leaves like a verdant Mr Twit.

'Come to the Jack in the Green Festival,' he says. He has a soft voice, with no particular accent, but there's a smoothness to his vowels. He talks like Beanie's brothers when they're trying to play down their background. I wonder if he went to public school like them. 'Come along, put leaves in your hair, nature in your soul. Release your inner druid.' He reaches over the wall, as far as he dares on those stilts on the uneven cobbles.

'And a special invitation for you, Fire Girl.' He passes me something. It's in the shape of a leaf, with hand-painted, curlicued script:

Free Pass. Le Petit Cirque Invites You to Our Jack in the Green Party. Admits One. Invites Only. Callooh Callay!

'It's a leaf-let,' he explains. 'You're pretty good, Fire Girl. Make sure you dress up, the leafier the better. I'd like to see you there.' He shakes my hand, and his grip is firm and confident. 'I'm Fabian, but friends call me Bee Beard. If you come to the party, you'll find out why…'

I shake his hand automatically, and he doesn't seem to notice my grimy nails, my chapped hands. His are none-too-clean, despite his accent. But inside I'm thinking, *Circus*? Did he say *circus*?

'It's *Le Petit Cirque*,' he says, as if he's read my mind. 'What did you say your name was?'

I nearly tell him 'Willow', but correct myself just in time. 'I'm Frog,' I say. 'Is it…a real circus?'

145

'*Frog!* What the bloody hell you doing up there? I've been trying to find you –'

Suz is back. My heart sinks.

She's looking madder than ever in her grimiest coat with a Barbie doll's head in a buttonhole. She hasn't been the same since I found her after the storm. I watch her as she peers at Bee Beard and me with suspicion.

'What ya doing, Frog?' Her voice is petulant; she doesn't like me leaving her.

The spell is broken; the birds, the butterflies in the garden, the leaf nestled in my hand.

Bee Beard adjusts his feet back in his stilts and smiles at me. 'A day to remember, so don't be sad, fellow leaf-lover. Come join the dance. Callooh callay!'

I watch him stride down the alley, hollering, laughing, shaking his bells. Then I look at Suz.

I can see by the look on her face that she's had her hand in his pockets.

The Longest Air Walk in England!

'I'm sorry…I said I'm sorry.'

Suz is still talking. She's been talking since the pickpocketing incident, all the way from the Old Town.

I wish she'd shut up.

She's saying something about getting me work as a living statue, she knows someone who knows someone who has a costume I can borrow. By 'borrow', Suz of course means steal. Being on the streets so long has made her shed any morals like a dog shedding hair.

'I need some space,' I say. 'Away from you.'

We are at the pier. Grumpy Guy has locked up and gone home. The little information kiosk is deserted, the Harley-Davidson gone. Taunting me, rising above us, is the *Hastings Pier Opening Soon!* sign, with its laughing golden lady; she's still holding her finger up to her lips and half-closing her eyes as if her lashes are too heavy. She's still holding that ruffed pig tucked under her arm and turning her face to the spotlight. *Grand Opening! Pop-Up Circus! And More!*

Through the grid-iron gate, I can see that they've started getting the stage ready for the show. There's a tightrope being built – two platforms, one at each end of the pier.

The Longest Air Walk in England!

Walk on Air over Water!

Be Amazed!

'I'm going in,' I say.

I climb the barrier very deliberately, knowing that Suz can't follow me. I know without looking that Suz will stay there, waiting and watching.

She follows me like a stray dog, I think, *and I don't need her. Why do I need her? What use has she ever been to me?*

I start to walk along the pier, away from her, feeling the decking bounce under my feet. Through the slats, the water gleams.

After a while I stop. Look back.

Suz's face is pressed against the gate, and she's pulling puppy eyes at me.

I sigh.

'I hate you, Suz,' I say.

I drag a stack of deckchairs closer to the gate, climb back over and let her clamber onto my back, piggyback-style.

'I love you, Frog,' she says, as she gasps her way over. 'I knew you'd come back for me.'

'Your feet really stink,' I say. Her trainers are rank with the reek of too many wet days and nights. I wonder when she last changed them.

She lands with a groan, and lies on the top of the deck-chairs for a moment, panting.

'I hope you know I may never get back over, Frog. I mean, I could totally starve out here.'

'We-ell,' I say. 'I suppose I could always push you chips through the gate.'

She doesn't answer. There's just the sound of her rasping and I wonder when she first started sounding like that.

I drag two deckchairs off the top of the pile and carry them halfway down the pier.

Across the bay, lights twinkle. The Ghost Train wails.

'We could sleep out here,' says Suz, settling herself into her chair with a huff of effort.

'You stole from that man with the beard,' I say, watching the water glimmer through the decking.

I see her shadow shrug.

'He had money.'

'I was making a contact. He has circus connections,' I say. 'You could have wrecked my chances, Suz.'

'Just a posh boy playing at circuses,' she sniffs. I hear rustling as she pulls out paper scraps from her bag to make origami birds. 'He's not the real thing. You're better than that, Frog.'

'I believe you're actually jealous.'

She laughs her gravel laugh.

'You are. You can't bear to think I may have made a friend. A useful friend,' I add.

Suz's deckchair creaks as she gets back up and shuffles off.

I feel her hurt and I am glad.

It's a balmy night. From the streets and houses, lights dance like fireflies. I picture all those people in their separate lit-up homes. And then there's Suz and me, on the edge of it all.

I clack my deckchair onto its lowest setting and stare up at the tightrope platform. From below, the structure that is going to hold the high wire looks a little like a claw. Something dark and grim: a hook or a scythe.

I shiver, even though it is warm.

I will be a performer, I think. It's what I want, most of all. I'll do it for my mother. I'll learn to fly. I'll learn the trapeze. I'll leave the Handbag and Daddy and their stupid baby far, far behind. I'll prove that I don't need any of them.

There's a cry from the end of the pier.

Suz.

Struggling out of my deckchair, I hear it again. She's calling my name, and I can't see her.

Why would she climb over the edge of the pier?

Oh my God – 'Suz!' I scream. 'Stay there. Hold on. Don't do anything stupid –'

It was me, I think, as I race barefooted over the bouncing boards. I did this. I should know she's fragile, I –

Shaking, I look over the side.

'Shit, Frog. You took your time. Help me, would you?'

Suz is straddling one of the struts, holding out her cardigan, which is bulging.

'Take it, will ya? Can't do everything round here.'

It's full of coins. I glare down at her.

'What the hell are you doing down there? I thought…
She gives a slow smile. 'Oh, you thought that, did you? I got you worried there, did I?'

'Oh, shut up,' I snap.

Later, I count the coins.

'They'll have been left there by the workmen and women,' Suz tells me. 'It used to be a thing, back before the fire. People would chuck coins over the side onto the girders underneath, where they'd stay, like a magpie's nest of treasure. Kind of like a wishing well,' Suz adds, sleepily. She's made more of her paper birds, fingers expertly folding and tucking.

'So you've just stolen all those people's wishes? Nice.'

I am still shaky with shock.

Beside me, Suz snores. The sound is strangely comforting, like a horse blowing out its breath. I can't see her now that the daylight's gone, but I know if I could, she'd look young as a child, nowhere near her twenty years. Sleep does that to her. Around her feet, her paper birds flutter like bright flowers.

I pick up a handful of them, and move to the side of the pier, hang over the edge, and throw them into the winking sea.

I watch one fly, get picked up by the wind, a bright jewel, watch it spin and fall. Below us, the sea slaps against the pillars.

If the whole world ended today, now, this minute, I think, there'd be only Suz and me, on the edge of the world, at the end of the pier. I watch the shredded light from the town dance in the water like gold confetti. Somewhere, a motorbike revs and ebbs.

Suz stirs and sighs, like she knows I'm still awake.

'This is where I'll be, Frog, when I'm gone. I'll be riding the back of –'

'A bird, Suz. You said.' But my voice is soft now.

''Night, Frog.'

''Night, Suz.'

Greasepaint

'It's easy when you know how,' Suz tells me, sitting on her haunches like a yogi. 'C'mon, chin up more.'

We're in our favourite spot, beneath the palisade, two metres away from sun and shingle and sea.

'How much longer are you going to be?' I complain. My skin feels tight from the face paint drying.

'I am transforming you, from Frog to…Queen of Flames,' Suz intones. She has her ubiquitous roll-up in the corner of her mouth, and her eyes are squinched up against the sun. She's in her element, though, I can tell, humming below her breath, dabbing the paint brush into a plastic cup of water from the public showers and mixing it busily. She's used the tray from a bag of chips as a mixing palette, and it's sliding with vibrant colours: indigos and greens and magentas.

'Hold still. Chrissakes, you nonce.'

She spits on the back of her hand and adds a daub of blue glitter.

'Sorry,' she says, when I make a face (difficult to move because my face feels like it's hidden under layers of tightening clay). 'Forgot you are so *precious*. You should have got some gold too. Really sets it off, you know, like you're on fire.'

'It was too expensive,' I say, without moving my lips.

Suz rolls her eyes. 'You don't mean you actually *paid* for this little lot. Oh Jesus.'

'I'm not like you,' I say primly.

'Stealing's not wrong when you're trying to *survive*. As long as it's not actually harming anyone. How do you think I stayed on the streets for so long? By street magic?' She nods to the almost empty clay pot in front of her latest chalk drawing. There's a couple of pound coins in there, but all of the rest are coppers. Enough for a coffee, if we're lucky.

I say nothing as she takes a tiny brush, its tip not much more than a single hair, and draws in some complicated shape by my left eye. Blows on my skin to dry it quickly.

'All right, all right, I know I haven't seen my dental hygienist for a year or ten, but no need to flinch. You're just as bad. Your breath stinks like a dog's anus.' She swills in some more blue as she speaks.

'Bat breath,' I mutter.

'Dragon dick.'

'Bull balls.'

'Bull balls? What are you *like?*' She rocks with laughter, and almost drops her paintbrush. 'Here, hold still and shut your eyes. I'm going to blow glitter over them. You can hold your breath if you want to,' she adds.

I feel her blow gently, and something soft sprinkle over my eyelids. When I open them, I seize the mirror she's holding out to me and stare deep inside. I am transformed.

Where my face used to be, there is a magical creature, half-bird, half-lion, with fierce peacock eyes and a roaring muzzle that she's caught right in the act of breathing fire. As I tilt my head in the sun, I shimmer like I've caught fire.

'Shall I do your neck too?' she suggests. She doesn't say anything, but you can tell she's pleased by my reaction. Afterwards, I rinse out the paintbrushes and do Suz's face, trying to copy the feathers and swoops and swirls, but it doesn't come anywhere close.

'Sorry, it's awful,' I say, handing her back the brushes.

Suz laughs. 'I love it! Your first attempt. As a performer, you'll have to get used to doing your stage make-up, you know. I'll give you lessons if you like. Maybe tomorrow…' She yawns and looks shifty, and I know that she's longing to smoke some spice. I can tell by the way her eyes are flitting towards the buckled old tin she keeps, tucked inside her sleeping bag.

I shrug, and go to rinse out the brushes. Suz is messy like that, never clears up after herself. There's always a trail wherever she goes, a feather here, trodden-on chalk dust there, a discarded Rizla wrapper, a grubby friendship band, a tinselled streamer from the saris she likes to collect and turn into ribbons.

'You're so good at all of this,' I say, when I get back. 'Why can't you get a job too, as a make-up artist or costume-maker? Maybe you could make hats for the shows!'

She shudders. 'I've tried jobs before. Can't last, not for a moment. Makes me feel like I'm being controlled, like I can't get up and walk away if I wanted to.' And she won't say any more. Just withdraws into that dark place again, that room she keeps locked up and tight. When she's like that, there's no talking to her. I give up and wander down the beach, looking for sea glass.

Popcorn

'Well, how do we get in then?'

'Are you daft? We don't pay, not at that flamin' price. You'll be getting us to buy Meal Deals next, paying a tenner for a bucket of puffed-up popcorn kernels. I could get those down the market for a few pence, for chrissake.'

'Well, you don't pay for those either,' I remind her.

Suz ignores me. 'We need to find out what time the shows

finish. C'mon, Frog –'

It's busy inside the cinema. Suz pushes through the Saturday night throng and people don't look at her, not much. She stands and squints at the times of the shows.

'9.30P.M., perfect. That one'll do. Screen Six. We need a crappy film 'cos there'll be more space. Got the time on you, Frog?'

I haven't of course, so I ask a boy about my own age, who takes out his phone and tells me it's twenty past. He's cleanly dressed in a shirt and jeans, and seems nice. Then his eyes slide to my dirty clothes, my black-rimmed nails, and I see myself reflected in his sympathy. I may as well be sitting on the floor, gazing at his newish trainers, because that's what it makes me feel like.

I watch him saunter back to his friends. He grabs two of his mates' shoulders and squeezes them, laughing. He doesn't look back.

'Chrissakes, Frog. You coming?'

Suz leads me back outside the cinema, but not before she's grabbed a handful of jelly snakes from the pick 'n' mix and shoved them in her pocket.

I refuse to eat one out of principle and she laughs, taunt-ing me by sucking up the snake, red, green and quivering, into her mouth and making loud, ecstatic *mmm* noises.

'Here we are. Stand back now. Be subtle.'

A door opens, and cinema goers spill out of Screen Six onto the street, blinking in the last threads of the sun. Suz and I slide inside.

'Shhh, now. We wait here, while they clean the place up. Then we go and choose a nice comfy place to sit. There's no way this film'll be packed, don't worry.'

We sit on the floor in the little passage, while the boy and the girl in uniform wander about the auditorium, sweeping up popcorn and picking up cups and 3D glasses. They don't see us, and I have the feeling that, even if they did, they wouldn't care. Both have earbuds and are plugged into their music.

After a while, they take the wheeled bin bags and trundle them away.

Suz and I sit down near the back where there's more leg room. We have the place to ourselves for the moment and Suz's pocketful of jelly snakes. I forget my earlier disapproval. It's utter heaven.

The film, as Suz predicted, is utter rubbish, and, as we don't have 3D glasses, is out of focus anyway. It's something about a father who is trying to save his family from an alien invasion of giant grasshoppers. The wife does a lot of shrieking and the two children are sickly cute. It's awful.

But we don't care, not one bit, because we can sleep, and it's warm and it's dry, and we're sinking into the velvety softness of the chairs, our legs over the ones in front. Suz passes me another jelly snake, and I eat it with my eyes closed, half-listening to the film family.

Female voice, high, panicked: *Oh my gooood, Martin, what are we going to do? What about the kids?*

Male voice, low, strong, reassuring: *Leave it all to me, Dinah. I can handle it. Stay strong for me, won't you, Junior? And you too, Princess.*

I slip in and out of weird dreams of grasshoppers and aliens and jelly snakes, all the time smelling the strawberry and lime huff of Suz's snake breath, which is a big improvement on the usual.

'We need to go, Frog. They're cleaning again.'

'One last show.'

By the time we're kicked out after the last show, I know the movie word for word.

'D'you think that Princess was ever able to stay strong?' I ask.

Suz snorts. 'Not without her daddy and Junior to help her,' she says.

The last thing the girl's mother ever saw was the giant grasshopper's mandibles. Unfortunately, Martin wasn't able to handle it quite as well as he'd hoped.

There's something different about Suz, and now I see what it is. She's wearing a new coat: a quilted silver jacket with a hood. She looks sheepish when I point this out to her.

'She won't miss it, Frog. Honestly, you should have seen her. She could have bought up the whole high street, just like that.'

'You took it from the back of someone's chair, didn't you?' I say. 'At the cinema.' I touch the collar. 'And it has fur, Suz. I thought you were supposed to be vegan?'

'Crikey, Frog. I'm vegan-esque. How many times? And it's faux. There's nothing wrong with wearing faux.'

'Oh, I forgot, you have no principles.'

'It's a luxury, having principles,' she reminds me. She pulls her hood up and plunges her hands deep inside her pockets. She looks like a little silver pixie.

She also looks warm.

Carnival

Suz shoves the lit devil sticks into two crumbling plant pots. 'Up there,' she says, jerking up her chin.

She means the thin roof high above us, the balustrade made of stone.

'Walk it,' she whispers, and her eyes look dark and wild. I shiver as she fixes my peacock tail to my costume, weaves feathers in my hair.

She has been different recently. Extra bright, extra energetic, extra happy. The black tins of cider are lined up along the beam in our squat and they are replacing the jars of lentils, pulses, almond butter. We live off chips, sharing them from the same bag. Sometimes we add winkles, gritty with sand and vinegar. You can get them for free if you hang around the fish stalls at close of day. We eat them together, picking them out where we've shaken them over our chips, with cocktail sticks.

'They're not actually life forms,' proclaims Suz. 'They count as mineral or vegetable.' And if it wasn't for her too-bright eyes, and the ever present smell of cider that hangs around her, I would think that she was back to her old self.

'Feet,' says Suz, and I watch as she wraps them with ribbon, criss-crosses it over and under. Crushes chalk with a stone and rubs it briskly on my soles.

My heart buzzes, the blood in my veins feels on fire as I climb. I have done this, I think, many times. I place my foot on the edge of the railing, stare straight ahead over the sky-line, and raise my arms either side of me. It is a calm, clear day; the recent storm has settled the weather, and the blue mist of sea is quiet as velvet.

'You need a pole,' she shouts. reaches up and passes me a broom handle.

I walk.

I walk, one foot in front of the other, feeling the edges with my toes. Time stops, and below me, the morning shimmers. Cars crawling like caterpillars, sun-lit windows, the mocking cry of the seagulls.

And I walk above all of this, a creature of fire and air.

When I climb down, Suz is applauding, her face dancing with sunlight.

'That was effing amazing, Frog,' she tells me. 'I believe you're ready.'

Tree Peacock

Suz peers again at the green leaf invitation.

'It does say *admits one*,' I say. 'But I'm sure you can come too.'

I remember how I felt with Bee Beard's eyes watching me. A mile high. Higher than his stilts. Higher than the tallest tightrope.

'It's an opportunity,' I say. 'Isn't it?'

Suz passes it back. 'You don't want me to go, right?'

'Of course I do. I never said that. I'll make them let you in.' I squeeze Suz's shoulder. 'I'm not going anywhere without my friend.'

Suz sniffs. I can't help noticing that her hair is even filthier than usual. 'There'll be lots of food there,' she says. 'We should take bags. Those sort of people put on a real spread. I've seen it before. They pretend it's all ethical this and organic that. But really it's just an excuse to gorge and glut and glamp it up. Artisan chic. Ethical glam.'

I stare. 'Bee Beard seemed really helpful and nice. This could be my chance, Suz.'

'Seemed really nice,' Suz mocks, in my boarding-school accent.

I hate it when she does that.

'We should take bags,' she repeats.

We find the tent by the organic bread shop.

Le Petit Cirque at Jack in the Green! proclaims a hand-drawn sign outside. Silver and yellow bunting flutters. Outside, the streets are filling with revellers.

People are setting up stalls on the pavement, selling green juice and luminous cider and veggie curries and patties and Green Man masks and hand-whittled wands and feathered earrings and beaded necklaces and chutneys and jams and magic spells. A tree druid sashays past, leaves fluttering.

Suz scowls as she looks at the circus tent. 'You sure you want me to come?'

'Of course I do,' I say. I look at her.

She has refused to dress as a tree, but is wearing her battered and ancient top hat. She no longer looks like the Artful Dodger, but now just carries all the ingrained grime of every homeless person. It is there in the shuffle that she has started to develop, in the stoop of her shoulders, in the glass-eyed gaze of her eyes.

People always stared at Suz, but now they're staring for all the wrong reasons.

Crouched in the littered street, leaves fluttering, I catch sight of myself in a shop window mirror. Suz has made me a full peacock costume, complete with emerald eyes and laurel leaf corset. She has used every scrap of fabric in her tat box, and emptied her glue gun, sticking strips of sari and sequins to sticks. Some passers-by turn and take pictures of me on their phones.

'I am a Tree Peacock,' I say. I lift my arms and twirl, and my tail spins around me, a million fluttering leaves and feathers. My face and neck and hands are painted with broad, sweeping brushstrokes of emerald and gold and russet.

159

Suz nods. Her eyes are flitting over towards the cider stall. I watch a giant green cat do the samba with a tribe of painted ladies, their butterfly wings pulsing with the drum-beats as they grind, grind, grind.

'Ready?' I say. The silver and yellow bunting flutters.

But Suz is dragging her feet, scowling.

I shrug. Unpin my leaf invitation from my costume. Take a deep breath and enter the tent.

'Helloooo!' It's Bee Beard, dressed this time in a crumpled linen shirt and shorts. 'Lovely to see you – Frog, isn't it?' He pulls me into a quick hug, and he smells so clean.

I spent an hour this morning, washing myself in the beach lavatories: my face, my armpits, even putting my feet in the basin and ignoring the sideways glances of early swimmers. I hope I don't smell of anything worse than squirty handwash.

If I do, Bee Beard doesn't seem to notice. I see that he has crocheted bees stuck all over his beard. 'I'm Bee Beard, as opposed to Tree Beard,' he explains.

He breathes warm cider and smoke all over me as he pins a woollen bee to my leafy bodice.

'Nice, aren't they? My girlfriend knits them for me. I do it with real ones too, of course.'

His beard tickles my skin as he fiddles with the safety pin, then stands back, satisfied.

'Do what?' I ask.

'Bee-bearding, of course.' He's shouting over the noise of drums from outside. 'We keep real bees at The Meadows, for honey. It helps when the circus closes at the end of the season.' He stoops down to pick up a leaf that has floated from my tail. 'Nice costume, by the way. Love the tail feathers.

'Let me introduce you to my girlfriend. Lala – meet Frog. She's a street performer, and she's bloody excellent. She's also

160

the most amazing, um, Tree Peacock?'

I look down at my costume, laughing. Suz has done a brilliant job. I am teetering in silver skyscraper sandals which Suz said she 'found' outside a nightclub.

Lala gives me a limp handshake. She looks utterly bored. She's wearing an off-the-shoulder black top and jeans.

'Lala doesn't do festivals,' Bee Beard confides. 'Thinks they're beneath her. Only tolerates them to pay off her massive overdraft, don't you, love?'

Lala scowls.

'So what act do you do?' I ask her.

She mutters something that could be 'aerial' and wanders away to the buffet. People are piling in now, pulling in their children, trailing leaf-bunting and balloons. Outside, I can see a woman sitting by a table of face paints, children queuing up to be turned into green Spidermen and fairies, and it makes me think of Suz. Where is she?

Bee Beard is shaking hands with a group of tree druids, all of them laughing and spilling plastic pints of luminous cider. The tent is packed with people now. I tug down my leaf corset and wonder what to do.

Then I see Suz, over by the buffet. She looks every inch a homeless person, clutching her carrier bag, in her dirty trainers and baggy old cardigan. She doesn't look creative and kooky any more, just grimy and street-worn.

She sees me and shouts.

'Oy, Frog. They've got a real spread. Free booze too.' She waves her bag at me; shoves another bread roll into it.

I shrink and redden. I can feel the tree druids watching.

Bee Beard's at my shoulder now. 'Hey, Tree Peacock! Come and say hello.'

'Interesting-looking creature over there,' he's saying. 'I wonder how she got in?'

He watches as Suz waves frantically at me. My heart sinks as she limps her way over.

'You know each other?' He's too polite to raise an eyebrow.

Suz plants her arm around my shoulder. I wish she wouldn't.

'Know her? Of course I know her. We're sisters, aren't we, Frog?'

I smile brightly at Bee Beard. 'I won't be a moment.' I steer Suz back towards the entrance, by the buffet.

'What on earth are you doing?' I hiss. 'Are you trying to spoil my chances?'

She's holding a paper leaf plate piled with slithering heaps of olives, hummus, falafels, stuffed vine leaves and salads. Bottles of cider poke their necks out of her pockets.

'You do know that's fish eggs, don't you?' I jerk my head towards her taramasalata.

'For god's sake, Frog,' she slurs. 'I'm vegan-esque, aren't I? How many times?'

'Maybe you should go now,' I say. I can feel Bee Beard and his friends watching us curiously.

'Am I embarrassing you?' She takes another huge mouthful of food, then reaches for more flatbreads and falafels.

'Well, a little. Yes, actually.'

'So why don't you go off with your new friend, then? I'm all right here,' she says. She burps, and coughs out some couscous.

I leave her eyeing up the Jack in the Green cupcakes, and make my way back to Bee Beard, who's helping his friend carry some bongo drums to the centre of the tent. His girlfriend leans against a table and takes out her phone.

'Everything all right?' he says.

'Mother – meet Frog. She's the fire dancer I was telling you about.' He's shouting over to a woman in riding boots and a gypsy headscarf. 'Frog, this is Tilly, my mother. She's the boss.'

Tilly is a young-looking fifty-something. She has good skin and even better teeth. Wide apart eyes and no make-up. Her handshake is firm. I wonder how my life would have been if Daddy had chosen someone like her instead of the Handbag.

'A fire dancer, you say? We don't have one of those.' She pulls out something from her gilet, and hands it to me. It's a card, edged with yellow and silver circus stripes. 'Here – come and see me to show me what you can do. We've been staying at The Meadows. We'll be popping over to Eastbourne for the summer, and then moving on to Paris…'

Paris.

I remember my promise to Suz. 'My friend is great at performing too. She can make costumes – do all sorts of things –'

I take a deep breath and point her out.

Tilly and I watch Suz as she sways to Bee Beard's bongo drums, paper plate in hand. One of her shoes has come off and she hasn't noticed.

'What a shame. We only have room for one more act,' says Tilly.

Her eyes are smiling, but there's a shudder in them.

The Green Man

It begins with the stilt-walkers.

There are five or six of them, combing and picking their way through the streets like oyster-catchers looking for limpets. Each walker is dressed head to toe in green, leaves fluttering from each extended arm and leg like newly sprung beanstalks. Black horns curl from their heads and their eyes stare out of magnificently painted faces.

There is a drumming and a hooting. People dressed as animals, kings and demons whoop, howl and grind. Someone blows a hunting horn, and Bacchus, the god of wine, is being pushed down the hill in a bathtub on wheels, glugging a stone jar of red wine. He has grapes in his beard and vines in his hair, and his student friends around him are pissing themselves laughing, and handing out free Green Man cider punch, which looks radiation-luminous.

I look around for Suz, and think I see her top hat bobbing. Imagine her tipping back the cider and sliding her hand under butterfly wings and leaf arms and green pockets. I sigh and follow the crowd as it weaves its way along the street. Dirty cartons, cups and paper plates that once contained green dahl, curried dabs, stuffed vine leaves and artisan Scotch eggs, apple juice and Green Man punch litter the pavements and swish around our feet as we walk.

By the time the crowd picks us up and swirls us through Old Hastings and up to West Hill, I am drunk with laughing and whooping. Bee Beard taps glasses with some men in long green evening dresses, and then passes me a spilling plastic pint of luminous green cider. I drink, and drink again.

'It's wonderful, isn't it?' he laughs. His eyes are bright. One of his friends knuckles his hand and dances off in his silky dress, high heels wobbling. They're dressed as tree elves, but have rugby players' bodies.

I feel nice and swimmy with cider and sun and drumming music. My leaves are drooping, but I don't care. I feel like dancing. I feel like flying.

I tap Bee Beard on his arm. 'What's happening now?' I ask. There is a buzz in the crowd, as if something is going to happen. I crane my neck, looking for a top hat, weaving its way through the crowd, but I can see no sign of Suz.

'Jack in the Green has to be slain to release the spirit of summer,' shouts Bee Beard, waving his cider so that some of it slops over us.

'Kill the Jack! Kill the Jack! Kill the Jack!' chants the crowd. A huge effigy of the Green Man is lifted by the stilt-walkers onto an unlit bonfire made of old crates.

'Where's the Green Woman?' shouts someone, and every-one laughs.

There's a platform rigged up on the green, and revellers are climbing up, dancers and drummers and singers. A troupe of Morris dancers performs to howls and stamps of approval, jangling their bells and waving green handkerchiefs.

'Your turn,' yells Bee Beard, pushing me up to the stage. 'Do your fire thing – quick!'

I stare at him. 'I can't – I'm not ready, I –'

'Make way!' he's shouting, in a surprisingly strong voice. 'Make way...for the Tree Peacock!'

And I have no choice but to be tumbled and shoved for-wards; his tree elf friends are laughing and spilling cider and lifting me, with my tail scattering leaf feathers. I am raised over the crowds, and people are helping carry me, and just once, just for a moment, I think I see Suz's hat, lost in the crowd.

And then I'm on stage, facing a green-faced, leaf-clad crowd.

I swallow.

'Here's the moment you've all been waiting for!' cries Bee Beard. 'The Wondrous, Splendiferous, Fire-tastical... Tree Peacock!'

And then I realise that the crowd has hushed, and eve-ryone is standing back in a sort of circle, and looking at me expectantly.

This is what Suz would call a Big Moment.

With hands that only tremble slightly, I reach down, hand my plastic cup to Bee Beard, and draw out my fire sticks.

'I need a lighter,' I say.

'A lighter! The Tree Peacock needs a lighter!' yells Bee Beard. A Morris dancer throws me one from the side of the stage.

Careful not to let my costume get in the way, and glad that there is no breeze, I flick the lighter and there is a whoosh as the Kerosene flames up. I think of Suz and lift up my chin and howl. Then I give the performance of my life.

I hurl the devil sticks high into the air, I toss them and reach and catch and dive and spin and swoop. Only once do I nearly miss one, and there is a hairy moment when I worry that my tail feathers will catch fire, but the laurel leaves on my costume are fresh and glossy, and won't take easily.

And all around, painted faces are smiling and staring and laughing, and there is clapping, and drum-beating and the stamping of feet. As the climax to my act I draw the longest stick dramatically from its sheath and tip my head back and swallow the flames, one after the other, over and over, as Suz has taught me.

Afterwards, people whoop, and Bee Beard high fives me, and his friends scoop me up and lift me high over their heads, and I am lifted onto the throne, and crowned Green Woman there and then.

Well, obviously that last part;s made up, but it feels like that. It really does. When I've finished, and I put my fire sticks away, I look about for Suz, but she isn't there.

If only she had been here to see.

Bee-Bearding

We share a banitsa, pastry flaking over our painted chins.
Fabian picks his off with a grubby finger and sucks it. For a
posh boy, he has awful manners.

'Well?'

'Well what?' I say. I am too busy tucking into all the
food he has ordered to talk much. We are in a Bulgarian
restaurant, tiny, narrow, busy. Inside it is packed around the
bar, but the restaurant section is quieter. There's a humming buzz of low chatter. A quartet band with violins
plays something slow and yearning. It reminds me of the
Romanian band that made me cry in the Art Café. A scythe
hangs above us, some relic of Bulgarian past. Its blade winks
and gleams.

'Love this place,' said Fabian. 'Like, it's really authentic,
you know.' He's pretty drunk by now, but I don't mind. I am
drunk too. And hungry.

I accept the last piece of banitsa and refill my glass with
the free water on the table. When the waiter returns, I point
to the bean stew. Bread comes, warm and wrapped in a white
linen napkin. My stomach roars, and Bee Beard laughs.

'Hungry?' he says. He doesn't seem to mind my unkempt
state. He looks just as bad, and so do most of the diners;
cider-flushed, tangle-haired and dropping leaves from their
homemade costumes, everyone's in good spirits, keeping out
of the cold until the fireworks start. A candle sputters on our
table. I feel warm and content.

The stew comes, and it is delicious. I seize fistfuls of
doughy, warm-from-the-oven, thyme-scented bread, and
mop up the gravy. Beans, soft as butter, wild herbs, sweet

potatoes, rich, tomato-scented gravy; it is incredible. When I'm done, I burp and sigh.

Bee Beard is watching me curiously.

'Where are you from?' he asks. 'It's just that you sound more Home Counties than Hastings. Are you in a commune or something?'

I laugh. 'No.' But I won't say any more.

I am not Willow Stephens now, I remind myself. I am Frog. I am the girl who plays with fire.

I lean forward, fix him with my brightest smile, and hope that my teeth aren't too dirty.

'So, can I join your circus?' I ask.

Beneath the table, the fingers on both hands are crossed. The waiter hovers, and I point to what seems like the biggest dessert.

Rule #8: *Always ask for more than you can eat. You never know when your next meal will be.*

'So can I?' I repeat.

Bee Beard finishes his glass of red wine and offers me the carafe. I shake my head. I prefer the cider, and have three plastic cups of it lined up on the table, despite the waiter's frown.

All right, so my manners are awful now, too.

'Come down to the farm tomorrow,' says Bee Beard. He pulls out a little card, and it is the same one that Tilly gave me earlier. He shows me the map on the back. 'I'll remind my mother to expect you, but you'll have to hurry. It's our last day of rehearsals before moving on to Eastbourne.'

I make short work of the apple tart I have chosen. I eat the mints that come with the bill. The taste reminds me how long it is since I have cleaned my teeth.

By the bar, people are starting to move. Bee Beard stands up. 'Time for the fireworks,' he says.

Catherine Wheel

I did go and look for her, I swear.

After the fireworks, after we have danced in the trampled -in trash of polystyrene trays and plastic pints and mud-clagged costumes, after we drank more cider under the star-shot sky and I've been introduced to all of Bee Beard's friends, and instantly forgotten names, and faces blur and fireworks arc and whistle and splatter-crackle.

After. After. After.

It is only when I peel a sparkler wrapper from my shoe that I think of Suz.

I don't know what time it is, then. All I know is that I am tired and drunk and happy. I have lost most of my costume, and it is cold, but I don't mind. It is like the early hours after the May Ball at school, when Beanie and I met up with the boys from the neighbouring school, and sneak-stumbled back, trying to persuade the irate groundsman to let us back in with our sixth form passes. Hitching up our evening dresses and running, clutching each other and hiccupping with suppressed laughter.

Suz. Fireworks. Alone.

I can't believe I didn't think of that.

I rip my tail feathers off, take off my shoes and start to run back down the hill path, leaving Bee Beard and his friends calling after me.

I helter-skelter back to our house, yank off the boards covering the broken windows on the ground floor. I am too tired and too panicked to go the roof way.

What if she's done something stupid? a little voice says. I think of what I might find hanging from the rafters and shudder.

Spinning like a dead fly in silk.

Stop it.

I try to breathe calmly, and climb through the window, leaving my silver case outside on the ground. I'm careful to avoid the jagged glass where vandals and ex-squatters have smashed their way through before the council boarded it all up. Inside it is quiet and hushed as a church. I know instantly that she is not there. I don't bother to check up in the rafters.

I stop only to shove on my DMs and grab my bag and an old cardigan. Then I push my bag out of the window, clamber back outside, and retrieve my devil sticks. I take one last look at the graffiti wall.

No grades or advice from Suz today; just the skill-less scrawl of someone's tag, a soulless squiggle, written over and over again, as if whoever made it was trying desperately to remember who they were.

There's the ghost of a chalk mark underneath, meant for some other tag, too many days ago.

Could do effing better, it says, in her confident scrawl. I smile.

Then I remember the sparkler wrapper, and start to run again, back towards the town.

It's hours later that I find her under the arches, by the sea wall.

It is sheltered from the wind and the rain by a curved roof canopy. Her head hangs, and she's huddled in her silver pixie hood.

I sit beside her. She groans, but doesn't look up. It's obvious she's on something. The spice is eating away at her, little by little. Her lips are dry and cracked as the tiles she's sleeping on.

It is too shadowy to see Suz's face, but I can tell she's asleep, her pouch spilling tobacco by those black-rimmed fingernails.

Far off, a gull screams. Suz coughs.

I shake her. 'Suz? Suz, it's me. Wake up.'

She moans and shakes her head, pushing further into her sleeping bag. I feel a stab of irritation. I have to audition before the circus moves on. I need to shower, find a costume, and work out how to get there. I need to persuade Suz to come with me.

'Suz, come *on*. Wake up and listen to me.'

I kneel down in front of her, trying not to breathe in her smell. I think of Bee Beard, circuses and honey. Imagine another night in the rain-soaked, chilly depths of the rafters.

Rats and pigeons live in rafters, don't they?

I try not to think of The Meadows.

Sounds like a haven. Like I've come home.

Try not to think of how even the word makes me think of ponies and cantering and sunbathing by the tennis courts in the summer term at school.

Try not to feel guilty.

'I've found us a circus, a real one, Suz,' I say, pulling at her.

'You can help make the costumes, do the make-up, anything you want.'

She shakes me off. She's awake now, watching me with shadowed eyes. 'You left me,' she says. 'You fucking left me.'

I don't know why I ever thought her eyes were like sea glass. Today they're dark as storm clouds.

'I'm sorry, I didn't think –'

I tug her again. 'Suz, come on, *please*. We have to be there by the end of today because they're packing up.'

I turn away because Suz is gasping at her spice. I am sick of darkness. I leave her under the arches, a huddled shape. I decide to leave for the circus there and then.

'Suit yourself then,' I say.

At this point, I still think that I'm going to come back for her.

The Circus

In the end, I follow the path through the woods. A few people pass me, walking their dogs. No one gives me a second glance.

Suz just shrugged when I asked if I could take her fire kit. She shrugged again when I promised to return for her.

I turn left, following Bee Beard's map until I come to the track that it says will take me to the farm.

The Meadows.

It is a word filled with sunshine and cider. I smile, and try to push Suz from my mind.

By the time I reach the turning, it is raining, in thick dull thuds.

The silver case drags at my shoulder, my DMs are clagged in mud. My carefully applied make-up smears on my sleeve as I wipe my eyes. I force myself to keep walking, because what else is there to do? Where else can I go? All the time, Bee Beard's card lies damp and pulpy in my hand.

They were laughing at you, sneers a voice. *What would they want with you? You used to be like them, but you left that girl behind, remember?*

Once, an owl lifts in front of me, its great tawny wings outstretched as if it owns the evening I stare as it disappears over the bank. I thought owls only hunted by night, but maybe I am wrong about this, like I'm wrong about so many things. The trees beside me bristle. I climb over a stile, sliding, slipping, thinking that I must be close. I trudge over the field, dragging the case and my bag. And then I see a sign at last:

The Meadows.

And behind it, misted in rain, big tops and tents, like silver and yellow ghosts. A circus. Some giant has dipped a brush in watercolour and splashed in the yellow amongst all the grey. A little patch of magic.

The circus. Where all runaways end up.

The best place to hide, after all, is in the spotlight.

Like a dreamer, I follow.

Pirouette

Something nudges me in the dimness, and I nearly cry out, but it is only a horse – a miniature pony, uninterested in anything but tugging up the trampled grass. He is fat as butter, glossy in the misted rain with his wire-and-straw mane.

Huff, he says, when I trail my hand along his flank. *Huff.*

I wish Spook was with me now. I miss him missing me.

Music draws me.

It is the same music that seems to follow me, at street corners, in cafés, at the edge of my hearing. Haunting, yearning, shuddering. And somewhere, a woman's throaty voice, singing, lifting, emptying.

There are farm buildings dotted around, a manège for exercising horses, a large barn, which looks like it's been recently fitted with a new roof. A large white farmhouse.

Near me are static caravans. Dotted around are wagons and trailers. I can hear the squeals of children. Somewhere, a baby cries. A young boy in Transformers pyjamas and flip-flops darts past on a scooter. I shrink back. He is only three or four. He slips back into the shadow of a wagon. There are a few broken wooden chairs outside, and a clothes dryer which is strung with pale tights of all sizes. Wooden steps, painted red. Inside the big barn, more music: fiddling fast, quick, light songs, chatter, laughter, clapping, applause, faster and faster, until the barn seems to throb with drumming, thrumming clapping fiddles, men's whoops and occasional whistles.

I pass dirty-faced children, catching and throwing each other on trampolines in the space between the caravans. I pass unnoticed, ghostlike. I wonder if I should call for Fabian. I am dizzy, shaky from no sleep and too much cider the night before. The bean stew and bread seems a long time ago.

A boy slips out of the barn, dressed in fishnets and tails, legs lovely as a girl's. He pulls his phone from his hot pants and starts swiping with his thumb.

I drop my case and bag in the muddy grass. Sway my way up to the barn door.

Inside all is light and warmth.

I see a ring filled with sawdust.

Men and women playing violins and singing.

A giant woman with the face of a Geisha girl.

I lean against a wooden pillar, exhausted. Leather and wood and the sweet scent of roses rushes to meet me, and I collapse in the sawdust.

Dancing Girl

Yellow. Silver. A small round tent topped with a blue flag.
  My mother turns to face me, smiles, as she pats her hair. 'Come,'

she says, beckoning me to sit on her lap. Her hair smells of rose oil and magic. She points to the picture on the wall.

'Home,' she says. 'Your home and mine.'

Alice in Wonderland

Sheets, cool and clean.

A painted door.

A map stuck with pins.

There is a little lamp glowing softly on the shelf beside me.

I unglue my cheek from the pillow and sit up, trembling. I don't know where I am. I don't know how long I have slept for. I am fully clothed.

My bags!

I scramble off the bed to look for them, because it's my whole life in there, my world, and then I see my things: the silver case containing my devil sticks, my cloth bag, my shoes – they're standing neatly on the floor next to some small trainers and a juggling pin. I breathe again. Sit back on the bed, which is a child's bed and built into the wall with cupboard doors.

There is a strong smell, a mixture of stale sweat and garlic and, strangely, roses.

The bed is tidy: a bright crocheted blanket and flowery, old lady sheets. A pillow without the slip. There is a book upturned at the end of the bed, a Manga comic with a bug-eyed warrior girl with pointy breasts. I wonder how old the child is.

There's a tiny washbasin set into the wooden sideboard, and a built-in stove and a kettle. Bottles of something dark line the window shelf, along with different-sized glasses and mugs. I open the lid of one and sniff inside. Smells pungent, of plums and spirit and apricots. *Rakia*, it says on the label.

The curtains are drawn tight – pretty curtains sprigged with violets and primroses. I wrench them open and see that it is bright and sunny outside.

How long have I been asleep for?

There are noises outside, sounds of poles clashing and banging. The sound of a lorry rumbling. *They were going to move today!* I think. *Fabian…*

I splash water on my face, straighten my clothes and grab my shoes. My hands tremble as I pull them on. It's important that I find Fabian, and get him to take me to his mother. Then I need to audition and, somehow, find time to go back for Suz. I'll make enough money, and then I'll take us both to Paris.

I imagine us both on the coach, and then showing her the sights. I've been there, of course, many times, on school art trips and language trips, and once with Daddy on business.

Just as I am about to leave, I catch sight of myself in a mirror and freeze. I can't go like this. I am covered in mud from where I must have slipped, climbing over the stile.

I rummage in all of the cupboards that I can find, but there's only child-sized clothes: joggers and hoodies and dungarees, and costumes – a sailor suit, a pirate suit, a clown.

Outside the window I can see lines of washing strung up between the caravans.

From the line, I've taken a pair of gold leggings, some thick knee-high socks, an orange T-shirt, and a revolting pink hoodie, studded with rhinestones. There are branded tops and vests and hoodies. Joggers with big designer logos and diamante-studded leggings and tights. Long harlequin

176

socks and stripy stockings and arm sleeves. A bear suit. A silver-sequinned leotard, ripped. Nike T-shirts. Kappa tracksuit. More pants. Bras. Holey ballet tights.

I am rooting through a line of knickers when I freeze.

A clown is hunkered on a plastic garden chair, under an outside lampshade. He has a mirror propped on his knee, the sort you hang in a hallway, and is drawing black teardrops under his eyes with a thin brush, which he dips into a little pot. On the grass is a cone-shaped hat. White. Black pompoms. He looks like the sort of clown you'd get in one of Beanie's *School Friend* annuals, the ones that her granny gave her from when she was a child. A retro clown, straight from the 1930s.

Something makes him turn, and for a moment it seems that our eyes must meet, he with his sad-happy face, his old man lines carved into thick white greasepaint. I shrink back under the washing line, dropping a pair of leopardskin knickers on the muddy grass. It's fine, though. He hasn't seen me. He just sighs heavily, then props his mirror against the table and picks up a tin of greasepaint.

I grab armfuls of whatever I can find, and am about to sneak back inside the gingerbread wagon when I hear a voice.

'It's wrong to steal, you know.'

It's a child's voice, high and clear. I spin round, heart thudding.

It's a girl, wearing an Aladdin's costume of silk pantaloons and a sequinned bra. She has pepperpot breasts and the plump belly of a child. Her eyes are swooped in makeup, pink and purple and blue. She looks magnificent and knows it.

We both look at the clothes I am holding.

The girl calls something that sounds like 'Baya', and a little boy comes running. It's the boy I saw earlier, still in his Transformer pyjamas. His brown eyes widen when he sees me; his lashes are as long and curled as a camel's.

The girl whispers something and he giggles.

'Thief!' he says. His voice is deep and hoarse, the voice of a man-boy.

From somewhere far off, a deep-throated woman sings at full throttle, warbling, commanding. I clutch the clothes to my chest, and try to sound assertive.

'I'm here to see Fabian,' I say firmly. 'He's expecting me.'

The children whisper and giggle again, and then the girl turns her head and shouts something that sounds like, 'Delilah!'

The clothes in my arms feel like they're burning me. The girl does a handstand, her pink trainers incongruous with her Persian costume.

'And what do you two kids want now? Always bloody interrupting me when I'm trying to do me work –' The voice breaks off. A man's voice. Gravelly. Liverpudlian. Out of place in this otherworld.

But there is nothing ordinary about the owner. I begin to feel that I am in the middle of a strange dream. I try not to stare; instead, try to peg the elephant suit back onto the line.

'They used to have an elephant here once,' the voice says, matter-of-factly. 'But she kept eatin' all me scones.'

It's a man dressed as a Geisha girl, with a pale white face and rosebud magenta lips. He's wearing a Japanese robe, a kimono, covered in shiny jade and orange flowers, a huge sash at the back.

He reaches out to shake my hand, and his hand is rough and warm, with beautifully painted nails. His sleeve falls back to show a muscle-thickened forearm, on it a blurry tattoo of a mermaid arching her back against a ship's helm.

Behind him, the two children run off into a caravan.

'Used to be a docker, didn't I?' the man says, seeing me looking. 'I'm Delilah, by the way. I was the one who carried you to Kit's room. You've slept all night and most of the morning.'

'Kit?' I say. I feel sure that I've heard that name before.

'I think you'd better put all of them clothes back, don't you?' Delilah continues. 'Then we'll say no more about it, will we?'

In silence, we peg up the washing, Delilah pausing at the leopardskin knickers to mutter, 'I wondered where they went.' He laughs at my expression. 'Only joking, love. I wouldn't get me little toe in those, let alone me backside.'

Something comes trotting, and it is a pig, small and pale. It is wearing a dirty clown ruff round its neck and, as I watch, goes to a step and rubs against the edge, scratching itself. It ignores us and trots off between two caravans.

'I need to find Fabian,' I say.

'Oh yes?'

'He told me to come here. To audition.'

'Oh, he did, did he?'

His eyes, which are carefully made up with pink and gold eyeshadow, are gently creped and hooded. Shrewd eyes, but kind.

'I need to speak to whoever's in charge,' I say. 'It's really important that I get to audition before you leave.'

It's what I want to say anyway. But the words don't come out. Instead, what comes out is an ugly sound: a gasping, gulping, snorting sound like an animal. Delilah waits until I've finished, patient as the moon, and then pats my back, over and over.

'There, there,' he says. 'There, there.'

Overture

I follow Delilah to the barn. Open the door, and slip inside into another world.

As we enter, the same clown I saw earlier pushes past us, sweating. He's carrying a pile of metal poles with a frowning man in a Cossack suit.

'They're supposed to have loaded these,' he's muttering.

The hay bales I saw last night have been stacked at the far end, and there are cables slithering over the floor, amongst squawking chickens.

Outside, someone starts up an engine. Inside, the last zithers of a violin.

In the centre of the ring, a girl in footless tights is spinning upside-down in a hoop. There are claps and shouts as she stops, and casually steps out of her harness. She pulls her pony tail out of its band, and shakes her hair.

Leaning against a pillar, tapping a pen against her teeth, is a tall woman with dark hair in a gypsy scarf and riding boots. By the ring, there's a small trampoline where children are practising jumping and catching each other.

A group of teenagers sits on the hay bales, chattering. One of them's Kit, the boy from the Art Café, at the pier auditions. It seems worlds ago now. I look down at my dirty, bitten nails, and wonder if he will recognise me.

I hope he doesn't.

The tall woman stands up and claps her hands, and I see that it is Tilly, Fabian's mother.

'OK, you guys, we'll leave the horse act, and call it quits.'

Delilah leans forward to say something to her, and she peers in my direction at the back of the barn, shielding her eyes to focus. I dig my nails into my palms. Wonder why there is no sign of Fabian.

Delilah's voice, beckoning me: 'Come on then, kid. Show Tilly what you're made of.'

'So what's your act?' Tilly asks, in her clear, ringing voice, and a Home Counties accent. She looks like the mothers in green Hunter boots who used to collect Beanie and her friends in their families' ancient Land Rovers, and shows no sign of recognising me yet. She waves at the other performers, and they move to the seats and start to unstack them, and unclip them from their metal stands. The musicians have stopped playing now, and are packing up their instruments as carefully as if they were tucking children into bed.

'Show me now,' she says. 'But hurry – we're short of time –'

As if to prove her point, there's a shout, and a girl throws down a bundle of wires from the top of a ladder. She shouts again, and it sounds like a curse. She has a welding mask on top of her head.

'It's fire,' I say. I clear my throat. 'I perform with fire.'

I can't believe how long I have waited for this moment.

I wish Suz was here with me. I wish I wasn't here.

I close my eyes, and see Suz, sitting cross-legged up on the rooftop, calling to me, and waving her rollie.

'*You can do it, Frog. Fire Girl. Phoenix Girl, Queen of Flames!*'

'You're the girl in the peacock costume? Fabian's friend?' There's an edge to her voice, her eyes sharp under the spotlight.

I nod. Wonder if the scene at the Jack in the Green Festival actually happened. I wish my peacock tail wasn't lying trampled somewhere in Hastings.

'Well, go on, then.'

181

She's polite and friendly, but that's because she's well-mannered. You can tell she's also impatient to get moving.

There are clatterings and shouts as the circus is dismantled around us; the wooden platforms that support the chairs are unbolted and stacked.

With trembling hands, I take out my kit from the silver case. There's a whoosh as the flames catch, and now Tilly is paying attention.

I juggle first, raising my head, and getting used to the feel of the sticks in my hands. Without music, and without a crowd to get pumped up, it is difficult, but I think of the noise and foot stamping of the day before, the singing and cider, and try to conjure up the same feeling. And then I'm a wild thing, dancing and twirling. Stamping out all of the rage, all of the anger and loss and hate and loneliness. I spin and I stamp and I fling fire, catch it in blackened fingers. My hands are strong and sure. My legs are thick and strong and defiant. I am fire.

She's watching, but giving nothing away. I can make out Kit, perched on a ladder, swinging his legs. He has his phone in his hand, and is in a dark hoodie.

I pause, panting.

'Can I use the wire?' I say. There's a tightrope strung across the back of the ring, low to the ground for practice. It looks as though two acrobats are just about to dismantle it.

She frowns, but nods.

I climb the short ladder. Then I face them all defiantly, fire sticks in hand. I have used Suz's face-paints to paint coloured stripes down my face so that it resembles her chalks. I have taken out her last piece of chalk from my Kit of Happiness and put it in my pocket for luck.

I close my eyes and grip the sticks more firmly.

I am doing this for you, Suz, I think.

I walk quickly to the middle of the rope, tighten my core as I lean my head back and swallow fire, one baton after another. I perform a half-turn like Suz taught me, and then half-dance, half-wobble, to the other end of the rope.

When I'm done, I let the batons drop onto the sawdust, spent. No one speaks. Then I raise my head.

Tilly turns to Delilah and beams. 'I think we've found our final act,' she says. She thrusts out a hand, firm and strong. 'Welcome to my circus.'

Bubbles

I almost cry when I get under the shower.

In fact, I do cry, it's literally that good. I can feel days of filth and horror sluicing off me, pouring down my back, over my skin. Tilly has let me use the one in the farmhouse, off her kitchen, and I squelch out yet another handful of shampoo, and push it through my filthy hair, try out each of the little bottles of shower gels and conditioners and facial scrubs in turn, until the shower steams with mint and juniper and lavender.

When I've finished I see that she's left me towels folded over the tiny basin, and they're big and warm and dry. When I bury my nose in them they smell of lemon and roses. I use them all, wrapping them round my body and hair and shoulders.

So clean. *So clean!*

I stare at myself in the mirror, rubbing away at the steam with a towel.

'Hello, Circus Girl,' I whisper, and smile.

'Everything all right in there?' Tilly's voice, and a tap at the door.

I move my shoes and clothes away with my foot, and push it open slowly.

Tilly passes me a small pile of what looks like ironing.

'Just some more clothes from Fabian's girlfriend,' she says brightly. 'We weren't sure if you had underthings.' She says it matter-of-factly, as if it's the most normal thing in the world to be passing over your son's girlfriend's knickers.

She pauses. 'And do you have anything you need to wash? We do have time. I can get Marika to put it on a quick cycle.' She passes me a carrier bag.

Blushing, I stuff all of my soiled things inside, and hand it to her.

'There are wellies outside, too,' she adds. 'It gets very muddy on the farm. Especially when we're packing up.' She turns. 'Oh, and before I forget – we're having champagne and cupcakes in the kitchen at five. We always have a little celebration before we leave. It's become a sort of ritual.'

I close the door and hear her footsteps in the passage outside, swift, confident.

I stare at the fresh clothes in my hands. She's added deodorant too, a scented roll-on, tucked inside a cleanly laundered sweatshirt. Slowly, I lift my arms and rub it on. Snap on a clean-smelling bra that isn't mine, and pull on soft cotton knickers. Push my head through the velvet softness of a top that is unstained. Unstreaked with chalk or sweat stains or grime.

I take the brush from the glass shelf and pull it through my wet hair, slowly at first, because of the tangles, then fast as it slides through slippery conditioner.

Then I pull on the knee-length socks, and fold the rest of the things into my emptied bag. Check that my Kit of

Happiness is still at the bottom. I leave the shower room, and find a pair of spotty wellies neatly placed outside the door. I put them on, and follow the sound of laughter to the farmhouse kitchen.

Fabian's there, sprawling on a chair next to an Aga.

'My Tree Peacock!' he says, and waves a glass at me. 'Come give me a hug.'

I let him squeeze me in a bear hug, and pull away, gasping.

He is drunk, I realise. He looks unkempt, as if he hasn't slept or washed since the festival. Beside him is the girl who did the aerial act with the hoop. I recognise her now as his girlfriend, Lala. She and Tilly look grim-faced.

'The wanderer returns,' laughs Tilly, but there's a brittleness to her voice. 'Cupcakes,' she announces. 'We all need cupcakes.'

I let Fabian pour me a glass of champagne, and he sloshes quite a lot of it on the quarry tiles. This is a real farmhouse kitchen, of the type that the Handbag would hate, and Beanie would approve of. The range is pumping out a smell of baking, and there are jugs of roses everywhere, spilling white and yellow petals over the giant scrubbed table and window ledges. An ancient retriever sighs on a rug, stretched out over Fabian's feet, and thumps his tail.

'Where's Delilah?' I say.

A television is on discreetly in the background, perched almost as an afterthought on a great pile of cookery books on the dresser. It's showing a twenty-four-hour news programme. Streams of migrant people are trudging endlessly over somewhere in Eastern Europe, Bulgaria or Hungary. They're trying to cross the borders, and hard-faced soldiers in steel-toed boots are stopping them.

I switch my attention back to the champagne and jugs of flowers.

Tilly pulls a face. 'She doesn't come to our cupcake feasts, the traitor. Prefers to camp out with the Romanian lot.' I notice she says, 'she'.

'I'm getting too old for caravans,' she laughs. 'I travel back to the farm when I can.' She doesn't look old at all.

There's the sound of knocking, the back door is thrown open, and the other performers spill inside, looking tired and sweaty.

'Is everything packed up?' asks Tilly. 'The horses too? Come on, let's get some fizz inside you. We leave in an hour.'

Fabian, on his chair by the Aga, looks almost asleep. I wonder why he didn't help the others.

'Cupcakes,' trills Tilly. 'Will you help me, Lala?' The sulky-looking girl helps her perch them onto large blue-and-white china platters. Tilly gets one of the acrobats to take the scones from the oven, and another to pile strawberry jam into an earthenware pot, and I realise that she's in her element. This is her home, and this is the way she likes it, being in command.

I accept a scone and pile dollops of fresh cream onto the plate which Kit offers me. He's sitting on a retro bar stool by the cupcake mountain, and there's a streak of white greasepaint by his right eye. I point it out to him.

'Sure it's not cream?' he says. He rubs it off and licks his finger. 'No, you're right, it's greasepaint.'

I laugh. 'How long have you been working here?'

'Since the Art Café. The pier work only starts in the high season, so I took this on as an interim. Mainly to save for uni.'

I notice again his faint accent.

'And you? What have you been doing since we first met? I remember your first, er, interesting performance.'

I feel myself blush. 'Don't. I was awful.' But then I am silent. I don't have the words to describe my life since then.

I pass him my glass to be refilled. 'I was a sort of street per-former,' I say at last.

I look across the kitchen, which is filling up. It is like the party I once went to at Beanie's house, when she had both her brothers back from uni, and her sister home from travel-ling, and they invited all of their friends around for a huge celebration. I sat there, in the middle of all the warmth and laughter, and I wanted to climb right into her life, and zip up the top so that no one could come and take me away. Except they did of course. Martyna came to get me in her car, mut-tering about being treated like a servant.

And the house mistress came to meet me at the school gates, and let me stay at her school flat, because I was one of the only ones who stayed at school that Easter.

The television's still showing footage of people in boats, people trailing carts and bags and children along dusty roads. Fabian's fast asleep and the dog's trying to climb onto his lap.

And suddenly, there I am. On the television.

I am on video, in my school uniform. It's from when I was in the final of the debating society competition. My hair is long, and dark, and spilling out of its plait, but there is no doubt that it is me.

My palms start to sweat. I take a quick look around the room. No one is looking at the television. I wonder if I have time to turn it off, if anyone will mind, or notice.

Kit is still talking, pointing to a photograph on the wall, a picture of two little girls of different ages balancing on huge rolling globes. He is saying something about Tilly's daugh-ters, but I am not listening. I am frozen, staring at my face on the screen.

Do I look like me? Is that even me, any more? I try to swallow the scone that is in my mouth, but it is dry suddenly. It is made of sand.

Tilly is raising her glass for a toast. She is standing with her back to the TV set, and surely now, someone must see? Tilly is saying something about the circus. We raise our glasses and drink.

I see the video switch back to the news studio. A woman in a stripy blouse is talking earnestly to the camera, and then a photograph of me as a little girl slides into view.

Aged eight. Summer's day. My birthday party, which I wanted to be a riding party. My best friend at the time came. She wore a dress with strawberries on and her breath smelled of sugar. I had to lend her some jodhpurs and teach her to sit on my pony, because she didn't have one; she'd never ridden before. That was before the Handbag ruined everything. That came later, when I was so much older.

The newscaster is talking again, and now the screen fills up with a huge recent photograph of me with my bright schoolgirl smile. This one is zoomed in close, just in case you didn't catch that chicken pox scar on the side of my nose, the way my nose is too big and my eyes are too small.

Kit is talking about the last jobs we need to do before leaving.

'I'll do anything,' I say, trying to keep his attention away from the TV screen. 'I'm strong. I've always been strong. I mean, I can lift things.'

He laughs. Behind him, my face is huge as a giant's.

'Glad to hear it,' cuts in Tilly. 'And you're adaptable, I hope? Not precious about doing just one type of act? With such a small troupe of performers, we need flexibility.'

My picture snaps off the screen, and is replaced by a report about climate change.

I breathe again.

'I'll be anything you want me to be,' I say.

Stooge

Dear Suz,

I had to do it — come here, I mean. You do understand, don't you? That I couldn't miss this opportunity — I had to go. I feel it's been ages since I last saw you. I've been sooo busy since we arrived in Eastbourne.

My main jobs are mucking out the stables (I actually helped build them, Suz. Can you imagine that?), stacking and unstacking the chairs each time there's a performance and rehearsal, and of course, practising for my own performance.

Turns out I'm to be a stooge.

A stooge is a person who aids and abets the performer by pretending to be a member of the audience. All the time they're really working for the circus.

The other definition of a stooge is an underling, subordinate or lackey. Not exactly a starring role. I vowed straight away that this wouldn't be for long. I mean, how the mighty fall! From Phoenix Girl to minion in less than a week!

I let Ana kit me out in my stooge outfit. Utterly dull. Just normal clothes with a bit of make-up to make me look older. I had to sit in the front row next to one of the acrobat kids, who was pretending to be my son. Even though he's only five years younger than me, and Chinese!

The performer I'm working for is the Great Garibaldi. He's basically a clown, but does a bit of magic too. He does a thing where I sit inside a counter and pop my head up through different holes as he lifts and lowers giant cups. The boy who is supposed to be my son then tries to guess which cup Mummy's head will be under. The twist is, Garibaldi starts to become angry and tries to chop my head off. So I have to remember the routine, and count very exactly, and move my head to the right position in order to make it work properly. I have no idea what it looks like from the audience perspective because I've never watched it in action. All I know is that the audience seems to enjoy it. There's always a lot of clapping and cheering.

It's all rather boring, and then there's Garibaldi's toenails.

He has the most revolting feet, which he never washes, and they literally make me want to heave, as I'm crouching awfully near them during the act. There they are, shifting and shuffling, and when he's standing still, he has a habit of scratching the back of one ankle with his other toenail, which makes this hideous rasping sound.

His toenails are long and grey and horny. I think he must have a fungal infection. Even writing this makes me want to be sick.

But it will all be worth it once they give me the starring role!

Miss you,

Frog. x

Ribbons and Corsets

I am perched on a red velvet sofa. It has great swirls of wood at each arm, like giant scrolls, and it is dirty and thready and patched all over with pieces of mismatched velvet. On one arm lies a sliding heap of corsets, their eyelets and laces all different jewel colours: purple and amber and turquoise.

In the lamplight, the costumes shimmer like ghosts.

Ana, the costume-maker, shuffles to a large wooden cabinet and riffles through it. I watch as she takes out a corset, hanging by its laces from a tiered rack. It's beautiful: swagged with teal-green velvet ribbons, the colour of a mallard's neck. It's green and black, with little satin-stitched metal holes for the criss-crossed ties.

Ana climbs onto a stool and places the corset reverently around a woman's ample waist. The woman bows her head and lifts her grizzled hair up, out of the way. Her hair is not typical old lady's hair; it is mad and wild and wiry. Ivy attacking brickwork.

Ana nods and grins as she draws in Silviya's corset ribbons, slow and tight. The performer closes her eyes and braces until it is done.

'Looking good, Silviya,' calls Delilah. She's reclining on a battered chaise longue, like the one we have in our library, the one that Daddy paid a designer to buy from an auction house in Mayfair.

I flinch as something springs lightly onto my shoulder, and then onto the table in the middle of the tent. It's Kahlo, Ana's tiny spider monkey, with a woven basket attached to its back with blue ribbon.

Kahlo chatters quietly in my ear, patting my cheek and neck with cool dry hands. I try not to mind.

We watch as Silviya is transformed. Ribbons and green chiffon are pinned onto the base of her corset with deft tugs. Ana spits pins, stitches and nods; all the time, her little monkey beside me silently chatters. Silviya spins round, her doughy arms held up, curved nails shining.

Kahlo the monkey jumps down and actually starts collecting up all the empty cotton reels and tossing them over his shoulder into the basket. Satisfied, he picks his way delicately over the rest of the table, gathering loose threads and pins and ribbon, still with the little woven basket strapped to his back.

Silviya gazes into the age-spotted mirror. The harsh lights throw into relief every line, every crease and fold. But she is beautiful. She stands silently as Ana pokes a brush into a china dish of grease paint, draws a gleaming red bow over that proud mouth.

Silviya licks rouge from her teeth and spits. She lifts her mermaid wig of real dog's hair, curled and brushed.

'*Dobur*,' she says. 'Good. This will do.'

Delilah stands up. 'Your turn now, love,' she says. She turns to Ana, who is nodding and waiting. 'This lass needs kitting up,' she says. 'For her first show, like.' She winks at me. 'Good luck, kid,' and she is gone, in a swish of fuchsia silk kimono.

Ana waits, smiling. She makes me stand on a wooden stool, and hold my arms out to be measured. Then she searches among the shelves and rails deftly, pulling out blouses and dresses and tights, while all the time her little spider monkey sits on a rail and chatters.

I wish I could wear a mad costume, like that silver lobster hat, its beetle body hugging the shape of the head, and its antennae spiralling upwards. Or the one that looks like a giant clam, its ribbed sides clasping the wearer's head like Princess Leia's side buns in the original *Star Wars* movie. There are costumes hanging from a wooden airer, its wooden slats reached by lifting and lowering knotted ropes; flesh bodysuits in shades of brown and cream and pink, costumes which sprout strange tubers of octopus leg suckers, moon craters and sea anemone-feelers. I touch a glittery flapper dress, pink and gold and burnished as a rose, but Ana smiles and shakes her head.

I take the clothes she hands me, and wonder why she doesn't talk.

Behind a screen, I dress, pulling on the cotton tunic dress in pistachio green and cream stripes, flat pumps, and a lemon cardigan. As a stooge, I have to look ordinary, just a regular member of the audience. When I'm done dressing, I look just like the mothers of the girls I was friends with before, the ones who drove Land Rovers and ran committees and drank secret gins and tonics. It is as if Ana has seen beneath the hard-faced, crop-haired girl I am now to the person I could have become.

I look like I've come home.

Later, dressed in my stripy dress, I squeeze past a dad with his toddler on his lap, and sit on a hard plastic seat. My 'son' is already in place, catching Pokémons on his iPhone. I stare into the ring and feel my heart skittering as I wait for my turn.

Warm lights made to look like burning torches throw shivering flames over the tent walls. A girl with headphones around her neck is up a ladder, fiddling with the lighting.

A sweep of pink spotlights. A drum roll.

Then, a spotted horse appears in a cloud of sawdust.

Astride it like an avenging angel, a wild woman, a Mer

Queen, is riding bareback with no bit or reins. Her hair is wild like the wind, her long thighs gripping the horse's flanks, strong as saplings.

It is Silviya, the woman from the costume tent.

She raises her arms in the air and clapclapclaps.

The horse bends its forelegs and bows, and the little group cheers and whoops.

'Behold, be astounded, by Mirela, the Magnificent Mer Queen!' shouts Tilly, in full ringmistress costume.

Silviya leans forward and whispers in the horse's ear. I lean forward to watch. The horse, which looks just like Spook, picks up its legs in a delicate trotting motion. Silviya guides it using only her hands and fingertips. With no saddle, no bit, no bridle, she gets the horse to spin and dance; to raise its heels and point its toes and march and trot and side step. All with only a whisper, a light stroke of command.

I love it.

With a mysterious motion of her hand on the horse's withers, she makes her horse 'swim', like a true horse of the ocean.

Without warning, from a puff of the Mer Queen's breath, the horse rears and spins in the opposite direction, snorts froth from its nose. It explodes into full gallop – making the front row gasp and cower – and then stops, in a perfect pirouette, before performing the same feat in each direction.

Then, up it rises in a terrible rear, legs pawing at the dust-moted air, plumes trembling.

The audience explodes as the boy beside me yawns.

Next, Lala, the aerial dancer. Seated around the ring are the fiddlers, zithering faster as she climbs the trembling ladder in the centre of the ring, the fringing on her dress shivering.

She hangs by her hair, her face a blur as she spins, faster and faster, her dress a flash of gold. I lean forward and sigh.

I want to do that.

Hair Spray and Rose Oil

Mother smells of rose oil and cigarettes. It's the most beautiful scent in the world. She doesn't talk to me – it's a serious business, getting dressed up. I can feel her cool hands as she tucks my hair behind my ears, smooths it with oil. She backcombs my pony-tail hard and it hurts, a little, but I don't care because she's watching me in the mirror and that little frown of concentration is all for me.

I hang my head upside-down like she tells me, as she sprays so much hairspray on that it makes me cough, but it's all worthwhile because she scoops back the hair, smooths it lightly, tucks, teases, tweaks, tugs, and now I'm not Willow Stephens any more: I'm Willow the Indefatigable, Gypsy Princess.

She does my make-up too, swooshing blue and green shimmer over my eyelids, leaning so close that I can feel her eyelashes on my cheek as she applies mascara.

'Now you look beautiful,' she says. 'Now you are a princess.'

And she laughs as she whirls me about the room in my gold tutu and my sparkly pink tights, my hair shiny and smooth and long as a mermaid's, even longer.

Martyna used to take me into town to have my hair cut. I kicked and screamed but she was used to tantrums. Her hands were firm as paddles. She'd brought up her five brothers who were a lot worse than me, she said. Couldn't I scream a bit louder because not everyone's looking yet? It's the tangles, she told the hairdresser. Hair too thick to be long, she was fed up with battling it every morning. Who did I think I was, anyway? A bloody princess?

Fancy Pants

'So what would you like to be, more than anything in the world?' asks Kit. We are resting between rehearsals, sitting on garden chairs in the sun. Kit has dyed his hair bright red, and is now applying the dye to my hair too. Delilah shudders when she sees it.

'Disgusting, that,' she says pleasantly, handing round mugs of milky coffee.

'Make it shorter,' I say, when the dye's taken.

'Are you sure?' Kit wields the scissors. He's in one of his silly moods, and I wonder if I should trust him with my hair. But then, it'll always grow back, won't it?

'I would like to be a pigeon,' I say. 'All those chips, and rooftops.'

'I was talking about jobs, stupid.'

I shudder. 'Ugh. Who would want one of those?'

'Well, not you, for a start. You would never need one.'

I look at him, and feel the freeze of scissors against the back of my neck. Kit's words come out, easily as ever. Flippant, thoughtless, throwaway. But now my old paranoia is back, and I am thinking of a hundred different meanings behind his words.

Does he know my background?

Is it just my voice that gives me away?

Has he seen or heard or read anything about Willow Stephens, the Missing Schoolgirl, who walked out on her rich daddy's wedding day?

I can't let him see that it's affected me. We're friends. Aren't we?

And Kit's back to chattering away about his dreams of becoming a lawyer, of going to Sofia University, and I retort with ridiculous ambitions of being an ice cream-seller, magpie-breeder, kipper shop-owner, and it is as if nothing's been said.

It's been so busy, exhausting but fun, even with the tension between Fabian and his mother, and the fact that his girlfriend seems to hate me. We have set up somewhere near Eastbourne, and have a small field, about the size of a village green, all to ourselves.

Tilly arrives early each morning, to exercise her beloved horses with Silviya, and check that everything's running smoothly, and no one is shirking their duties. My back and shoulders ache from all the lifting and carrying. When I'm not practising or performing, I help Delilah with the cooking, or hang around with Kit. Fabian likes to sleep in. Sometimes he doesn't come home at night.

When my hair's done, Kit holds up a mirror, and we peer into it together, his and hers matching hair, cropped short, tomato red. We look awful, but free and careless and happy.

More importantly, I don't look like the girl called Willow. Not one bit.

Bunting

The tea tent is fluttering with grey and yellow bunting. Outside, the sounds of families drifting to the ticket booth to buy early bird tickets, the squeals of children running as Kit chases them in his toy clown car, beeping his giant horn.

Inside, Tilly is poring over drawings and charts, her hair knotted up in a green headscarf, severe black spectacles slipping down her nose. Wax crayons and Staedtler fineliners and pencils are all over the table, on its tastefully garish sunflower-yellow oilcloth.

Delilah is in her *Cook Knows Best* apron, a cerise-pink fan sticking out of her black Geisha bun, bulk-making scones. Her latest cupcake creations sit neatly in trays in various stages of icing; she is trialling piña colada flavour, although Tilly says that it is common. She's stabbed yellow cocktail umbrellas into some of them, and Tilly reaches over and plucks them out briskly.

She looks up when she sees me.

'You've inspired me, Frog,' she beams. 'Come and look.'

I lean over her drawings, and there are various sketches and mood boards, showing a girl with outstretched arms, showering flames behind her; a giant peacock with a tail made of fire, horses with flamed and feathered plumes.

I remember the pink-plumed horses at the Handbag's wedding, Spook tossing his pink-feathered head. I imagine how long that would have taken her to plan.

'That's lovely,' I say. But it isn't.

Tilly is not great at drawing. I imagine Suz, head bent over her drawings in this sunny marquee. Then I feel a stab.

I haven't thought about Suz for ages. Not since we first arrived here.

'Phoenix Girl,' says Tilly. 'The next show's all about fire. We're going to take it as a theme. Create more costumes, themed cupcakes, horses with flames as plumes.' She takes my arm. 'It's all down to you, Frog. I was inspired by your costume at the Jack in the Green Festival. It was…remarkable. I'm sure you won't mind me stealing a teeny-weeny bit of the idea.'

'It was Suz's idea,' I say. I watch Tilly as she carefully shades in a tail feather. She draws like she's filling in one of those colouring books for adults.

'Mmmm?'

'Suz. My friend. She designed my costume.'

'And a bloody good costume it was too. You looked bloody fantastic in it.'

Fabian's back.

He walks carefully between the tables and I know at once that he is drunk. He sits himself at the counter and picks up a cupcake. Takes a cocktail umbrella and spins it between his fingers.

'Well, these are rather nice.'

'Are you going to go through the books with me, like we agreed?' says Tilly. Her tone is as careful as her son's walk.

'Are you going to make me, Mother? Do I have a choice?' He takes a huge bite of cupcake. 'Now that's more like it. Needs a splash more booze though, Delilah, my sweet.'

'Don't be ridiculous, Fabian,' Tilly snaps. 'And where's the bloody signage for the tea tent?'

'Where's the bloody signage for the tea tent?' Fabian mimics. He walks unsteadily towards his mother's table, and leans over her shoulder, breathing heavily. 'Wasn't there a girl with you – before?' he says.

I realise that he's talking to me. I look up at him, and am shocked by his appearance. He looks like he's slept in his clothes, and his eyes are pink and wet. He starts laughing silently. 'You really are the limit, Mother, stealing someone else's ideas. I suppose you're going to pass them off as your own?'

'I don't mind,' I say. But I do really.

Suz should be here, sitting at this table, licking the buttercream off piña colada cupcakes and drawing her wonderful, mad, vigorous worlds all over the sheets spread out on this spotty, dotty oilclothed table. For a flash I want to sweep the whole tablecloth and its contents onto the floor, snap every one of Tilly's expensive pens and crayons, and scribble over her awful, careful drawings.

But I don't do that.

Instead, I smile sweetly and say, 'I love it.'

Night Music

Silviya's home is tiny but cosy. It's hung with framed photographs in colour, black and white, and brown sepia, covering every spare piece of the wall. There are babies being balanced on strong men's arms, a man holding up a baby elephant, blank-eyed twins on tightropes, fierce monobrowed women swallowing fire, a blonde lady in a catsuit hanging by her hair. The more modern ones show family groups: smiling husbands and wives and children standing in kitchens, in gardens, amongst horses and dogs and tigers.

'My family.'

I stand awkwardly in the stuffy room, which is full to the brim with Silviya's children and grandchildren. At its centre, the woman who sings every evening sits on a wooden chair, her hands on her knees, her hair drawn back under her scarf. Baya and his sister perch on the arms of the sofa; smaller children climb onto knees and laps and the backs of chairs.

'Come, come, little bird.'

I am given a wooden chair, taller than everyone else's, as if I am somehow special. I move it back, so that I am not on show. The old man next to me says something in Romanian and laughs toothlessly. I look across at Delilah, and she nods and smiles.

'This here's the real circus,' she says.

After we have all been passed food – little plates of pastries, still warm, buttery and crumbly and filled with cheese; plastic dishes of garlicky dips; fruited breads with seeds and olives; paper plates of chopped spicy sausage – the woman in the middle – who Delilah whispers is Silviya's daughter, Marika – lifts her head and sings.

She is unaccompanied by the musicians. Just as before, her voice begins soft and throbbing, then rises into a keening song of longing. Her family around her close their eyes. Silviya nods and smiles, tears wet on her cheeks. The children are still; even the babies are quiet in their shawled nests.

I look at Delilah, and she is weeping too, careless of the make-up that is coursing in shimmers down her cheeks.

I think of Suz, hiding in her homemade cave. I think of Tilly, bright and hard amongst her bunting and cupcakes.

And I wonder if my mother ever sang to me.

Feathers

Silviya turns round, and her eyes are tender and heavy. She is stripped bare of make-up, her face shiny with cream.

'Come closer, little bird,' she says. 'I am going to tell you a story.'

Behind her, the mirror shimmers with a thousand costumes, a thousand dreams.

Her hand clasps mine, and feels warm and oily. I pull up a stool and we sit, knee to knee, the distant violins lilting with the night cries of children in the dark.

'I used to gaze at you for hours,' she says, stroking my hand in hers. 'Your eyes, so dark, so knowing. You tried to climb, even before you could sit. I would lift you under the arms when your neck was strong enough, and your little legs would scramble, trying so hard to climb up my belly to be lifted high. If I placed you down, you would scream and holler, enough to wake up the whole park. You wanted to be lifted and to be seen, even then, even at a few days old.'

'You…' I say. Silviya has taken off her corset, and her body floods out into her favourite orange and turquoise robe. She looks like an empress, regal as a queen.

'I had no choice but to give you up. Your father and me, we were from different worlds, different lands. I tried to live as he wished, but at night I lay in our bed, feeling all that house, all its empty rooms, around me, and I wanted nothing more than a crocheted blanket, a window full of stars. I had more space than I had ever had before, all the time I would ever need, yet I had never felt more imprisoned.'

She leans closer, till her breath strokes my cheek.

'You and me, we were born to fly,' she says. Then I watch

as she unhooks her robe, and releases her wings, which have been crushed and folded at her side. At last I see the reason for her corsets. She gives them a shake and laughs as many coloured feathers scatter and drift.

'Join me,' she says, standing up, and pulling my hand. 'I'll catch you if you fall.'

Then we whizz around the room on pretty-coloured wings and soar out into the night sky. Oh, and live happily ever after.

Obviously.

I wish Silviya was my mother, though. She'd be strong, and tough, and wouldn't take any shit from anyone.

I wouldn't have ever had to run away.

Illustrated Girl

I am being transformed.

'Is this the final time?' I ask, as Delilah scratches and scuffs.

'I bloody told you, yes,' she mutters.

Delilah doesn't like being interrupted when she is at work. She's copying my tattoo from one of Suz's drawings. It's one from the few scraps of paper I kept when she replaced my money. The drawing I chose is a phoenix, stretching its wings across my shoulders, dripping molten fire across my back.

I am lying tummy-down on Delilah's bed, and around us are the tools of her trade. Her tattoo needles are neatly lined up, along with all of her coloured inks, with their strange and wonderful names: magenta and lollipop, hunter green and banana cream and fleshpot. In front of me, the television's on, 'to distract me,' Delilah said, but I don't need distracting. I feel excited, as if I am reinventing myself.

'Are you sure?' Delilah asked, before our first session.

'Yes, I'm sure,' I said. Because each mark made, each drop of colour scuffed in, makes me feel like I am a new person, like I am being scribbled out and remade, whole and new. I am something definite.

Today, she's doing the colours: filling in each carefully drawn outline with jewel shades.

The gardening show on the TV switches to *Crime Solve!* Delilah looks up as the title swims around with its serious-looking font.

'Oh, I like this one,' she says.

Behind the title of the show, people's faces float, and it's not clear whether they are victims or perpetrators. The music starts, it's a heartbeat, faint at first, then getting steadily louder and faster. It reminds me of that gruesome story by Edgar Allan Poe: *The Tell-Tale Heart.*

The presenter (blonde, female) arranges her legs elegantly around the table, and perches on her seat, grave-faced, coffee mug in hand. Behind her, rows of volunteers are busy answering phones and tapping on keyboards.

And there I am.

My schoolgirl-head and-shoulders shot swims into view next to the presenter, and now the presenter's trailing her fingers over me, like I'm the weather, a cold front that's approaching from the west.

Delilah's needle hovers. I hold my breath.

Will she recognise me?

The presenter's saying something about my multimillionaire father. She mentions the word 'devastated'. Her co-presenter strolls on, equally serious-faced (black, male, handsome). He says that Willow was a 'bright and popular schoolgirl' with a 'bright future'. He says the word 'bright' a lot, as if I'm something that needs toning down, or they're running out of adjectives.

'Big mystery this one, isn't it?' says Delilah. I relax.

It is very strange to view myself in the third person. It is even stranger to see the actor that they've chosen to play me in the reenactment. It is as if I'm dead and have come back to gatecrash my own funeral.

The girl is too thin and too tall. They've also got my hair wrong. She's dressed in a bridesmaid dress that is deliberately black and a little long. I grow cold as I see my own bedroom, my bed with its heaps of pillows and folded Welsh blanket and Egyptian cotton bedlinen. Just seeing it makes me want to cry. There are all of my artfully abstract photographs of my ponies and horses. My first pony, Storm, from when I was five. Big Bonnie. And Spook. My beautiful, gorgeous Spook. Hanging from my dressing table are my necklaces and beads and vintage handbags. There's the bag of letters that Beanie and I would write to each other, even when we were going to see each other soon, over the long school holidays.

My heart grows even colder when I see what Almost-Willow is doing: she's opening her bedside drawer and taking out a large pair of scissors.

Suddenly I don't want to watch any more.

Delilah yawns and picks up a different size needle.

'It's a strange one, isn't it? About that girl. Can't really tell if she's the victim or criminal!'

Almost-Willow's face is in close up, and I shiver. She looks vindictive. Now she's in the Handbag's room. And now she's cutting the buttons.

'Just look at that poor girl!'

But Delilah isn't talking about Willow Stephens, little rich girl. She's shaking her head at the Handbag – Kayleigh-

Ann, who's being played by a skinny actor with big boobs. Almost-Kayleigh-Ann is pouring her heart into her role, sobbing into Almost-Daddy's arms, her ruined dress in the foreground.

I watch Willow climb down the wisteria and run through the woods. I watch her hitch a lift with a Santa Claus lorry driver. I watch her dodge the fare on the train to Paddington.

All the time, I'm thinking, *Do I know her? Is she really me?* I can't get Kayleigh-Ann's sobbing out of my head.

Delilah's needle scratches and scuffs, and I begin to feel a little sick.

Then there are the interviews.

'And there the trail ends,' frowns the presenter. 'We know that this disturbed schoolgirl is somewhere on the south coast; that she spent some time sleeping rough in Hastings, where evidence suggests she has turned to a life of crime. You see her here, tying up a fairground worker with Christmas fairy lights, along with an unknown female, believed to be a busker. In true *Thelma and Louise*-style they have terrorised the streets of Hastings, stealing and breaking and entering to survive.'

Terrorised, I think. Suz would smile at that.

'We believe that Willow may be in a state of psychological disturbance; that she is being influenced by her friend. She may even have forgotten her old identity, and be confused. We have reason to believe that she has assaulted a police officer –'

Here, the camera cuts away to show a shaky mobile phone video of me and a large yellow dog, leaping onto a police officer's chest, me smacking her with a dead seagull. There I am, turning to look at the screen, with my droopy-eyed clown face. With my knee on the officer's chest and my painted face, I look less like a schoolgirl and more like some kind of deranged action figure.

206

I glance at Delilah through the reflection on the screen. She's watching very intently.

'We have eyewitnesses who say...'

And here, on camera, is Terry the Disney dad, complete with lemon shirt and swirly tie.

'She was clearly mentally disturbed,' he's saying. 'Concocted some cock-and-bull story about being on a game show. We believed her. Why wouldn't we? Gave her a place to stay out of the kindness of our hearts. She abused that. Stole from us –'

Well, a banana and a packet of crisps, I think. Terry's making me out to be some sort of unhinged psychopath.

Afterwards, Delilah lets me look before she mends me with bandages. Each swirl, each feather, makes me bleed, is dotted with pinpricks of blood, but she has stripped me raw and remade me.

'I love it,' I tell her, and she hugs me close, those big hands holding me like I am something precious and loved.

'There now,' she says.

On the television, the female presenter leans forward and looks earnestly at us both.

'If you see this girl, it's important not to approach her but to phone this number immediately. Her father is offering a large reward for her return. We are expecting a significant amount of interest in this case. As always, our team is on hand twenty-four-seven to handle any calls.'

Here she mentions a sum that makes me dig my fingers into my palms and Delilah suck in her breath.

Shit.

I touch my dressings; I can't wait for them to be unpeeled so that I can be revealed, finally, as the Phoenix. But I feel like I'm already playing with fire.

Trapeze

It is Lala who teaches me to fly.

Fabian finds me writing my journal up in the crow's nest.

'Who are you writing to?' he asks.

I hide my notebook. 'No one. Nothing.' *(It was you, of course, Suz. I haven't forgotten you, although you've probably forgotten about me by now.)*

'You're always writing,' he says. He smiles, slow as a cat. 'Let me see. Is it poetry? I rather like poetry.' The ladder bounces as he climbs up.

I sit on my book, and don't know whether to feel annoyed or pleased that my private time has been disturbed.

In the end, I decide to feel pleased. After all, it was he that found me, gave me my first break and bought me dinner at the festival. I owe him. But I don't trust him. His eyes are too bright and knowing. He drinks too much. I sense the darkness in him, just like the spice held Suz.

But he makes me laugh. In all that darkness, there's a child trying to get out.

'I spy, with my little eye, something…high…that will make Frog…fly,' he sings.

I stare at him. 'What do you mean, Bee Beard?'

He jerks his head up at the apex of the small big top. There it is, glinting silver, hanging, at rest.

'I know you want to,' he says, and neither of us is laughing now. 'I have seen it in your face. I know that look.'

I swallow. 'I have always wanted to fly,' I say simply.

'Good. Your first lesson is today. Nine o'clock.'

I'm still gaping at him. I have no idea when that is. I haven't worn a watch or owned a phone in the three months since I ran away. He rolls his eyes and checks his own phone. 'That's, like, in three minutes.'

'But...why?' I say.

'Lala's old neck injury's giving her trouble. She sprained it again, trying out a new move. Mum's furious. Said it's about time we had a back-up.'

I am not sure about Lala. She has pretty much ignored me since I joined Le Petit Cirque. When she looks at me, if at all, she makes me feel like I am an insect grubbing around. A worm under her shoe.

Still. *Flying.*

All at once I am transported back; the years peel away, like pages in a diary:

'Go on, little one!' my mother's eyes smile. 'Fly! Up you go!'

And she's throwing me, higher and higher. Up, up, into the clouds that are apricot-dipped; and beneath me, her head is up-turned, waiting for me to fall.

Ringmistress

'It's awfully good of you to step in like this,' smiles Tilly. 'Lala should have been more careful – she's always taken far too many risks.'

She casts her eyes around the tea tent, straightens a strag-gling line of bunting.

She's already dressed in her ringmistress costume: pol-ished riding boots and midnight-blue velvet frock coat with copper epaulettes and embroidered frogging. Suz would adore it.

She doesn't like Lala, I realise. Doesn't want her for a daughter-in-law. *She likes me because we're the same. We have the same accent.*

Would she like me so much if my father swooped up in his GAS 1 reg Porsche? If she saw Suz and me shoplifting, street-drawing, squat-sleeping?

'I've told Lala to teach you. I can't pay her as much now she's not performing of course, so she's sulking, I'm afraid. But the show must go on!'

Tilly smiles brightly. She doesn't look like she's been sleeping much. I wonder if she worries about Bee Beard, when he's away 'on business'.

'Are you sure you're comfortable in the tack room? I can fix you up a bed in Lala's caravan if you like. Now that Fabian…'

Her voice trails off, then she seems to rally herself.

'Pass me that newspaper, will you? I need to fix my face for the troops.'

She always talks like this: like she's the commandant in charge of a platoon.

Tilly leans into her make-up mirror and starts to apply lipstick. It is when she reaches for the paper that I freeze.

There's a full-page picture of me. It's open wide, picture up, one of the nationals too, not just a local one.

The CCTV footage is blurry, but it's me all right, in my mustard-yellow coat and cropped hair.

HAVE YOU SEEN THIS GIRL? the headline shouts. And *CONVENT GIRL TO CRIMINAL.*

Tilly puts her lipstick down and tears off a long strip of paper. It is the piece with my photograph.

She holds the newspaper up and seems to frown for a fleeting moment.

I start to feel the familiar signs of panic: the hammering

heart, the cold ice of sweat, the pressing down on my lungs. Will she recognise me? Will she recognise the girl in the photograph?

Tilly presses the paper to her lips and kisses it to blot her lipstick.

Then she screws up the paper and tosses it onto the table.

'Let me know if you have any concerns about Lala,' Tilly says. 'Wish me luck with the show.'

'Break a leg,' I say automatically.

The minute she is gone, I snatch the ball of paper and shove it into my pocket ready to read and burn later.

I take a calming breath and look around at the artfully casual tea tent, with its local art and jam-jar flowers and spotty napkins. She'd be like me, I think, about Kayleigh-Ann's wedding. She'd go round the guests, plucking tasteless fascinators from balayaged heads, replacing gold-swagged chairs with nice rustic hay bales. I imagine her mother-of-pearl polished nails popping all of Kayleigh-Ann's naff balloons with a long, sharp hatpin.

I try not to hear the little voice in my head:

She's no worse than you.

Cloud Swing

'Christ almighty, what is *wrong* with you?'

'I'm sorry.'

Lala is sitting up on the tiny platform, scrolling through her phone. She signals to Zella, the lighting technician up in the crow's nest.

'I cannot wait all day.'

I blush, try to collect myself.

'Sorry.'

She scowls down. 'Come on up, please.'

I begin to climb, trying not to mind how the ladder wobbles. I am strong, though. All the shunting and carrying of staging and equipment has seen to that. I climb, one hand after the other, up the swaying ladder. Above me, Lala waits. The ladder's attached to her platform. The platform's attached to a steel frame, and also ropes that hang from the apex.

'Why now?' I say, when I am up at the top.

She shrugs. 'No reason.' She pushes her phone into her jacket and zips it shut. Her eyes are pale-lidded without her swooping gold make-up; it makes her look much younger. Her hair is lighter too, the long glossy ponytail that she uses for performances gone. There's a cluster of pimples on her forehead, which is pinched into a permanent frown.

And then there's the neck brace.

Just looking at it gives me shivers, as if it's a warning. Delilah is always full of dire tales of gore and horror: the Chinese acrobat crushed when he lost his balance and fell from the Wheel of Death; the circus elephant that went rampaging through the streets of Honolulu after kicking its handler and the ringmaster to a pulp in front of hundreds of little children.

Lala becomes businesslike, as if this is a job she has to do, and she may as well get it out of the way. I don't care, though. I crouch on the swaying platform and feel the blood buzzing through my veins. No one knows that this is where I come every night, when most people are asleep, and there is only the sound of crying babies or ghosting owls, and the distant hum of traffic. *I climb up here, Suz, and this is where I write to you, did you know?*

I have my mother's photo tucked into my pocket next to my heart. It's in my blood, I think. This is where I get close to her. This is where I belong; finally know who I am.

'Ready?'

I nod, and Lala shows me how to dust down my hands with resin. I know how to do this; I have watched the acrobats many times. The dust clouds and vanishes. Up here, even the air feels alive. The pigeons feel it too; they're shivering their feathers with the magic of it.

'Hold here – like this.'

Lala takes my hands and shows me the correct position. I am shocked at how callused hers are, her palms hardened and rough below her fingers. You sacrifice beautiful hands, being a trapeze artist. There is pain behind the beauty and grace.

For the first time, I fasten my hands around the trapeze bar. It is worn and scruffy-looking. It has been well-used, the binding around the bar grubby and frayed. I look up. The side ropes near the bar have been wrapped tightly with black tape, similar to what you'd put around a tennis racket. It smells of effort and hard work and pain.

My heart begins to race, and automatically I think of my pills. But there are no pills, not any more. *That girl is gone, remember?* I stare ahead, at the opposite platform. I don't look down, even though I can feel the yawning space below us; I smell freshly raked sawdust and resin and sweat and the scent of rose oil that always seems to linger.

'Hold on,' I say. I feel inside my pocket for Suz's chalk. Feel its reassuring silkiness.

Now I'm ready.

I stare straight ahead as Lala clips me into the safety harness. The nets are stretched below, too. I can hear the Chinese acrobats having a discussion in low voices.

'You need to slow your breathing, stay calm.'

There is concern in Lala's voice. I can't let her think that I am too weak for this. I am not that girl any more. I think of my tattoo spreading its wings across my back. I am powerful. I am strong. I can fly.

'OK? Focus. Get ready.'

She holds me steady around my waist. 'Look forward,' she says sharply, when I turn to her. 'I will say when. You keep your eyes in front at all times. Focus. Focus. Keep your body straight. The momentum will do the rest.'

I nod my head, my mouth dry. For a fleeting moment I am wondering if this is a good idea. Then I think of my mother's voice. *'Fly, little bird! Higher, higher!'*

'Ready? *Hup!*'

Her voice is sharp, and, with a cry, I let go.

And then there's air and space and whooshing speed and the thudthudthud of my heart in my head and there's nothing below me or around me or above me and then –

'Good.'

Lala catches me as I return to the platform, steadies me as I stumble a little.

'OK?'

I can't speak.

When I turn to her, panting and trembling, there is a half-smile playing around her lips, and then she switches it off. Becomes businesslike again.

'Again. This time, keep your body straight, but try to relax.'

I do it again and again, until the palms of my hands are raw and red, and my shoulders burn and my body is drenched with sweat. And each time, it feels more and more right; my arms feel strong and sure; my body and my thick, sturdy wrists were born to do this.

If only Suz could see me now.

214

Tumbling

My body is changing, subtly. My shoulders are broader, well-muscled. My abdominal muscles are corded with steel, my triceps hard as stone. My hands though are a mess.

Lala shrugs when I show her. 'Circus hurts,' is all she will say. But she calls Kit for the first-aid pack.

I flinch and shudder as Kit pulls away my bandage.

'Oh god, I can't look,' I say.

He turns over my hand and pours brandy over it – I hiss with pain. He takes a swig and laughs. 'You can always pee on it,' he says. 'That's what Russian athletes do.'

But I am whimpering too much to answer. I watch as he takes a bottle of something brown and sticky and unscrews the lid.

'What *is* that?' I say.

He smirks. 'Friar's Balsam. Cough mixture. It will help build up calluses. Ready?'

I nod, throat tight. Clench my teeth as he pours the mixture straight onto the tear in my flesh. We watch as it bubbles and seals itself with a skin-like white powder. The pain is fierce fire, but somehow makes me feel high and exhilarated. It makes me want more pain, because then I feel buzzy and alive. Kit cups his hand under mine and holds it still while it heals. Lala waits, scrolling through her phone, scowling.

It is time to be bandaged, and then I must go through it all again.

'*Hup,*' barks Lala, and I jump up and let go, keeping my eyes forward, my body straight.

'Now, waitwaitwaitwait.'

It's such a rush, all that air and space around me. It's worlds better than the feeling I got being on the rooftop, or hanging from the tallest tree. I focus on looking ahead at the other platform, where one day Lala will wait, ready to catch me.

'Legs up!'

At her command, I lift my legs forward and up, clench my tummy muscles and force them through the gap, until they're up and over the trapeze. I feel the padded bar beneath my knees, feel the blood rushing to my head, and my heart buzzing with the thrill.

'There you go, nearly there,' she calls, as I near her platform again.

I have hardly swung away from her when she shouts, 'Hands off!' and I let go like a flying angel, like a bird spreading its wings, like a child running downhill. Kit laughs and takes pictures on his phone but I am hardly aware of it because

oh my God, I'm flying

I'm flying

I'm flying

and the world is just one huge

rush

before

'There you go, that's perfect. Now the bar. Legs out. Legs up a little bit. And drop!'

And I fall, into the safety net, legs out and bouncing hugely, and

Ican'tspeakIcan'tspeak

for laughing.

Lala shrugs. 'OK, I suppose.'

Cavorting

Lala teaches me how to do neck hangs, hair hangs, toe hangs, and how to smile through the pain. All the time, she rarely speaks, other than to issue commands, and that worry squiggle in the middle of her forehead gets a little deeper. When she is not on her phone, she and Kit are often together, talking in Bulgarian in low, fast voices.

Delilah fusses over me like she is my mother, feeding me up with meat.

'You need protein, our kid, with all that cavorting through the air,' she says, when I protest at her latest offering.

'But it's liver,' I say, pulling a face.

'Sheep's liver, fried up with salt and paprika. Best thing for growing muscles,' she says. 'Don't want you fainting in midair. You'd make a big splat right in front of where the kiddies sit, have you thought of that?'

I have thought of dying, of course I have.

But I am obsessed. Being up in the air makes me forget who I am, who I was. I have always been running from something, but now I am finally flying. The only thing that is real is nownownow.

Each morning I am first up. I spend hours stretching, doing planks and pull-ups and leg lifts. By day I rummage around Eastbourne's tat shops for scraps of fabric and old saris and dancewear that I can give to Ana to transform into makeshift costumes for my act. I still perform my fire dance, each matinee and evening, and each night it gets wilder and wilder till I dance myself into a frenzy and try hard to lose myself, as the violins blur.

Afterwards, exhausted, I splash ice-cold water over my

face from the outside tap, and look into the spotted mirror hanging over the trough. I stare deep at this stranger's face with her shocking red buzzed hair and taut cheekbones and corded neck, and I wonder who on earth I really am.

When I can't sleep, I climb up in the crow's nest, and write to Suz. Sometimes I visit the horses and breathe deep their warm scent of leather and hay and home.

At night, I sleep in the tack room. Tilly has put up a narrow camping bed for me behind a pinned-up blanket in the tackroom, and I am surrounded by saddles and plumes and different types of bits and leading reins and bridles. I have made a hole in the gap between two of the boards in the wall behind my bed and stuffed my Little Kit of Happiness and journal inside it. Over it, I have hung the chalk drawing that Suz left me; both of us soaring over a toadstool city, riding a giant magpie.

My favourite stunt is back-somersaulting, letting myself fall backwards through space to catch the bar with my ankles upside down at the last second. Timing is everything: if I thought about it too much, I would miss the moment, and fall.

When I have finally mastered the back somersault, Lala waves me over.

I crouch on the platform, trying to catch my breath. I can't wait to go and get a shower and file down my calluses, soak my hands in baby oil for a while.

Lala's voice is matter-of-fact, but what she says sends me soaring.

'You are ready to perform,' she says. 'Tonight.'

Sequins

Ana hands me my costume: plastic-wrapped, shiny, special.

Then I see inside. At something that makes me hiss in my breath.

It's The Dress. Lala's.

It's the gold sequinned one that Lala wore for her act. When I look at Ana, she presses it into my hands.

I touch the plastic. 'Mine?' I say.

Ana laughs toothlessly, smiling and nodding. Beside her, Kahlo begins picking up pins and sticking them into her basket, chattering. I stand at the full-length mirror, and hold out my arms. The other performers come and go, collecting hats and wigs and laundered costumes.

Shivering a little, I draw the dress over my arms. It is backless, and fitted expertly so that nothing pops out mid-performance. It's what Beanie and I would do all the time, borrow each other's clothes. When we were little, we'd often sneak into the prefect's dorms, lifting their bottles and creams on their dressing tables, sniffing their perfumes.

I clench my abdominals then, and focus on my face, staring at my eyes until I can let go of the mirror with my other hand. I want to put make-up on, swoop out the shadow until it looks like a golden peacock. I pick up the eyelashes that Kit made, the ones with tiny real feathers that he made for Lala's birthday. He stayed up all night in his wagon, spraying each feather with gold glitter.

I lift my arms and imagine I am in the spotlight.

I am the Phoenix. I am the golden girl. I am beautiful and I am strong and I can fly.

'It suits you.'

Kit is watching me in the spotted mirror. He is hunched over the dressing table in his black hoodie, applying the rest of his clown make-up.

'Shit, Kit – you frightened me!' I laugh.

I watch him for a moment as he circles his eyes with kohl. He seems edgy tonight, spilling powder, dropping his brushes.

'Like it?' I say, spinning around for him.

'You look fabulous,' he says, but his eyes don't smile. I wonder if it is because I am taking over Lala's act until she mends. They always seem so close.

'Are you sure she doesn't mind me doing this? Her show, I mean?' I say, turning around again so that Ana can stitch up the rip. She has attached little silver bells around the bodice and hem, in the fringing, so that I tinkle as well as shimmer.

'You are a fallen phoenix,' says Kit. 'Or something. The storyline behind Tilly's shows isn't always clear.' In the shadows, his face looks hollow and somehow very serious and sad. 'You try to reach the sun, but it all turns stormy, and then you fall. Caught like a bird in a cage,' he whispers.

I shiver. 'Don't,' I say. 'That's horrible.'

I change the subject.

'How do you know Lala?' I say. 'Just from the circus?'

He shakes his head. 'We go back a long way,' he says. 'Our families know each other, in Plovdiv.'

He picks up a paintbrush from where he's dropped it.

'Her little boy's back in Bulgaria,' Kit says. 'She is trying to save up money to bring him over.'

'She has a child?' I think of her silences, the way she is always on her phone. No wonder Tilly's not keen. 'But circus work doesn't bring in much money, does it?'

Kit turns back to the mirror and begins to fill in his clown smile. 'But what if it is all you know how to do?' he says.

There is a breeze, and Lala comes in. She stands in her

wellies, arms crossed over her chest. She's wearing a fringed shawl that looks like it's one of Silviya's, wrapped around her throat and neck brace, and she's shivering, even though it's not cold, not at all. She's wearing Kit's tweed cap on her tousled hair. I have time to notice that before she comes over.

I freeze, still holding the eyelashes in my hand. I feel foolish all of a sudden, in her dress. I place the lashes back on the table.

'Let me,' she whispers. Her eyes dart over to Kit.

Ana stands aside and Lala zips up the dress. Her hands are cold as she hooks up the clasp. The dress is tight, suddenly, like I can't breathe. I can feel Lala looking at me as I lean forward into the mirror.

I feel her breath on my cheek, and think of Suz, blowing pixie dust over my face, all those weeks before. The mirror wobbles a little, and the remaining heaps of beads clatter to the floor.

'Thank you – for everything,' I say.

Lala stares at me for a moment. Doesn't answer.

She ducks out of the tent flap and is gone.

The movement stirs the breeze and makes the false lashes on the little plastic table flutter like dreadful spiders.

Arabesque

I am ready.

My body buzzes with a thousand bees. I jiggle about, then try to focus on my stretches. Every five minutes, I leave the tent to check up on the line of people joining the little ticket wagon. Kit is already entertaining the children in the queue, whizzing up and down on his little toy car.

'Honk, honk,' he says. 'Honk, honk.' Each time, his vintage car horn squirts bubbles at the children, who shriek and then clamour to follow him.

I run beside him to catch him up. 'There's quite a crowd,' I say.

Kit seems distracted. He has forgotten his red nose, and I pick it up from the dashboard and put it on for him.

'I expect they'll get to see quite a show tonight,' he says. His eyes slide to one of the ring boys, whom I don't recognise. This one is leaning up against the side of the Portaloos, looking uncomfortable in his spangly tights. A customer goes to ask him something, and he shrugs his shoulders and points vaguely towards the car park.

'Well, break a leg,' I say, but Kit is gone, beeping his horn manically as the children chase after him.

There really does seem to be a lot of people, which is strange for a matinee. The car park is full. One car near me has its door open, and a woman is talking to its occupant in a low voice, balancing her coffee on the roof.

I duck under the tent flap and make my way over to the holding area, where performers wait and warm up before their act. The pot-bellied pig runs in and scratches himself vigorously against a unicycle. Delilah is smoking an electric cigarette, talking to one of the maintenance workers. She gives me a wink as I pass.

'You look fricking amazing,' she mouths, and I smile.

I feel fricking amazing. I go through my stretches once more, sliding easily into the sideways splits this time; pull myself forward onto my toes, feeling strong and supple. My feet are bare – 'better to feel your moves,' said Lala – and I have bronze-coloured footless tights under my gold sequinned dress. It is totally backless, to show off my dramatic tattoo, which is now fully healed, its colours rich and fresh and vibrant. When I move my shoulder muscles, my phoenix moves too, as if alive. Its great beak curves around the back of my neck, and its tail feathers curl and twine over my vertebrae, shifting and moving as I twist.

The music changes.

The clowns' bicycle act stops, and Garibaldi does his thing with the new stooge.

Almost my turn.

There seems to be an awful lot of new front-of-house boys. There's another that I don't recognise; he gives me a hard stare as I pass, and scratches at the top of his fishnets. He looks awkward in his tailcoat and high boots. His face is young and red and sweaty.

The Chinese acrobats prepare to do their tumbling. As their finale, one of the girls – the youngest – climbs right to the very top of her sisters, flips onto her hands and quivers, just slightly, as she balances. Below her, the banked-up girls tense and smile, their bodies contorted into impossible positions.

The lights snap off, and the harsh white spotlight is on the one at the top, who can't be more than five, and nobody breathes; no one digs in their hand to take another mouthful of popcorn.

But she flips lightly into a seated position, waves, and the audience applaud, relief spreads.

My turn.

I dance out, force the grit from my throat, try to remember to breathe. And then I'm climbing high up the swinging ladder, waving and arching to the audience as Lala has taught me, smiling my painted smile. I reach the platform, where I've spent so many nights scribbling into my journal, and then my hands are on the trapeze bar; I grip the familiar curve of it through my bandaged hands. Next, the resin – pat, puff! Like a professional, my costume swinging and shimmering, the straps just digging into me a little where Ana's sewn in the modesty strip.

I stare straight ahead, wait for the violins below to pick up my rhythm. Focus.

Breathe.

Tighten my grip.

And then.

I am flying, over the blurred crowds, the packed seats, the cameras flashing.

I swing, count to three, hear Lala's voice in my head shouting *'huuupp!'* and then I'm hanging, ready to let go, ready to swing back onto the platform.

Remember to focus, I think. It feels wonderful, this whoosh of air, this swoop of freedom. I am a bird –

Watch me fly, Suz. Watch me fly! Suz's paper birds flutter and fly, bright and beautiful, her laughing eyes the colour of sea glass –

Something's wrong.

There's someone standing up in the front row, someone who has been there all the time but I didn't register, was only concentrating on my routine. The woman's blonde and stocky. She's dressed in mufti, T-shirt and jeans instead of her usual too-tight skirt, but I know her. I'd know her anywhere.

Scally.

She's there, in the front row, and now she's speaking into something in her hand; she's squeezing past a bald father and his two children. A flurry of spilt popcorn. She's stepping over the barrier, in her plain clothes, her too-tight jeans, her hair messily held back.

Scally looks up, and her eyes widen as they meet mine.

She's found me.

And by the time I see that there are others rising up out of their seats, I am falling, tumbling in mid-air, into the safety net, and I'm gasping, bouncing,

and the music

withers

and

dies.

Catch Me If You Can!

I lie, bouncing in the net, and there's Scally peering down at me, one eyebrow raised sardonically.

'Here we go again, lovey,' she says in her Manchester accent. 'Come on, up you get…All right, all right,' she shouts, over the excited chatter that has replaced the fiddles. 'The show's over.'

'Stupid thing to say,' I whisper.

'What's that, love?'

'Stupid thing to say, in a circus.'

And then I close my eyes, but not before I see Kit's eyes slide away from me, like he can't meet my gaze.

And that's when I know.

'It was the reward money, wasn't it?' I shout as the ring boy, now stripped of his spangled tights and frock coat and back in his yellow luminous police jacket, grips my arms tightly and marches me to Scally's car.

But Kit's gone. He slipped away like smoke, like a lie, as Tilly and Delilah tried in vain to get the audience together and settled back down in their seats.

Ha! Good luck with that! Not much chance when the show's moved outside.

The constable holding me is the one I saw by the portaloos earlier, of course. How cunning Scally is! It was all carefully planned, wasn't it, so that she knew I couldn't run?

'I'm sorry!' I shout to Delilah. She's standing there, holding Kahlo, her mouth dropping open. 'I'm sorry I lied, about *everything.*'

I'm not sure I even know myself what is true any more.

I sit in the back next to the male officer, who still has traces of greasepaint by his ear. I long to take a tissue and rub it off for him. Instead I smile at him brightly. He doesn't react. Just stares straight ahead, occasionally looking out of his window.

'Lovely legs you got there, Constable,' remarks Scally from the front. She's driving, a half-smile on her face, manoeuvring the car with short deft turns of the wheel. Her fingernails are filed short.

'Shurrup, boss,' mutters Lovely Legs. He scratches the top of his thigh, and I wonder whether he's still wearing his tights underneath his regulation police trousers.

The indicator tickticticks. We stop at the lights.

'Don't you try any funny-business, lovey,' Scally warns. I take my hand away from the handle. It will be childlocked anyway; I suppose she'll have made sure of that.

It's ages since I've been in a police car. The last time, I think I was thirteen. They found me in a garden shed at the bottom of my friend's garden. I lived off apples from their tree, and managed to squeeze in and out of the dog flap. I knew the girl and her family had gone away on holiday. She hadn't stopped boasting about going to Dubai all term.

She wasn't really my friend. I made that part up.

I stare at the back of Scally's head, at her rooty, bleached hair, and wonder what she really thinks of me. Does she think I'm mad?

The police station room she puts me in has a fluorescent light that flickers. I hate that. All of a sudden I have a head-ache, and it is one of those screeching, pulsing ones that begins and my temples and sends little spikes and jabs into my brain.

I lean on the table and lay my head on my arms. I miss Delilah. I wonder how Kit knew. It must have been my jour-nal. Had he been reading it? Had he found it in my room? Had he seen me in the newspaper too? Or on TV? Did eve-rybody know who I was, after all?

'How much?' I ask the police officer on a chair in the corner. She looks up.

'Sorry?'

'How much did he put out for me, this time?'

She sighs. 'Thirty thousand pounds, I think.'

Enough, then, to pay for tuition fees at a good university. I remember Kit's impatience when we were talking about our dreams. I should have listened. I only ever think about myself. Is that who I am, then? Is that what you think of me? The spoilt little rich girl who doesn't know she is born? Needing everyone to run around after her, to validate her existence…

But there has only ever been one person I needed to come and find me.

The door opens, and it's Scally again. She nods at the of-ficer sitting down, who gets up and leaves.

'I need you to come with me now, Willow,' she says, and there is a sigh in her voice. 'There's someone wants to see you.'

She leads me down the corridor, and I am counting the naff pictures on the walls, and counting the tiles on the floor, and then I am in a small waiting room, and she's right, there *is* someone to meet me.

'Hello, Daddy,' I say.

Interval

He stands, shadowed against the window, checking something on his phone. He slides it into his pocket when he sees me.

'You look different,' he says. 'Your hair…'

I wait. My heart's tripping.

He's come, I think. *This time, he's actually come to find me.*

'Why, Willow?' he says, and he doesn't sound angry, only tired.

I can't speak; I just wait for him to come closer. My fingers dig into my palms, feeling the ridges, the hardened skin, the calluses. I slow my breathing. Watch him walk forward into the light.

He clears his throat. 'Shall we sit down?'

I know then that it's not going to be any different. Nothing's changed. He doesn't come to hug me, doesn't crush me into his arms because he's been so worried, he's missed me so much, he's been desperate to know where I am, what I've been doing.

He doesn't do any of that.

We sit together on the sofa that has been put there for this purpose. It's a grotty green, with coffee cup stains on the arms. A Monet print hangs behind us: sun-dappled people in a flowery garden, sugar-sweet. Somewhere, a photocopier cranks. All this I notice, while the space between us yawns wider than decades.

Daddy clears his throat.

'Well,' he says.

'Well,' I agree.

Silence tightens like a terrible chat show.

I look over at the window, and wonder if I have the energy to try the sash and how high the drop is. I wonder what they'd all do if I scrambled down, Spiderman-style, and webbed my way through the streets, to some secret cave. Would they all chase after me? Would it ever stop?

'Kayleigh-Ann was very upset at what you did to her dress,' he says.

Buzzzz. Wrong beginning.

'I'm sorry.'

I trace the callus on my hand, circle it, think of Kit pouring over balsam. Nothing will change, I think. It is always going to be like this.

Daddy shifts gear. 'Kayleigh-Ann's been looking after the horses,' he says. I almost laugh at this. Well, good for her! What a star she is. Not letting my horse starve to death. I bet she's been looking after our house too, wondering what little changes she can make now that the difficult stepdaughter's off the scene. But I don't say this. Instead I make an effort.

'How's Martyna?' I say.

Daddy looks surprised. 'Oh, she's, well, fine. Just as usual.'

'Do you ever speak to her?'

'Pardon?'

'Do you ever speak to her?' I say, and I am surprised at how my voice sounds, harsh and broken. 'Do you ever ask her about her family?'

'What do you mean, love?' He scratches his head. He's not sure where this conversation's going. Nor am I for that matter.

'Did you know she has family, back in Poland? That she probably hasn't seen since forever? That she cries, sometimes, in the kitchen?'

'What are you talking about, love?' He's looking at me now, but I don't want to look at him, because if I do, I feel like I would scream and punch him. And then they'd probably lock me up. Put me somewhere nice and safe and secure and finally give up on me.

It would be a relief, probably, for all of us.

Daddy sighs. You can tell he has no idea how to continue with this conversation, that's he's itching to get at that phone, which has been buzzingbuzzingbuzzing in his pocket.

'She's lonely,' I whisper. 'They're all of them lonely.'

Daddy stands up. Is he going so soon? Is that it? This delightful little father and daughter moment over so suddenly and sweetly.

But no, it's not over. Not by a long shot.

'There's something I need to tell you, Willow.' He hesitates. Walks over to look out the window again. 'It's about your mother.'

I stiffen. And all at once I am buzzing, but not in a good way. Because hardly ever in my life has Daddy mentioned my mother. He's always avoided it, coughed, changed the subject. I shift round to look at him, but all I can see is the dark shadow of his back against the window. Outside, between the rooftops, the evening is settling over the sea.

Breathe, I tell myself. *Just breathe.*

And Daddy's voice as he speaks to the window is that of a stranger spinning stories. Except I don't think this one's make-believe.

'I thought she was beautiful,' he says. 'I met her when I was interested in buying up fairgrounds. I was just diversifying my business into carnival attractions. Always knew there was some money to be made.

'She was working the Waltzers, spinning them fast, to make the kiddies squeal. I'd had a few drinks by then. It had been a long day. When she saw me watching, she pulled me inside one, laughing, said she'd show me how it was really done. I knew she was trouble, but there was something about her dark eyes, her strong arms, spinning, spinning me – she had the strength of a man, despite her petite figure. It was like she…bewitched me.'

Daddy hesitates. I dig my nails deeper.

'We went and had a drink, and then we…got close, outside the arcades. I thought that was it – it was just something in the moment. I'm not proud of this, love. I was in my thirties and should have known better but, what I'm trying to say is that…your mother was no circus girl. She was just a girl who worked the Waltzers. That picture you have. It's all fake. She had it done at the photographic booth at the fairground. Even the snake's fake. It was all set up. You could choose any background you wanted…

'I thought nothing of it, just a mad moment when I'd had a drop too much to drink. And then, nine months later, there she was, she'd found out where I lived. She turned up on the doorstep with this baby in her hands. She was laughing and crying, rain streaming down her face.

'"It's yours, Gary," she said. "Doesn't have a name. Not yet. I need a place to stay. I'm at rock bottom."'

I look up then. 'Stop it,' I say. 'Just stop it.'

But he's gazing out of the window, at a pigeon ruffling up on the roof. And he doesn't stop. I can't make him stop.

'I took her in, what else could I do? Tried to make a go

of it. I had everything a man could want: cars, designer suits, a stunning house. But I was lonely, and I couldn't seem to settle down with anyone. It was like there was something missing.

'I really believed that we'd make a go of it, your mother and me. I tried. I helped out with the bedtimes, the nappy changes, feeding you your first food. But she…was distant. As if a light had been switched off inside of her. At first I thought it was postnatal depression, but then I found she'd been meeting other men behind my back, disappearing when I was away on business, leaving you to the au pair, coming home drunk.

'The last straw was when I found her with the gardener, when she'd left you alone in your cotbed, screaming to be fed. I told her to leave.

'The last words she said to me were…were…'

But I already know.

'Don't,' I say. 'I don't want to know any more.'

I feel cold and shivery. When I look down, my nails have forced open the rip in the palm of my hand. I don't feel a thing.

'Stop it,' I whisper.

But Daddy's still talking; it's like a stopper has been released and all this poison is coursing out, acid-burning everything in its path.

'She threw back her head and laughed at me,' he whispered. 'Said that you weren't mine, never had been. That she only said that because she found out that I was loaded, that I was the best plan she had once she'd got herself into trouble.

'She didn't even stop to go up to you. You had been put down for your afternoon nap, and had woken up hungry. You were three years old.'

He looks up, and his face is that of a stranger. I don't want to look at it.

'I named you Willow,' he says. 'Your mother didn't even bother naming you. After she left, I went to your bed, looked down at you, snuggled round that little stuffed monkey she'd won for you at the fairground, and it was like something had shifted inside me. I couldn't let you go. I had my responsibilities. But things were never the same after that. Every time I looked at you, I saw her.' His voice breaks. 'And I saw *him* too, whoever he was.'

He comes close, tries to take my hand. I flinch it away. I make my legs stand me up from the sofa.

'So, can we go home now?' I say. It's like I'm forcing my voice out through treacle. Like one of those dreams where everything slows down and you can't get your limbs to perform the simplest tasks, like walking forward or focusing and especially not running.

Daddy hovers, hopeful, blinking at me through his pale eyes.

I pat his hand. 'It's fine, Daddy. It's totally fine. Thank you for telling me. It must have been hard, keeping all of that a secret for so long.'

And I put on my brightest smile.

Bright as glass. Sharp as a scream.

Leopard Act

So what's a girl to do, after learning that a) her glamorous circus-performer mother is nothing but some fairground slapper whose baby was something of a hindrance to her afternoon fumblings with the (delete as needed) gardener/ chauffeur/pony-nut delivery man? Not only that, but *dah-*

dahhhh! Turns out her father doesn't love her either, because the very sight of her reminds him of said fairground-trash mother.

What *is* she to do?

Answer: run away of course!

And the way I went about it this time? You'd be proud of me, Suz, you really would.

There is admin to get through, before I can escape. The police officer with the kind eyes leads us through into a room with no windows. Daddy shuffles.

'Is all of this really necessary?' he asks.

'Your daughter Willow has been found in possession of a credit card belonging to a Ms Christine Jones, believed stolen. She also travelled on the South Eastern Line without purchasing a ticket, and committed two acts of deception and fraud when she handed over your personal bank card to a homeless woman known as Naz. As well as wasting police time, these are serious charges,' the officer says patiently. She has a line of script inked on the inside of her wrist as she fills in the forms. I wonder what it says.

'Yes, yes, I know all that,' Daddy is saying impatiently. In a moment he'll get out his chequebook and try to pay her off. Offer to buy them a new police training centre or something. Or say that he knows a top lawyer –

'I know a top lawyer –'

There you go.

I stare down at my hands. The rip in the left one is really throbbing now, and I am glad. It sharpens things. Cuts through the dream-treacle of my mind. I wish Kit were here to make it better. Or Delilah, with her kind, sad eyes and terrible treats.

'Ready to go…'

I glance up. We're on the move, it seems. Daddy's worked his magic again, just like last time. Just like all of the other times.

Daddy's car purrs down the lanes. Is that a cliché? I suppose it is. We're being driven by his chauffeur. I realise I don't know his name; I've never bothered to ask. I look at his face in the rear-view mirror. I can see a dark eye, a cheekbone. A mole in the shape of a triangle beneath his eye. I wonder if he has a wife and family. I wonder if he has children. I wonder if Daddy knows his name.

Beside me, on the seat, is my bag. They had made me wait in the police car while Lovely Legs fetched it from the tack room. I am still wearing my costume under the rain mac that the policewoman lent me. I take out the Kit of Happiness, and empty it of everything but the head girl badge, the photograph and the button. The photograph I rip carefully into tiny pieces. Flutter them out of the top of the window. It feels like the time I cut my plait off: like another piece of me has blown away.

Soon, there'll be nothing more left of what used to be me.

Soon, I'll be nothing more than scraps in the wind.

I place the chalk, the button and Beanie's head girl badge into my coat pocket. Keep checking, intermittently, that they're still there.

Rain slides to and fro on the windscreen. The wipers push a dead fly to the side and back again. We pass a woodland, and then a couple of pubs, and then a farm. I stare at the rip in my hand, fascinated.

'I need to stop,' I say abruptly.

Daddy turns around.

You can tell he's suspicious; his pale blue eyes wrinkle in his tanned skin. I expect he's been on a few more Caribbean holidays, since I've been away. Made up for lost time with *her*.

'We've got a long drive, love. Need to make tracks. Stefan's had a long day.'

So he *does* know his name. Imagine.

'I really need to stop. To go to the loo, I mean.' I change tack. 'It's my *period*,' I say. 'It's really heavy, and my stomach hurts, and I really need to change my –'

The car skids a little in the rain as we draw into the car park of a country pub. *JUGGLER'S ARMS*, it says on the sign. This will do nicely.

Daddy gets out first. 'I'm sorry, love,' he says. 'But I can't let you go in alone. It's not that I don't trust you…'

What a stupid thing to say. Of course he can't trust me. But I smile nicely. 'It's totally fine, Daddy,' I say. 'Shall we get a drink, since we're here? And perhaps Stefan can come, too?'

Daddy keeps a tight grip on my arm as we push past Sunday drinkers and families complete with grannies and daughters and mothers-in-law, all rosy-faced from gin and tonics by the log fire.

'You can leave me now, Daddy,' I say, as he hovers outside the ladies. 'I'll have a lemonade, please. I'm not going anywhere.' I watch as he stands on guard outside in the little lobby while Stefan moves to the bar to order drinks.

'I'm not going anywhere,' I repeat.

But of course I am.

The instant I'm inside the washroom I move to the window. It opens easily, but is far too small for me to climb through. I might have been able to once, but not now. Not with my trapeze-toned shoulders. I go inside a cubicle anyway, thinking that I may as well go to the loo while I'm here. I am totally calm. I know that an opportunity will present itself to me. It's just a matter of when.

I resist the temptation to pee on my hands, even though

236

I'm hearing Kit's voice telling me, *Go on, it's what the Russian acrobats do*, and I flush the chain, wincing at the sharp pain in my palm.

I stare into the mirror above the washbasin. Think how recognisable I am with my vermillion red hair and the weird coat they lent me at the police station. I take off the coat so that I'm standing in my gold show costume. I still have my stage make-up around my eyes. I take a paper towel and wipe away a few smears, pinch my cheeks and lips so that I don't look so pale, and then wait until someone likely comes in.

A lavatory flushes, and a stoop-backed old lady comes out, someone's grandmother out on a family treat. She is wearing her best clothes: a matching cardigan and skirt and a lavender flowery scarf. She stares at me, then gives a rich throaty chuckle.

'Who are you, dear – you're not a strippergram, are you? Are you waiting to surprise somebody?'

I nod vigorously. 'Yes,' I say. 'Shhh – don't say anything.' The old lady winks at me, and then is almost thrown backwards as the door swings open.

'Mum! We were getting worried about you…' The woman's voice trails off as she sees me. She is wearing a floor-length, faux-leopardskin coat, and sunglasses on top of her head.

'It's the strippergram, dear – she's going to jump out and surprise somebody.'

The old lady throws her hand in front of her mouth. 'Ooops, sorry. Wasn't supposed to say. What am I like?'

I giggle. 'I know, it's exciting, isn't it? I wondered if you would mind helping me, though. It's just that I've never done this before, and I really, really want it to be a surprise…'

They lean forward eagerly as I explain my plan, and describe Stefan in minute detail.

Minutes later, I am waltzing out of the ladies wearing the leopardskin coat, a lavender-scented scarf wound around my red hair, and a pair of fake designer shades clamped firmly on my nose. As I pass Daddy holding his spilling pint and a half of lemonade, my fur coat whispers and swishes. He is staring in bemusement at Stefan, who is being dragged away from the bar by a little old lady and a middle-aged woman, with goosebumps on her bare arms.

The door opens, the pub-fug snaps to cold drizzle, and I am free.

Wheels of Fortune

A taxi's waiting in the car park.

Without thinking, I pull open the passenger door and get inside.

'Mrs Jones?' asks the driver.

I nod quickly. The pub door swings open, and a family is spilling out, rosy-cheeked with wine. A teenage boy helps his grandmother down the steps.

For a moment, it seems as though the taxi driver's changed his mind; he's staring through me, taking in my grubby face, my leopardskin coat.

I check my wrist for a non-existent watch. 'I have a train to catch,' I say tightly.

I think I can see Stefan's head over the family.

The driver turns on the meter.

'Where to?' He winds down the window, and I wonder why, until I realise that I must smell bad.

Unsavoury, that's what he'll be thinking. I haven't had a shower since before my show.

To Paris, I think, and start to giggle.

He stares at me strangely. I make my voice sound normal, and tell him, Hastings.

He unclicks the indicator and finds his place in the traffic. All the time his eyes are watching me in the mirror. The radio's on, some local station, with an over-bright presenter with a regional twang. Music starts, a track that was popular in another lifetime, when Beanie and the girls would sing along to it in the dorms. It grates. I wish he'd turn it off.

The driver's eyes meet mine. 'What wrong with you?' he asks. 'You ain't going to be sick, are you?'

'I'll be fine,' I say. I try to stop myself shivering.

He nods, changes lanes. Switches stations.

I look out of the rear window for blue flashing lights.

'So, what are we to do about this growing phenomenon of teenage girl runaways? Is it exam pressure, or are they just trying to get attention?'

'Well, Trissie, it's a real problem in society, isn't it? A spate of copycat runaways, ostensibly trying to shed their old life and all its subsequent responsibilities, but, in reality, they're afraid; they've never had to make any real decisions, not like when we were young, and…'

'And of course there's a huge reward that's been put up for knowledge of her whereabouts, isn't there?'

'Of course, Mr Stephens is known to be a very wealthy man…'

'…somewhere in the region of…'

Too late, I realise what this presenter and her guest are talking about. Daddy or Scally can't have informed the press yet about my being found.

'And we believe that Willow's physical appearance will have

changed significantly by now, is that true?'

*'Someone with her psychological template will be switching ap-
pearance all the time. Possibly very short, almost brutally short hair
— we know that she was very attached to her long locks, that they
were linked in some way to her name, so this would be one of the
first things to go. And dramatic, outlandish acts of...something to
symbolise her new freedom. A tattoo, perhaps...'*

The taxi driver's looking at my left shoulder. I cover it up,
hurriedly, even though my tattoo doesn't show. Wish I wasn't
wearing such an obvious coat.

The guest speaker, someone from some university, an
expert in fugitive psychology, is still talking. I imagine the
presenter leaning forward interestedly, hands clasped over
crossed legs.

*'I believe Willow Stephens to have significant attachment issues.
It seems she was abandoned by her mother when an infant. Brought
up by a string of au pairs and a largely absent father. Boarding
school, of course, can trigger emotional disorders in the very young.
So, to put it simply, Willow will be very needy, desperate for attention. Basically, she'll attach herself strongly to the first person
she meets.'*

He makes me sound like a duckling, cheeping after its
mother. The driver's looking at me in the mirror. We stare
into each other's eyes.

Too late, I realise that this isn't the way to Hastings.

Double Swan Drop

'Stop the car,' I demand. 'I want to get out. *Now.*'

The childlocks are never on in a taxi. Just as he slows at the lights, just as he reaches out his hand, I throw open the door and half-dive, half-roll out.

It is easier than in mid-air, trickier than on a trampoline.

I land on the roadside, on my side, knees curled. A perfect landing. People crane their necks out of their cars as I jump up, scramble, run.

I keep to the back roads, hunkering down, ever watchful. Once, I hitch a ride. Once, I fall, slithering down an embankment when I think I see a blue light. And all the time the same thoughts pound through my head as I run:

I must get back to Hastings.

I must get back to Suz.

'Suz!' I yell. 'I'm back. I'm *back*, and I'm sorry. They're after me, Suz. I need you.'

That's when I see it: the board that says, *FOR SALE. Deluxe executive apartments. Stunning sea view. Glass atrium. Roof terrace. Spacious. Ready September. Open house: 4–8p.m.*

I duck inside the wooden security fence, avoiding the little cabin that you're supposed to walk through, coloured flags rippling. *Haven Homes*, it says. *Rooms with a view! Only 3 left!*

Everything's changed. They haven't put the windows in here yet; tarpaulin is stretched over scaffolding planks. Inside, they've stripped the place of Suz. No more graffiti. No more *Could do effing better,* scrawled in chalk.

They're building a swish atrium, all glass walls and ceilings and funky cube design. It sits glinting in the evening sun, surprised-looking on the Edwardian building.

I know at once that she's not here. Everything's stripped back. There's a brand-new staircase. Floorboards that smell of new wood and new money.

I freeze.

In what used to be our hall-open plan living area-tip-fire pit, there's a woman handing out drinks, dressed in a red and navy suit and scarf combo, like an air steward.

People are milling and murmuring: a family with a clutch of small kids, several well-dressed couples, an elderly lady with helmet hair.

'Thank you,' I say, taking a glass of Buck's Fizz from the air-steward woman. Her eyes rake me: my leopardskin coat, my cherry red hair. I smile back at her, hard.

I shove past a pearled, polo-necked lady with helmet hair and out onto the brand-new landing. Past the newly installed lift and into a room labelled *Show Home*. A kitchen of gleaming granite. Plates of smoked salmon blinis and glasses of Buck's Fizz. Out of habit, I take four, stuff them in my mouth and drain a glass. Louis XV ghost chairs. Wallpaper illustrated with giant trees. Up the stairs: beaten metal and orange beech.

Behind me, footsteps. The kitchen is filled with buzzing people, noisily exploring the fridge and walk-in larder.

'Excuse me. Sorry. Excuse me.'

Suz isn't here; of course she isn't. Not unless she's found half a million pounds from somewhere to buy a slice of our old house.

I risk a backwards glance, and there's Air Steward, determinedly clacking after me.

A dead end. Only a balcony, newly sanded and painted. Ahead, the sea winks white fire. I climb over the window ledge. Crouch. Look back briefly. Helmet Hair's mouth

242

hangs, showing half-masticated blini. I wave back at her.

It's easy to climb up to the roof – *our roof*. My circus training makes me spring like a cat, tumble like a tiger –

'*Tigers don't tumble.*'

'*Doesn't matter. Semantics, Frog. S'just semantics.*'

I scramble down the fire escape, take one last look at our house, and then I'm running again.

Freakshow

I find her by the train station, shouting. There's a line of people waiting for taxis, and their faces are turned away from her; you can tell they're trying not to look. Suz doesn't look like Suz any more. She has transformed too. She's wild-eyed and wild-haired; her dress – which looks like a man's cardigan – is buttoned up all wrong, showing her belly where it gapes.

I walk up to her, and she sees me without any recognition.

'Suz. Suz, it's me, Frog.'

'And you can fuck off too, ya pompous ass!' she bellows, twisting around me to shout at a lady with her two children shrinking into her. A group of teenagers are openly laughing, taking pictures with their phones.

'Come on, Suz, let's get you out of here,' I say, glad that I'm wearing my shades. I take her arm, and to my surprise she lets me lead her away from the gathering crowd, over to the car park at the back. 'Up here.' I help her climb the steps to where there's a small park, with a scruffy-looking swing and a couple of lonely benches.

All the time, I'm listening out for sounds of police. Maybe one of the bystanders called them, to stop a public brawl.

'It's Frog,' I repeat.

Close up, I am even more shocked at her appearance. I study her as she attempts without success to light her roll-up. Her hands are jerking and twitching uncontrollably. In the end, I light it for her, and she sucks in, greedily, slumped now and quiet.

I wait till she's smoked it all. Then she turns to look at me. There are sores around her mouth, greenish grey shadows under her eyes. She twitches occasionally – her chin, her shoulder, her leg – as if she can't stop.

Then, 'Frog, is it really you?' she says. She begins to cry, great ugly snorts that she doesn't bother to clear away. 'You left me,' she keeps saying. 'You only went and bloody left me.'

I don't know what to say.

'It was the fireworks,' she whispers. 'I hate those things, because it reminds me. It reminds me.' But she won't go on. She won't go there again.

Instead, she squeezes my arm. I try not to care that she is filthy, really filthy, with nails blackened from weeks of not washing. No signs of soot and chalk dust.

I take her hand, and it is ice. 'Where are your rainbow fingers, Suz?' I try to smile.

She shakes her head. 'I've not been so well. I've been us-ing too much spice. Drinking a bit too much. My chalks and drawings got nicked. I don't really mind. I've been too sick to draw much, anyhow.' She raises her head, and touches my cheek with her cold finger. 'You clean up really nice,' she whispers. 'Real nice.'

She coughs then, a great racking cough that rattles and clatters with sickness. It goes on a long time, and when she's finished, she leans her head against me, exhausted.

'I hope you made it to the circus, Frog,' she says. 'Did you? Were you a real star? Did you wear my costume?'

I start to tell her of the things I've done, the things I've seen, but when I look down at her, she's asleep on my shoulder.

Hairy Jack

'Can't go back, can't go back to my place, Frog...full of workmen...It has a freaking *chandelier*, for chrissake.'

Suz is shivering and mumbling, huddled against the wall in the leopardskin fur coat. Behind it are St Clement's Caves, and I think I know a way to get inside. I check up and down the tiny street; shrink into the wall to let a jogger pass.

It is easy to prise the grille away with my fingernails and a sharp stone. I bend it back, pushing away the ivy. Opposite, there's a narrow house with a clapperboard front and a balcony. It has cherry-patterned curtains at each window and a little wooden sign on the door saying *Seagull's Landing*. Thankfully, it seems to be empty. No one is watching us.

'Come on, Suz. Quickly.'

She's far too visible in that coat, standing shivering in the rain. I get a flash of irritation. Why can't she hurry?

Just as I am about to draw aside the grille, a rain-washed dog walker comes, with two fat labradors. It takes an age for one of them to squat on its haunches and for its owner to rummage about for a plastic bag to scoop up its mess. I stand with my back to the wall, wishing that we didn't both look so bizarre. Suz is standing in full rain now, in the middle of the alleyway, face upturned to the sky. The rain thrums. Bounces like pins on the puddles. The dog walker — it's a man, under his hood — casts a glance in our direction. I can feel him wondering about us.

This time it is me that is urging Suz through the gap. I let her use my knee to climb up, trying not to notice how thin she's become, her shoulders sharp even through the faux–fur coat. I push and squeeze her through at last, and hear her land with a gasp of pain on her bad leg. That coat's going to stink like wet dogs.

It takes forever for Suz to shuffle painfully through the tunnel. Another turn, and green and purple light sweeps the walls. We have reached Smugglers' Worlde.

'Shhh,' I warn. I help her step over the barrier rope into the main cave system. Ahead, a glass case displays a scowling head of a wrecker with a ticket in his mouth.

Smugglers' Worlde is closed at this time, of course, but there's a droning noise coming from somewhere. We take another passageway, and Suz clutched me tight. A man in headphones in vacuuming dust off a plastic skeleton that is hanging in chains in a green-washed alcove. We need to find somewhere to hide before he spots us. And what about the morning, when the caves open up again to the public? We won't be able to stay in the main caves for long in case someone notices us and realises we haven't paid. We are far too conspicuous — and Suz stinks. She smells of loss and street grime and hopelessness and old socks and dried-on sweat and oily hair and hardship and too strong cider and too few showers. She smells like someone who has given up.

I move her away from the cleaner, who has his back turned to us as he grapples with the skeleton. It is easy to slip past him and over the barrier into the *No Entry* tunnels. Ahead, there's a low rope, and in the cordoned-off area, a large fibreglass model of a cove and cliffs, with lots of little plastic figures dotted over it. I hustle Suz through, and together we crouch behind the moulded cliff, two Gullivers in Lilliput.

It's dark behind the cliffs; there's a hollowed-out space, right at the back. Above us, silhouettes of tiny figures keep watch on the clifftops: wreckers, forever watching the rigid waves for their plastic shipwreck. Hairy Jack's voice crackles out of the speaker, telling of wreckers and guineas and murder, and then stops abruptly. The cleaner must have switched him off.

'This'll do for now, Suz,' I whisper. 'Keep down and keep quiet.'

It's so dark in the back of this recess that I feel sure that no one will find us. Suz is shivering violently, but she doesn't speak. I help her off with her coat, and settle her down on the floor. Tug off our wet trainers, glad of the strong, fusty smell inside these caves. I tuck myself up beside her. My stomach growls. The cleaner will be gone soon. Then I'll see what I can forage.

Behind the counter, there's an entire box of torches for sale. I help myself. A fleecy jacket with the Smugglers' Worlde logo hangs from the door behind the front desk. I take that too.

Inside the staff kitchen, I find:
- A half empty litre bottle of Coke.
- A nearly full packet of chocolate Hobnobs.
- A kettle and things to make tea.
- A fridge containing a plastic bottle of milk.
- A plastic Tupperware tub half-full of tuna pasta salad.
- And, joy of joys, an unopened family-size packet of KitKats.

247

I find a carrier bag and stuff bits inside, but leave some things in case the staff get suspicious. Someone will miss their lunch tomorrow. I wish Suz was with me, so that we could make tea, but I'm far too jumpy to wait around for the kettle to boil. I'm afraid to switch on the light in case it triggers some kind of alarm, or I'm caught on CCTV, and despite the torch, shadows press in on me, making it hard to breathe.

On the way back, I swoop my torch around, trying not to think about wreckers. I half expect Hairy Jack to come dragging his latest victim through the tunnels, the floors glinting with spilled blood and spilled coins.

I think that I have almost reached our new home when my torch shines onto a huge figure, carved into the sandstone. He clasps invisible hands as he gazes sightlessly back at me. No eyes. No hands. It's St Clement himself. Somehow, I have got into the chapel at the very heart of the cliff.

Suz's voice drifts, from long ago. I flash my torch around, trying to work out which passage to go down, trying not to think about how the figure's face looks a bit like the one in *The Scream* painting by Edvard Munch.

And when the torch beam finds a door, I breathe again, because I'm positive I remember passing one near to our clifftop display.

Almost back. Don't think of St Clement's ghost dragging itself behind you. Don't think –

Something makes me open the door.

Something makes me shine my torch inside.

And what I see staring back at me is so shocking,

that I finally

finally

let out the

scream

I have been holding onto for so long.

Costume Change

The room is full of people.

When I've picked up my torch, I see a crowd of frozen faces scowling back at me.

My torch picks out the red lips, the crudely chiselled cheekbones, the heavy brow of a wrecker standing in front of me.

Waxworks.

There is a large crack across this one's rigid forehead, where he must have suffered a fall, the rest of his face contorted into a smuggler's grimace. Swooping my torch around, I realise that all of the waxworks are damaged in some way: eyes gouged, cheeks caved in, limbs missing.

I slow my breathing and force myself to push past them in search of blankets. The waxwork right at the back is missing half his head. Wishing it wasn't so icy inside the storeroom, I remove his jerkin, his shirt, his breeches. He has a pistol tucked into his belt, and something makes me take this too.

Grabbing a bundle of sacks from the floor, somehow I make my way back to Suz.

Our new bed is scratchy, but at least it takes the chill out of the stone floor. Suz's feet are bare, grime-nailed and bluish cold in the torchlight. I tuck the fur coat around them, touch her damp cheek. She's sleeping deeply and I try to persuade myself that this is good.

After I've covered her with the fleecy jacket too, I dress myself in the smuggler's clothes and push the torch into a crevice, where it washes the cave wall with low light. Above us, the pistol glints from its ledge.

If it were real, I'd shoot every shadow.

WANTED: missing schoolgirl/fugitive/fire-eater/air-walker. DESCRIPTION: strong, man's shoulders, tomato-red buzz-cut hair. Note in particular her thicker-than-average ankles, which are a definite giveaway. She may be spotted creeping amongst shadows in her unmissable smuggler's-jerkin-and-breeches combo. If seen, DO NOT approach. She may be armed and dangerous.

Seagull's Landing

I wake, wet-eyed and dry-mouthed. I was dreaming again of my mother. But this time, as she threw me higher and higher, when I looked down, her face was blank and empty, a torn-out hole. And when I wake up, I realise something that I should have known a long time before.

Because each time, when my mother threw me up, into those clouds, I never once remember her catching me.

Somewhere, I can hear gulls screaming: *Kyaa-kya-kya-kya-kya-kya-kya…kyau.* High-pitched. Blood-curdling. I follow the sound, half-remembered images of pirates and smugglers cutting through the dream-fug of my brain.

If the birds have awakened, it means it's morning.

People have moved into the house opposite.

The sun is out, finally. Pushing back the ivy, I take a deep breath of fresh air.

A movement catches my eye. A towel, bright against the balcony. A cafetière of coffee on the little café table. The flutter of a spotty tablecoth.

250

The front door of Seagull's Landing opens and a small boy appears with a little dog on an extension lead. I shrink back as it comes right below me, and listen to the tinkle of its pee as it takes forever to urinate against the wall. The boy's about seven years old, with a shock of blonde hair.

For a moment, it seems as if he's looking straight at me.

'Tarquin, croissant or pain au chocolat?'

A man's voice. I imagine its owner, turned-up collar, ruddy-cheeked, CEO, provider. Someone like Beanie's father. A woman comes onto the balcony to check the beach towel and lay out napkins and plates. A little girl in a floral dress skips around her, all ringletted hair and bare feet.

Trying not to think of biting into flaky, buttery pastry, I sigh and make my way back to the caves.

'Suz? Suz. Wake up. I have breakfast.'

Suz moans and shakes her head.

'Come on, Suz. You've got to eat before the staff get here to open up.'

They mustn't hear us crackling packets and crunching KitKats.

I push a KitKat under Suz's nose to tempt her – 'It's definitely veggie, Suz' – but she moans and turns her head away.

She must eat. She can't go on much longer without eating. I imagine her shrinking away to nothing until she's a ghost forever haunting these cave cliffs with the spirits of dead smugglers. She'll become her own story. I shiver.

'Please, Suz. Drink some milk then.'

It's not exactly vegan, but I keep my fingers crossed she'll not think of that, and to my relief she does sit up a little, and allows me to press the bottle to her mouth. I use the sleeve of the fleecy jacket to mop up the spilt milk running over her chin. I feel like I'm looking after a baby, a mother's relief when she's fed a little.

I finish off the tuna pasta salad and tie the tub inside the carrier bag, hoping there aren't rats.

'Do you need the toilet, Suz? Probably ought to go now before they open up.'

It takes forever to get Suz to her feet. She holds on to me heavily, and I see that she's bent double and whimpering.

'Hurts, Frog. It's my belly. Cramps something awful. I need…'

I know what she needs. I'm not going to get it for her. Can't let her go into that dark place.

'Would you…?'

'I can't, Suz. Please don't ask me.'

She begins to cry, whimpering, gasping, but quietly, like she's a small child.

'Hurts so much.'

I lead her to the washroom. It's tiny, with whitewashed cave walls, a baby changing mat fixed to one wall, a row of basins squeezed onto the other. I help Suz off with her coat, but she pushes me away when I offer to help her in the loo.

'I'm not that bleeding decrepit. Chrissakes.'

I pee and hover, wondering whether to flush. Do the cleaners come in early? There's no sign of that blue disinfectant they squirt around the pan, so I assume they'll be in before the caves open up to the public. I decide to flush.

I do my best to wash at the tiny basin, squeezing out liquid soap and sluicing my face, my neck, my armpits, as best I can. I try not to think how wonderful it would be to have laundered clothes and fresh underwear. Try not to listen to Suz heaving and retching and groaning in the middle cubicle. I don't want to think about what all that spice and cider's done to her body.

252

At last she comes out, looking a hundred years old. She pushes me away, sticks her whole head under the tap and drinks like a dog.

Suz shuffles off back to our den, dragging her fur coat behind her, crunching several tiny smugglers in her wake. I pick them up, and shove them in the pocket of my smuggler's coat. It won't do for us to leave any trace.

I lie back against the cliff, thinking of the cafetière sitting on top of its spotty tablecloth.

I would literally kill for a mug of coffee.

'Wouldn't you just *die* without Prosecco?'

The mother's voice, laughing. It sounds like something that Beanie would say.

I can hear them, laughing and fussing and scraping chairs on the tiny balcony. I move closer to the grille. Kneel down to listen.

There are noises of something being dragged, something else being unzipped, and then the stomach-rumbling scent of barbecue fluid. A rustling noise. I imagine the woman pulling out goodies from a Waitrose Bag for Life.

'Where's the beers, chaps?' The father's voice. He'll be fair-going-grey, with florid cheeks and carefully unkempt stubble. A man whom his wife will still find attractive. He'll be into rugby in a big way, and make sure that Junior is too.

Children's voices, squabbling about which flavour crisps, and then their mother, chiding them, but with a smile in her voice. Rustling sounds as they start to open packets.

Slowly, the scents rise and curl their way through the grille: I imagine organic pork and sage sausages, ribs plastered in homemade satay sauce, free-range beef burgers thick

253

as slabs, frying onion, herb-crusted lamb. And all of the time, that scented, coiling smoke.

My stomach groans as I lick my lips and listen. Gulls scream as laughter rises over good beer and even better wine and organic crisps and quinoa salad.

'What's that smell?' whispers Suz. She's shuffling towards me on her knees, eyes wide in the gloom. 'I wondered where you went, Frog.'

'Shhh,' I say. 'Go back to bed. I'll be there soon.'

I name them the Bear family. Father Bear, Mother Bear, and Junior Bears, in their little house through the leaves.

Too bad they don't realise that Goldilocks lives opposite.

Sneak Thief

I hover beneath the balcony, waiting and listening. I think it's about one in the morning, but I can't be sure. Time slows when you're a creature of shadows.

There has been no light in the house for at least an hour. The last drinkers have drifted home from the pubs.

They'll be asleep, under their Cath Kidston duvet covers. I have waited a long time. Father Bear insisted on some last-minute star-gazing from the balcony, and each time I thought the coast was clear, there would be a sudden rustle of crisps, the clink of a beer glass. Whispers in the dark.

I grasp hold of the wooden struts either side of the porch and pull myself up onto the roof; I hoist myself over onto their balcony.

There's food for the taking, some of it even bagged up.

They obviously made a start on clearing up but got too tired, and left it till morning. In the violeting dawn, I help myself to three sausages, half a burger and sticky spare ribs from the top of the kettle barbecue – shame to let the seagulls have it – and wrap them in a wad of paper napkins which they've helpfully left out under a Prosecco bottle on the table. Next, a bag of apples, and a couple of bananas. I leave the half-eaten giant packet of organic crinklecut crisps, afraid they'll crackle like gunshot in the caves. Finally, half a chocolate buttercream cake, covered over with a dew-drizzled plastic salad bowl. Probably from a farm shop somewhere.

It's difficult to climb down with all the stuff, but I manage it with a bag looped over my arm and over my back. I make a sling with a beach towel and shove in a couple of abandoned bottles of beer too, and a mostly-full litre bottle of lemonade. Then I scramble back over the railings and sneak-thief back across the alley to my cave.

It is all too easy.

If only I didn't feel as though I were being watched.

Back in our nest beneath the plastic cliffs, I gorge myself on bites of organic burger followed by rich buttery mouthfuls of chocolate cake. Follow each mouthful with a warm fizzy swig of yeasty beer. Burp and sigh.

But when I try to show the food to Suz, she pushes it away, shivering.

'I'm vegan, remember? I can't eat it, Frog.'

Her teeth are chattering, and I feel a spike of fear.

She needs medicine. We need proper food.

For that I'll need to cross another line.

Street Act

The chemist's shop is busy, but that's a good thing.

All of the stronger medication is behind the counter, on a wall rack, but there are vitamins, and paracetamol and cough medicine, all within easy reach. I have swapped my smuggler's clothes for my plain hoodie.

The girl behind the counter is very young. She can't be much older than sixteen, and looks like this is her Saturday job. It is Saturday? I have no idea any more. Time has slowed into a watery, dreamy stream of looking after Suz: freezing at every sound as I support her to walk to the toilet, trying to coax her to eat something. If she doesn't start eating soon, I'll need to take her to hospital, but every time I mention that, she shakes her head violently. Sometimes, I think that she has given up. There's a darkness inside her that has settled like a cat, needling its sharp claws to get comfortable.

I want the stronger medicines. The ones for fever. The ones to blot out her pain.

I make myself smile at the girl. Her name badge says that she is called Aleysha.

'Hi,' I say. I see her eyes flicker over me, taking in my bizarre clothes, my dirty hair and nails.

'I'd like some of your strongest sleeping pills, please, and some of those painkillers.'

The girl's face hardens. 'You need a prescription for those,' she says. She's not as young as she looks.

I point to the products on the rack behind the counter, name a brand which I've had before, when I used to get anxious over exams and couldn't sleep. If Suz could only sleep dreamlessly, I'm sure she'd feel so much better.

Aleysha pulls out a couple of packets. 'These are the only ones we sell without prescription,' she says. 'Would you like a consultation with our pharmacist?'

I turn to the little waiting area. Four or five people are sitting on plastic orange chairs, staring at me. I begin to sweat.

'She won't take long,' Aleysha is saying. 'Only ten minutes...'

The pill cartons are on the counter, next to throat pastels and lip balms in different fruit flavours.

'No,' I say. 'No, thank you.' I grab the cartons, and whatever else is in my hands and back away, push past the queue of customers out of the shop.

Someone grabs my arm, and it's a man, tall and burly in a bomber jacket.

'I've got her for you, love,' he shouts. 'Want me to ring the police?' He's already taking out his mobile phone.

'Hand it over, love. Come on.' The pharmacist is standing behind him, reaching out her hand.

I drop the packets, wriggle away and run, breath screaming in my ears.

It takes me ages to pluck up the courage to try again. I can't go back without anything. I need to provide for us, need to bring in money. Hours later, the only things I have for my efforts are a couple of boxes of coloured chalks and a packet of wet wipes, which I have stuffed in my pocket.

I sit watching the sea, expecting that any minute someone will plant their hand on my shoulder, steer me away to face my crime. Each face I see, I imagine that they know me; they've seen my photo; they know the reward. The next one, I think. The next person – that lady in the wheelchair, that kid with the earbuds, the old man with the older dog – they'll be the one whose face will light with recognition.

But no one looks at me. I might as well be invisible.

It feels strange to be back at Hastings. At this time of day, the seafront is mainly populated by elderly ladies, enjoying the afternoon sun on their faces as they make their way slowly along the promenade or sit side-by-side on benches, staring out to sea. I wonder why the sea pulls people like a television set, an open fire. What is it about the ocean that makes you feel you could gaze your whole life away, just looking at it?

'Got the time, please?' I ask a passerby. It's a woman with a small dog. She takes out her phone and tells me, but not before I've seen the look on her face. I scare her. I am what no one wants to become.

I lay out a piece of cardboard and take a piece of chalk. I spend the morning drawing random shapes, and rubbing them out when I get fed up of them. I draw clown faces and dancers and acrobats. I draw Lala in her aerial hoop, hanging upside down, hair loose and free.

'That's nice, dear,' says an old lady when I've finished colouring in a picture of the pot-bellied pig in his white ruff. She hands me two shiny, new pound coins. 'I used to long to be in the circus,' she says, when I thank her. 'Far too fat now,' she shrieks, looking down at her ample figure in its zip-up sundress. 'A fat tightrope walker – imagine that!' Her friend nudges her in the ribs, and they waddle away, chortling. They've been eating large bags of chips on the scratchy, greasy wooden bench beneath the canopy. Something glints. It's a phone. One of them must have dropped it when she was rummaging in her bag for coins.

I grab it and turn to shout after them. Then I notice that it is open to use. No code. Full battery power. I slide it up my sleeve and slip away.

Side Show

I carry my loot along the narrow streets, back to our secret cave entrance.

I flit my eyes up and down once, to check no one's looking. Today, the Bear family's balcony is crammed with holiday paraphernalia: wetsuits, bodyboards, hula hoops, waterproofs, buoyancy aids, lifejackets, cricket sets – a whole life of determined family fun. *We* will *have fun,* it says. *And this is how we do it – look!*

Daddy-Who-Isn't never took me kayaking or bodyboarding or surfing. But I had an awful lot of additional lessons to make up for it. Extracurricular activities till there were no hours left. I expect he wanted to tire me out so that whenever I came home for the holidays, he didn't have to talk to me, this stranger he had to pretend was his daughter.

'You left me, Frog. Where have you been?' A plaintive voice comes from the corner seat.

'I'm back, aren't I?' I say carelessly, but I try not to see that she's thin as coat hangers, still lying propped in the same position that I left her in.

As I lean forward to straighten her bedding, I notice a sharp smell coming from beneath her coat.

'I'm all wet, Frog,' she says, and starts to cry.

I crouch beside her, kiss her cheek, stroke her hair, but inside I am frightened. I try to laugh it off. 'Bloody hell, Suz. Have you been on the beer again?' I grab the last of the paper towels from the washroom, and remove her reeking bedding, make her roll to the side while I pull off her sodden things.

Suz makes little effort to help, just keeps looking at me with those huge dark eyes. 'I'm sorry, Frog,' she whispers.

I pull out handfuls of wet wipes and then dry her, tenderly, with the fleecy jacket. Everything needs to be cleaned. Everything needs washing. I do my best with what we have, and make up her bed again, tucking the fur coat back around her.

'I'm so cold, Frog,' she says, teeth chattering.

I try to laugh. 'Still cold? Why, you're all bundled up like the Starks of Winterfell. Look, are you sure you don't want anything to eat? I can get some more milk from the staff fridge...They've locked up now. It's quite safe.'

But she's shaking her head vigorously, and I leave it.

'I forgot to tell you – I have a plan, Suz.' I squat down in front of her and smile. 'I think we should go to Paris. No one knows us there, and I have enough money. It'd be a fresh start, and I think I know how we can get hold of passports...'

But her breathing's slowing, and I see that she's asleep, finally, her small hand clutching mine.

I sigh, and sit down on the floor next to her. We remain like that for a long time.

We can't live like this much longer. We need provisions. We need to leave.

There is only one person that I think can help.

Carousel

I still remember her number. Jab it in quickly before I change my mind. I am crouching up on the bank, trying to get reception. Any minute now I expect to see Father Bear come out of his man-cave, ready to protect his family. The fact that their balcony appears empty makes me feel worse, not better.

She picks up on the first ring, like I knew she would. An unrecognised number is far too interesting to someone like her.

'Hello, Beanie,' I say.

I listen to her gasp. 'Oh my god! Oh my *god*. Willow!' Her voice lowers to a hiss. 'Wills, where *are* you? Where have you *been?* There's literally the whole *world* after you —'

I look outside at the whole world. It really seems to be minding its own business.

'That doesn't matter,' I say. 'Listen, I need your help. Will you meet me?'

This time, there is only the tiniest of pauses. Beanie will dine off this story for weeks. She starts to whisper rapidly. 'Listen, Wills, I'm supposed to be supervising Prep, so I've got to be quick. Can you text me the details?'

'No texting,' I say firmly. I don't know how it works, but I need to leave no trace on this phone. I must delete the call log after.

Beanie listens closely as I tell her where we're going to meet.

I see her before she sees me.

Long-legged, chic leather jacket, blonde-dipped, messy-on-purpose hair. She has put on shades, perched on her retroussé nose, as if *she's* the fugitive. She hitches her hold-all onto an elegant shoulder, peering out over the fairground. Then she turns and makes her way casually to the carousel where I am waiting for her. She slides herself onto the zebra in front of my tiger. Takes her shades off and stares and stares.

'Is it you, Wills? Is it really you?'

And '*Ohmygod*, your face is, like, literally *every*where. The police have come to search our school. They went through all the dorms in plastic suits like it was CS-fahking-I...'

And, 'Why don't you go just go *home*, Wills?'

Because my mother was never a mother, and Daddy is not my dad.

Because I'm not wanted there, and never have been.

Because, because...

'How are you, Beanie?' I say. She looks well. She was always pretty, but she's even prettier in mufti. She smells of lilies and Marlboro Lights as she reaches over the tiger's head to hug me.

She shakes her head. 'I still can't fahking believe it. And you look so different, Wills. Like really kind of scary.' She reaches over to touch my buzz-cut. 'But pretty too,' she adds hastily. She lowers her voice, rummages into her huge bag. 'I've got the things you wanted,' she stage-whispers. 'All but one item. I couldn't find you an old iPhone, so I got you an Android instead. Sorry.'

My mouth twitches. 'That's all right, Beanie. And thank you.' I hug her back, and she looks gratified.

I can't believe I used to be in awe of her. Before I know it, Beanie starts talking about the wedding. The carousel starts up and Beanie waves a sheet of tokens at the man. I am so used to hitching a free ride in the days with Suz that it feels really strange, being above board, and I wonder how long it is since I've actually done something legal. Her head bobs up and down, and the animals' nostrils flare scarlet as they champ at the candy-sweetened air. Our hands clutch at the twisted poles, gilt-painted. Beneath me, my tiger paws at her zebra.

'Why did you do it?' Beanie shouts over the jangly music. 'That was really mean, Wills. When we arrived, all of her friends were rallying round her. They found all of the buttons except one and just stitched them back on like nothing had happened. But she was really sobbing, Wills. You could tell under all of her make-up.'

I say nothing. Think of the little button with its shred of silk fabric, in my pocket. Think of Kayleigh-Ann with her swollen eyes and false lashes carefully glued back on by her friends.

'But why? Kayleigh-Ann's all right. She's kind of fun. And your father, well he just lets you do what you want, doesn't he? Not like mine.' Beanie pulls a face. 'If I have to hear one more piece of advice about my personal statement…ugh!'

I stare at her. It's like she's talking a foreign language. Uni and personal statements and dormitories. None of these have any place in my new world.

When the music stops, the carousel-worker glares at us. I help Beanie with her heavy bag as we jump off. Beanie buys me coffee and a bag of doughnuts to share, hot and spiced and sugared. She flings cash around, carelessly happy. A pretty pucker as she sees me looking.

'Oh fahk – sorry, Wills. I keep forgetting. Here –' And wonderfully, magically, she tugs out a wad of crisp looking notes, rolled inside a hairband. 'Two hundred,' she breathes into my ear. She has sugar on her lip gloss.

She pushes my top aside to get another look at my tattoo. 'Me too,' she laughs. She shows me the subtle line of script along the inside of her slender wrist. 'You do look kind of scary, Wills.' She grimaces. 'Look, I have to go – I'm meeting Lars, my new boyfriend. Anything you need, just phone, OK?' She taps the front pocket of the bag.

She air-hugs me, touches my cheek as if feeling whether or not I'm real, and then leaves, blonde hair bobbing.

She's shouting something at me, the sea breeze ripping away at her words: 'You can keep the Little Kit of Happiness, Wills! Love you!'

And then she's gone, taking with her the last thread of my old world.

It's only later that I realise I didn't call Kayleigh-Ann 'the Handbag'.

Cirque de Paris

It is dark by the time I get to the coach station.

There's just one thing to do before I get back to Suz, and then everything will be OK. We can escape – finally start our lives.

I hand over the crisp notes that I've peeled from the thick wad that Beanie gave me. The money is all there, just like she promised. I don't know where she got it from. Beanie always had an endless supply of cash, just like I used to.

'Two tickets to Paris, please.'

The lady behind the glass partition doesn't look at me suspiciously, doesn't glance at her colleague and press a fugitive alert button beneath the counter. She just yawns and pushes the tickets through the gap.

'Coach leaves Monday morning, 6A.M.,' she says. She couldn't be more uninterested.

I snatch them and place them carefully in the zipped front pocket of my bag. And as I jog back along the path, my feet pound the rhythm:

Paris. Paris. Paris.

I can't wait to get back and show Suz.

Stand and Deliver

Suz tries to smile when I show her the Paris tickets, but you can tell she isn't interested, not really. She brightens up when I show her Beanie's medicine hoard, though. There's a paper bag stuffed full of medicines: paracetamol, sleeping tablets. I don't know where she's got them from, but judging by the amount of cannabis her brothers always had a supply of, I'm not surprised.

I watch as Suz tries to pop a sleeping pill out of its casing, then sigh as I help her.

'Falafel?' I ask. 'They're totally vegan.'

I take the food out of the bag that Beanie's made up for me. She's really pushed the boat out, as far as the Ideal Kit for Fugitives goes, I'll give her that.

There are rolled up T-shirts, all beautifully laundered, deodorant, mini travel bottles of shampoo, shower gel, moisturiser, toner, hand lotion, conditioner. I imagine her carefully decanting it all, and smile. Like I'm packing for an expensive skiing holiday or a place in the sun. Lip balms, in three cocktail flavours: malibu, coco-loco and gin fizz. A small box of Lil-let minis, each individually wrapped in pretty candy-coloured paper. I am touched by her thought-fulness. Spare socks. Sensible, comfy boy-shorts.

And then, the *crème de la crème*: two passports.

I flick through to look again at the photographs at the back. One is of Beanie herself, fair hair braided from when she went to Guatemala that time with school. It will have to do for Suz. If you squint, Beanie's braids almost look like dreadlocks, and anyway, they hardly ever check your passport on the way out to France, do they? Beanie says that coaches just get waved through.

The other passport is a friend of Beanie's brother. She looks nothing like me, but she does have very short hair.

'Just post them back when you've arrived safely.' Beanie had said. *'Or I can come and get them when I visit! It'll be totally fun!'*

We have everything we need for Paris, and a new start.

Maybe things are finally looking up.

Sunday. Only one more day until Paris.

I am eating a KitKat when I hear the voice.

'Do you see those chaps up on the clifftop, Tarquin?'

I know that voice. It's Father Bear, keen to educate Junior. I imagine him crouching down next to his son, all ruddy cheeks and upturned collar. I hold my breath, thankful that Suz seems to be sound asleep in her nest of clothes. Hairy Jack's ghost voice hisses from the speakers overhead. Somewhere, the thin wail of a baby.

'Now, remember what I was telling you about customs and excise laws, Tarq?'

I think I hear the boy yawn as his father launches into a long and not particularly accurate description of by-laws and dragoons. I wonder what they thought when they discovered that the seagulls had taken not only their leftovers, but their beach towel too. I've folded it under Suz's head as a pillow.

When they've gone, I breathe again, and tuck the KitKat wrapper quietly into my smuggler's jerkin pocket so that we don't leave traces.

'Da-aad.' The loud high voice of a child. 'Dad, there's a girl there.'

I whip round, heart thudding.

A boy is staring straight at me, mouth open.

It's Tarquin, his head a giant silhouette behind the little plastic horsemen. He's climbed over the No Entry barrier and is breathing heavily, huffing warm air into our space. Up close, he's a mini version of his father, with the same shock of Boris-blonde hair and upturned collar on his polo shirt. I can see the glint of his teeth, his shadowed frown.

Somewhere, his father calls his name.

Go, I think. *Please go.*

We freeze, the boy and me. From the speaker, Hairy Jack lets out a cackle of laughter.

'I know you,' Tarquin says. 'You're the girl from the telly.'

He leans closer, peering through the tiny figures, eyes bright with interest. I don't move, but inside my heart's skittering.

'We watched you on the news last night. Your friend was being interviewed, and she said that she was worried about you –'

I go cold. Struggle to my knees and see the flash of fear. His eyes flit to the pistol in my belt.

'What did you see?' I ask. 'What did she say about me?'

I am aware that he's inching away from me, this filthy girl in her smuggler's clothes, but I can't think straight, my mind's frozen.

'Tell me,' I insist. I grab his arm.

'She said that she was worried about you,' he stammers. 'Your dad was on there too. He was crying – owww, let go of my arm!' He's speed-breathing now, his narrow chest is rising and falling, quick and fast.

I release him, heart tripping. She told them, I think. She betrayed me. But pumping around my head too, the boy's

267

words, high and accusing: *He was crying…He was crying…He was crying.*

I watch the figures on the clifftop shudder as the boy pulls away and disappears into the gloom.

'I bet it was you who stole our barbecue things,' he calls, when he is safely out of reach. 'Dad! Daaaaaad!'

We haven't got long.

We'll just have time, I think, if we make a dash for the tunnel now – I just need to scoop up all of our things, and wake Suz up. Only have to hide out until the coach leaves tomorrow…

Crying. Daddy was crying.

Escape Artist

I swoop everything into my bag, higgledy-piggledy. The Kit of Happiness falls onto the floor, and I stuff that in too.

'We need to get going, Suz, we can't stay here any longer. They're coming for us –'

Suz flinches as I shine a torch into her eyes.

'Hair spray,' she rasps. 'It's the best thing for fixing chalk.'

'What are you on about, Suz? Honestly, come on, we have to hurry –'

But when she tries to get up, her legs give way immediately, and she starts to whimper. 'What's wrong with me, Frog? I can't make them move. My legs aren't working.'

And it's true, they're wheeling and twitching, as she sits on the floor and shudders.

'There's nothing wrong with you,' I say, and fear tastes

like copper change in my mouth. 'It's because you've been lying down too long, that's all. Your legs are out of practice, aren't they?'

I try to lift her, and she weighs no more than a child. 'We'll go to Paris, remember? Where you've always wanted to go? Well, I saw a sign by the pier – there's a new circus there that's looking for new acts. I think I'm finally ready, Suz. I can do my fire-eating act, and the trapeze too...'

And all the time, I'm listening, checking over the top of the cliff for the sight of an enraged Father Bear.

He'll get the security guard first, alert the staff about the danger to his son, and then he'll insist they call the police.

'We've got to go,' I hiss, grabbing Suz by the arm. We won't be able to walk out of the main exit now. We'll have to head back through the tunnels. Hope no one sees us climb out of the grille. Suz looks dizzy.

'I don't – I can't –'

'No time for that now. Hurry!'

I remove her leopardskin coat from her too-sharp shoulders, make her lift her arms as I pull on one of Beanie's sweaters, zip her into a hoodie, soft and sweet-smelling with its designer logo.

'Nice,' she murmurs, rubbing her cheek against it.

'Don't fall asleep again, Suz. We have to go – now.'

I shove the rest of our food into a carrier bag, and try to pull Suz up from her nest.

I know immediately that it's not going to work. Suz staggers a few steps, sighs, then sags. The only way I'm going to get us both to the coach station is if I carry her.

I have barely reached the first tunnel when I hear them.

'That's the pistol she used to threaten my son!'

I left it on the ledge, next to a plastic wrecker manhandling a tiny keg up the cliff face. They'll be climbing over the cliff top now, swinging their torches around our recent home.

Did I clear up all our evidence? Will they find anything?

Suz is a dead weight, even with my trapeze-trained shoulders. She sighs and slides.

'Where are we going, Frog?'

'Shhh!'

Father Bear blunders into our tunnel.

'Are you in there?' he calls. 'We know that you are. I won't have anyone frightening my son, d'you hear?'

Suz shrinks in my arms, eyes squeezed shut. 'Make him go away,' she whispers, and her voice is that of a much younger girl.

Torchlight sweeps the cave floor.

I stagger up the left-hand turn and stumble straight into a wagon full of caskets. In front of us, waxwork wreckers are knocking back ale in the midst of their ill-gotten gains.

That's when I make a decision.

Now You See Me

I have hidden Suz amongst the barrels and sacks at the bottom of the wagon. Beside us, a fibreglass donkey hangs its head. I lean to kiss my friend, and she is all bones and hollows. No one will notice her there, I think, just another bundle of rags.

'I'll come back for you, Suz, I promise,' I tell her.

But she's already asleep.

They've found me.

The electric light snaps on and I force myself not to flinch.

'I've called the police,' Father Bear shouts. 'We know you're the one they're looking for. You need to give yourself up now. Be a good girl.'

I breathe through my mouth, light as possible. I can't have a panic attack now. Please don't make me.

Next to me, an old crone in widow's rags opens her mouth in a silent yowl of fear. Her teeth are yellow stumps behind frozen lips. My smuggler's jerkin is hot and itchy, my hands sweaty as I try to keep them still. I have positioned myself right at the back of the storeroom, behind a scowling browed smuggler, cheeks flushed rec with drink,

'She's in here somewhere. Shine the torch in their eyes.'

'Are you sure all this is necessary, sir? We pride ourselves on our —'

But what he prides himself on I never find out because they're already moving amongst the waxwork figures, shining the beam in their gurning faces.

I can't blink. I must not blink.

Tarquin's father's in the second row now, pushing his way through, breathing heavily. He's so close that I can make out the logo on his polo shirt: *JC Cording & Co Ltd.* An expensive brand. Daddy once bought an entire shooting outfit from their shop in Piccadilly when he was trying to impress a client.

Please don't let him notice me.

He shines the torch into the eyes of the waxwork widow and she stares back frozenly.

My turn.

I stare back until my eyes water, and the pores on the sides of his nose blur and so do the gingery hairs in his carefully maintained stubble and then

and then

Blink.

Triple Twist

'I've found her –'

I push him with both hands and knock waxworks down: the wreckers, the drunkards, the weeping women, the dragoons, the revenue men. My breath screams as I race for the door, barge past surprised tourists: a man with a baby strapped to his chest, a girl in a wheelchair, a boy with a head torch.

'Stop that girl!'

And as I wend my way towards the ticket counter, towards the main exit, all I am thinking, the only thought that keeps pounding at me, is

I

can't

leave

Suz.

But I can't go back until the caves close, because if I do, they'll find her.

I don't know how long I wander, ducking into shadows, like a night creature afraid of the sun. In the end, exhausted, I find myself climbing inside one of the rotting fishing boats, the same one that me and Suz tied the fairground man up inside, a million years ago.

I haven't long to wait, then I'll go back for her. Shrink into the shadows, through the slatted sunlight, and sleep.

I dream of my mother, as I knew I would. She is dark and beautiful, shining in her gold dress. Her arms are raised high over her head, as if she is about to dive. I see that she is standing on a platform, above a pool of fire. Flames coil about her ankles.

I shout to her, to let her know the danger, and for a while it seems that she looks straight at me with her beautiful eyes. But then she twists, a graceful movement; she reaches round and unzips that sinuous spine. Her neck writhes and lengthens; she shrugs off her glamorous shoulders, and her dress shimmers into snakeskin chevrons.

She sheds one skin, then another,
and another,
until I see that,
after all,
she is only a snake,
which turns and
flickers its tongue,
then slithers
away.

Finale

I don't know how I first know that something is wrong.

Maybe it's the sympathy in the donkey's plastic eyes, or the heavy silence as if the frozen drinkers are holding their breath. Or maybe it's the fact that Suz really doesn't seem to have moved at all; she's still in exactly the same position.

I place a hand against her cheek, and snatch it away.

Everything stills.

Suz is cold. Her skin, when I touch it, is stone.

A mirror, I think. I need a mirror –

I don't know why I think that. It's like I'm a mad thing, fumbling through rags and bags, and even in Suz's coat pocket, even though I know there isn't one anywhere; it's been weeks since we wore make-up.

But all the time, in the back of my mind, I know that I am only putting off what I already know.

Suz has slipped away.

Suz has left me.

Transcript of Telephone Conversation between DS Tracy Scallion and Willow Stephens, Monday 15 August 2016 at 4.07A.M.

Scallion: Willow? Are you crying, love?

[pause]

Scallion: Willow, tell me, lovey. Tell me what's wrong.

Willow: I'm not...crying. I...

Scallion: Tell me what's happened.

Willow: ...won't wake up...

Scallion: Who won't wake up, love?

Willow: [incoherent]

Scallion: Shit.

Call ends.

They're coming for me, Suz.

So we haven't got long, OK?

They're coming for me as I knew they would do, in the end. We had such a time together, didn't we? And I'm sorry that you never got to see Paris. But Paris isn't all it's cracked up to be, not really. The boulevards are terribly long, and everything's so far apart, and not nearly as friendly as London. And it's awfully expensive. Nine Euros for a café noir! And the French aren't remotely totally vegan, Suz, not at all.

Honestly, you'd have hated it.

Budge up, Suz. I know that you're dead, but you're taking up an awful lot of room at the bottom of this wagon. But it's really rather comfy, isn't it, after sleeping in a bus shelter?

You don't half pong, Suz. Have I ever told you that? But it's strange how I don't mind one bit. I wonder where you've gone, now that you've left your physical being? Are you up there in the sky, Suz? Are you perched in your favourite spot on the rafters of that strange old house that you loved so much, or skimming over the ocean, like a breeze?

Who sang a line like that? It was from a film, I'm sure. It was that old movie with Dustin Hoffman as Ratso. The film that killed me, every time I watched it.

We hardly ever got to do anything normal like watching films, did we, Suz? We were always making plans and dreaming. Or we were foraging about, trying to survive the day.

But I wouldn't change a minute of it, not even

at the end. Because you were what I needed, Suz.

You were my breath of fresh air, my wake-up call.

And I want to say thank you. You can't hear me, of course, I'm not stupid. I know that you're not inside there, not any more. I felt that the moment I touched your cold cheek.

You've moved out. Paf! Just like that.

But I know where you'll be. And I wish I could say my final goodbye, Suz. I wish there was time to wave you off.

There are noises inside the caves, the sound of running footsteps.

I'll tuck you in. Kiss your cheek. I'm sorry that I've made it all wet, Suz, I know you won't mind.

Ball breath.

Dragon's arse.

Your feet are so cold, Suz, but I don't mind. And I know that you're not sorry that you're dead. I'm happy if you're happy. I'm only glad that I got to look after you, in the end, and to say sorry.

Because I am sorry, Suz. So sorry.

Goodbye,

Frog xxxxxxxxxxxxxxxxxxxxxxxxxxxxxxxxxxxxxxxxxxxxxx
xxxxxxxxxxxxxxxxxxxxxxxxxxxxxxxxxxxx

(AKA Willow. I'm sorry about that, too.)

Hurly Burly

There are sounds, faraway. Shouts. Footsteps. Lights buzzing on. When I look over the top of the wagon I can see green and purple mood lighting sweeping the cave walls, the swoop of torchlight. Father Bear would have called out all the troops, to protect Junior from the mad and dangerous fugitive. I wonder what he'll make of Daddy, and if they'll ever meet?

Ooops. Daddy. Keep forgetting.

I lean over and give Suz's cheek another, final kiss.

'Goodbye, Suz,' I say. 'They're coming for me now, so I really do have to go.'

I rummage around, find the Little Kit of Happiness. Tuck it under Suz's arm.

'I don't need it anymore,' I say. 'Not where I'm going.'

I take one last look at her face, peaceful, childlike, still. Then I grab my bag, and climb over the rope.

Someone's shouting my name. Scally's voice.

But I am fast and I am strong. It take me no time at all to scramble up the tunnel and make my way through the grille to the seafront.

Running Girl

Roof-running's easy.

Doesn't matter that it's a gable end, a railing. You hang, and the morning hangs with you.

Your terrain is gutters, ridges and gable ends. You share your world with gulls and rats and swallows.

I start with the confection of houses on the seafront. The Victorians have made them simple to climb. It is easy to take a running jump at the wall of a bay window, and push off with my foot to reach the railing on its roof. Below me, a dog walker gapes. I laugh, a choking laugh. I am mad, free. Suz, are you watching me? Are you?

My fingers grasp the edge of a balcony. I pound over ridges and ledges; grip chimney tops. Once, I slip. My body learns, rights itself straightaway. I vault over parapets, railings. Focus. Breathe. Leap. Land. Feet gripping, belly clenched.

Around me, windows glint pinkfire.

Sometimes, chimney flashing cuts.

Sometimes, window moulding crumbles.

Sometimes, the world stops.

A yawning space.

A voice says, *Jump*.

A world between worlds.

Certain as a cat, I leap.

Wide as houses, free as space.

I am Circus Girl. I am strong. Catch me if you dare. The streets are my circus now, the rooftops, my stage.

I pause, poised perfectly. I clench, pause,

hold

the balance point.

Then it re-begins: the runningdrummingthudding-poundingheartpumpingheartstopping thrill of it all

and I can't stop, can't ever stop, because while I'm still running, it feels

it feels

like you're

still
alive.

Dream Tours

It isn't far to the coach stop. Six o' clock, the lady said. I can still make it.

I have to make it.

I am exposed here. It's still too early for the holidaymakers to start descending from buses and trains and boats; there's only me, a few delivery people, and a couple of bold-eyed seagulls.

A man shouts something at me, and I flinch, thinking that he's coming after me, a plain-clothes officer after the dangerous fugitive that is on the loose. But it's fine, he's simply warning me out of the way of his mate's lorry, reverse-turning out of a side road.

Panting, lungs burning, I jog the few hundred metres to the coach stop.

The coach waits in the bus bay and fifty old ladies chatter like birds, waiting to get on.

Dream Tours, the sign on the coach says. *Paris*.

I take a breath.

It's still here. I haven't missed it.

A car cruises by. Its lights are turned off, but I know that it's an unmarked police car. Everything about it screams it, from the man and the woman in the front seats, pretending to drink coffee from cardboard cups, to the glint in its letters on the rear number plate. That will be where they keep the infrared camera, for spotting fugitives like me. The BMW sits low at the back, because of all the kit it has to carry. I begin to sweat.

Dream Tours. Dream Tours. Dream Tours.

It's like a beacon, pulling me.

The old ladies chatter and fuss. They're dressed in their best clothes for their trip: dresses and jackets and brooches, but with new white trainers, for walking.

The driver looks bored, waiting. She's scrolling down her iPhone, leaning against the front of the coach while the Dream Tours guide ticks off the ladies on her clipboard.

I pass her my ticket. Wait with drawn breath as she takes forever to find my name.

Sarah, I've put. *Sarah Bean.*

She takes my ticket and nods me on board. It is as easy as that.

Outside, the police car's engine starts, and it cruises back along the seafront. The last old lady is helped onto the coach. There's just the cases to put in the hold, and we'll be off.

I lean my face against the glass. Beside me, on the seat, is Beanie's bag, where Suz should be. I wipe my eyes with my sleeve, but it's no good; I need to find the wet wipes, because that kind-looking old lady across the aisle is starting to stare, and I can't draw attention to myself, not now, not when I'm so close.

I unzip the bag and find the wet wipes in the inside pocket, but there's something attached to the sticky label that keeps them moist. Something that makes me freeze when I look at it. A pink envelope with a pony's face on the front.

A letter.

It's in loopy writing, with carefully filled-in dots above the i's. I know at once that it must be from Kayleigh-Ann.

Dear Willow,

If you get this, I want you to know that it has nothing to do with your dad. He doesn't know. I've been trying to think how to get in touch with you for ever so long, Willow, even after what you did at our wedding. I just wanted you to know I don't care about it, not at all. It was all perfect, in the end, but not as perfect as it would have been if you had been there too.

I know he's told you that he's not your dad, but he is, Willow, he really is. I see it every night, when he sits in his scruffy old chair and asks me to pour him another whiskey. Yes, he's probably drinking too much, but don't we all, when all's said and done? We've all got our vices.

I love him, Willow. And he loves you, even though he isn't much good at telling you that. Men! They're crap at feelings. It might not be PC to say that, but I reckon it's true.

I've started an Open University course. I'm reading all sorts of books, trying to improve myself like in that old film — Educating Rita. I've read The Woman in White, Pride and Prejudice, To Kill a Mockingbird. It was hard at first, because I was always rubbish at school, not bright like you, but now I love it. I've got my own bookshelf in the library, filled with my very own books. I've put candles and fairy lights on the shelves too, and sometimes I just gaze at them instead of watching television, because it can be lonely, when your dad's out working late, and books are such good company, aren't they?

Anyway, I know I'm rambling on. I've never been much good at getting to the point.

I haven't told your dad I'm writing. Beanie said she'd deliver this letter for me. If you don't answer it, I'll understand, and I promise I won't tell where you are. Me and Beanie don't want you to get caught, not if you don't want to. But I want you to know that there's always a home for you here, and a little sister too, in a couple of weeks. I keep my fingers crossed that she'll get to meet her big sister!

I'm looking after Spook for you, but he misses you, Willow. He hangs his head and looks fed up, and even refuses the pony nuts I give him as a treat. He loves you so much, Willow.

Spotty is the same as ever – i.e. stupid but fast. He still used to try to throw me at the top of Poacher's Leap, before I got too big to ride him, but I've got him in hand. Honestly, give him an inch! We all miss you.

I'm sorry we couldn't be friends, Willow. But I want you to know that I think about you, every day. I can't bear to think of you out there all alone. Please come home. I'll keep out of your way, I promise – it's a big enough house!!!

And your room's exactly the same as you left it. I made Martyna clean around all of your little collections and not touch any of them.

I hope so much that you're safe and happy. I read this letter out to Spook and he seemed to understand every word. He's even kissed the bottom of it for you!

If you wanted to reply to this, I expect there's a way to do it without telling anyone of your whereabouts. I'm sure I saw that on a programme somewhere.

Anyway, look after yourself.

Love,

Kayleigh-Ann x

P.S. Kisses from Spook: xxxxxxxxxxxxxxxxxxxxxxxxxxxxxx
xxxxxxxxxxxx

There's a sort of smeary bit of smudged ink at the bottom, where it looks like she could have rubbed Spook drool over the page, but I can't really see properly because my eyes have gone all shiny.

I stand up, just as the doors are hissing.

'Excuse me,' I say to the tour guide. 'I really need to get off. There's been a mistake.'

Miss Vertigo

The pier is empty at this time of the morning, its decking freshly oiled for the holiday season. It looks clean and empty and new. There are no buildings – no little huts selling post-cards and fudge and candles. Only the information office, covered with posters and flyers of future events.

Tightrope Extravaganza.

The Leap of Death.

Miss Vertigo.

I get my breath back after climbing the railings. Above me, along the entire length of the pier, from beginning to end, is a tightrope, strung up on scaffolding, ready for the opening ceremony.

Behind me, cars close in, and this time, even before I turn around, I know that it's Scally. She shouts something, but I don't listen; I'm staring up at the ladder, taking off my shoes. There is no resin to dust my feet with, so I take my chalks from my pocket and crush them against the beautifully oiled boards. Powdered pinks and lilacs and yellows. I dust down my hands and feet, stare up and –

284

'*Focus,*' says Lala, *intense eyes gleaming*. '*Always, you need to focus.*'

I begin to climb, one hand over another. My body feels strong. My mind feels free. I can hear the terns wheel and the gulls cry and the sea pulling and pushing at the shingle below.

More shouts. Somebody is rattling at the padlocked gates. I laugh, soundlessly. I have come home. This is where I've always wanted to be, where I belong, with the wind and the sea and the shrieking air. Confident now, I continue climbing until I reach the top of the platform. It is different to being up in the circus big top. Here, there is the extra push and pull of the wind. It is picking up now, after all of the calm, sunny days. But I don't mind; don't even feel fear as it tugs at my newly grown hair, my smuggler's costume.

I love you, Suz.

I imagine you, somewhere far off, on the back of a seagull, dreadlocks fluttering, I imagine you, happy and free and flying. You'd never have been happy in this world of jobs and money and personal statements and career plans and applications and timetables and exams and institutions and systems and controlcontrolcontrol.

You were just Suz. A free spirit.

I stare out to sea, wind flapping more violently now, tearing at my sleeves. I wish I still had the costume that she made for me: mad and wild, with the beautiful, embroidered sari streamers that rippled and danced. A madder-than-mad world, according to Suz.

I am ready for my final performance.

I take a step forwards, ease my foot on the wire. It is thick and feels strong; there's just enough give to make it feel safe. I have never done this without a safety net. My feet, first one foot and then the other, grip the cord, sure and strong.

Keep focusing, dumb ass.

So I do. I smile and stare at the flagpole at the other end of the pier, rippling, tugging. Best not look at that, not while it's moving. I raise my gaze to the top, where a seagull stands still as stone.

There. That's better.

Beneath me, my feet carry me forward, my arms outstretched, tummy taut as wire. I imagine steel ribbons running through the very core of me. Noises and whirrings drift up from behind, but I don't think of them. They're sawing through the locks.

I laugh. Continue my final walk. There is nobody to watch it, not yet, only the bead-eyed gulls, and the hushing sea. We are in collusion. They understand the wind and being free and the weather. They understand the need to fly.

A sudden gust, and my arms wobble down sharp right, but I realign myself, take a few breaths as I settle back on the wire. I am in the zone.

Footsteps, thudding. I feel the boards vibrate, but I am a million miles away, up in the air. I am walking on air. A voice, and it is Scally, as I knew it would be. My one rock in the storm. A cliché, but then sometimes clichés are closest to truth, aren't they?

Because she's always been there too, I suppose.

'…down…don't…stupid…'

The wind rips at her words, tears them into little pieces. I am over halfway now. What does she think she's going to do? Climb up here after me? Not in that skirt, surely! The thought almost makes me laugh, and laughing's not good, up on the wire. Smiling, yes. Keep that smile fixed, harsh and bright and glaring. Sear it into the spotlight because it's the only thing you can do when your life's been one long performance.

But not now. My face is relaxed, and I'm smiling because this is what I've always wanted.

My foot slips. There are gasps from below, and I think I hear my father's voice –

Do I still call him Daddy? Do I?

– and someone else, higher, faster, frightened. So she's come too, this time. But I find I don't mind. All of that bitterness and vengefulness seems like it belonged to a different version of myself. Someone very young and fearful.

I am Phoenix now. My backline flutters, and I imagine the wings soaring off my tattoo, reaching out beyond my shoulders, shadowing the pier, darkening the sea. I wish I could juggle fire. If I still had your fire kit, Suz, I could add to my act, swallow and gulp and breathe fire while juggling devil sticks and –

'…Wills…please…'

A voice, high and shrill. Beanie's. Oh god, they're all here, then, come to catch me at last. But I find I don't mind, after all. All that running, all that chasing, when the only person I was running away from was myself.

Almost there.

But I don't want this moment to end. It is my last performance, and it's all for you, Suz, every bit of it.

'*Careful!*'

This time I do fall. It happens so quickly, a gust of wind that makes me gasp and lose my footing, the sea spray – or is it rain? – salting my face with cold prickles. I cry out and topple, hands flailing wildly, but one lucky grab and I'm back, hands gripping the wire, hanging like Kahlo, gasping in the wind. I look down, and they're all there: Scally and Daddy and Kayleigh-Ann. Behind her there's Beanie, with what must be her new boyfriend. Below me, Daddy's face is tight and white, really white. I see pure dread and fear, the fear of a father for his first child. And that's when I know, that's when I realise the real truth, the truth behind all the stories, the secrets, the lies.

Scally, she's there too, ever stalwart. Thank you for keeping me company on my journey, even though you never knew it. And Kayleigh-Ann, hands wrapped protectively over an ever-rounding belly, sobbing with fear as she tries to comfort my father.

The show must go on.

So I finish my little show, glad now of my strong shoulders, my powerful arms, those sturdy wrists of mine. It is a breeze to swing myself over the last bit and reach the end platform. There's no need for applause. I have everything I need in the looks of relief on their faces. I half-clamber, half-slide down, and there's Daddy, climbing up to meet me. Daddy's all broken but he gathers me up and hugs me till we both break into tiny pieces. And he grabs me so tight, sobbing so hard, that I start sobbing too, and when I see Kayleigh-Ann, with that uncertain smile, rivers of melted mascara down her cheeks (I will *so* have to teach her to do better make-up), I reach out my hand and pull her into the hug too.

'I'm going to call her Iris,' she whispers into my shoulder. 'After the ones that grow by the lake, under the willow trees. I've always loved your name, Willow. I wanted one just as nice.'

'I'm sorry,' I say. 'I'm sorry for everything.'

I have to be handcuffed, of course, it's all procedure, and this time I don't struggle, just let Scally lead me away, Daddy and Kayleigh-Ann following closely, because now I've got what I've always wanted. And all the time I'm looking back over that wide, morning-bright sea, and somewhere, over the bouncing water I hear you, throwing your head back and laughing.

'*You did it, Frog! You effing did it! I always knew you could…*'

And then you're gone, soaring away over the dancing waves on the back of that damned seagull.

Goodbye, Suz. Hope you enjoyed the show.

You're free as a bird now; the darkness has gone. I think of all of the times that I thought I wanted to fly, too. I wanted to chase after dreams, wanted to be in the spotlight, wanted so much to have attention, all eyes on me, even while I was running.

But in the end, it was never about the flying, was it, Suz?

In the end, all I ever really wanted was to be caught.

www.rocktheboat.london